MARSH, Ngaio, 1899-

Black as he's painted. Boston, Little, Brown [c1974]
260p.

I. tc.

Books by Ngaio Marsh

ARTISTS IN CRIME
DEATH IN A WHITE TIE
OVERTURE TO DEATH
DEATH AT THE BAR
DEATH AND THE DANCING FOOTMAN
COLOUR SCHEME
DIED IN THE WOOL
FINAL CURTAIN
A WREATH FOR RIVERA
NIGHT AT THE VULCAN
SPINSTERS IN JEOPARDY
SCALES OF JUSTICE
DEATH OF A FOOL
SINGING IN THE SHROUDS
FALSE SCENT
HAND IN GLOVE
DEAD WATER
BLACK BEECH AND HONEYDEW
KILLER DOLPHIN
CLUTCH OF CONSTABLES
A MAN LAY DEAD
NURSING HOME MURDER
TIED UP IN TINSEL
VINTAGE MURDER
WHEN IN ROME
BLACK AS HE'S PAINTED

BLACK
AS
HE'S
PAINTED

BLACK AS HE'S PAINTED

NGAIO MARSH

LITTLE, BROWN AND COMPANY · BOSTON · TORONTO

FIRST AMERICAN EDITION

To6/74

Library of Congress Cataloging in Publication Data

Marsh, Ngaio, 1899-
Black as he's painted.

I. Title.
PZ3.M3539Bl3 [PR9639.3.M27] 823 73-22307
ISBN 0-316-54666-6

Published simultaneously in Canada
by Little, Brown & Company (Canada) Limited

PRINTED IN THE UNITED STATES OF AMERICA

For
Roses and Mike
with love

The author's warmest thanks are due to Sir Alister McIntosh, K.C.M.G., and P. J. Humphries, Esq., for their very kind advice on matters ambassadorial and linguistic.

Cast of Characters

MR. SAMUEL WHIPPLESTONE: FOREIGN OFFICE (RETIRED)

LUCY LOCKETT: A CAT

THE AMBASSADOR FOR NG'OMBWANA IN LONDON

A LADY
A YOUNG GENTLEMAN
A YOUTH — OF MESSRS. ABLE, VIRTUE & SONS, LAND & ESTATE AGENTS

CHUBB: HOUSE SERVANT

MRS. CHUBB: HIS WIFE

A VETERINARY SURGEON

MR. SHERIDAN: NO. 1A, CAPRICORN WALK (BASEMENT FLAT)

HIS EXCELLENCY BARTHOLOMEW OPALA, C.B.E.: THE BOOMER. PRESIDENT OF NG'OMBWANA.

AN A.D.C.

MR. AND MRS. PIRELLI: OF THE NAPOLI, SHOP-KEEPERS

COLONEL COCKBURN-MONTFORT: LATE OF THE NG'OMBWANAN ARMY (RETIRED)

MRS. COCKBURN-MONTFORT: HIS WIFE

KENNETH SANSKRIT: LATE OF NG'OMBWANA. MERCHANT.

XENOCLEA SANSKRIT: HIS SISTER. OF THE PIGGIE POTTERIE, 12, CAPRICORN MEWS, S.W. 3.

A MLINZI: SPEAR-CARRIER TO THE BOOMER

SIR GEORGE ALLEYN, K.C.M.G., ETC. ETC.

RODERICK ALLEYN: SUPERINTENDENT, C.I.D. HIS BROTHER.

TROY ALLEYN: PAINTER. HIS WIFE.

INSPECTOR FOX: C.I.D.

SIR JAMES CURTIS: THE CELEBRATED PATHOLOGIST

SUPERINTENDENT GIBSON: SPECIAL BRANCH, C.I.D.

JACKS: A TALENTED SERGEANT, C.I.D.

DETECTIVE-SERGEANT BAILEY: A FINGER-PRINT EXPERT

DETECTIVE-SERGEANT THOMPSON: PHOTOGRAPHER

SUNDRY POLICE, NG'OMBWANAN EMBASSY GUESTS AND SERVANTS, AND FREQUENTERS OF THE CAPRICORNS, S.W.3.

Contents

BLACK
AS
HE'S
PAINTED

I

Mr. Whipplestone

The year was at the spring and the day at the morn and God may have been in His Heaven, but as far as Mr. Samuel Whipplestone was concerned the evidence was negligible. He was, in a dull, muddled sort of way, miserable. He had become possessed, with valedictory accompaniments, of two solid silver Georgian gravy-boats. He had taken his leave of Her Majesty's Foreign Service in the manner to which his colleagues were accustomed. He had even prepared himself for the non-necessity of getting up at seven-thirty, bathing, shaving, breakfasting at eight—but there is no need to prolong the Podsnappian recital. In a word he had fancied himself tuned in to retirement and now realized that he was in no such condition. He was a man without propulsion. He had no object in life. He was finished.

By ten o'clock he found himself unable to endure the complacent familiarity of his "service" flat. It was in fact at that hour being "serviced," a ritual which normally he avoided and now hindered by his presence.

He was astounded to find that for twenty years he had inhabited dull, oppressive, dark and uncomely premises. Deeply shaken by this abrupt discovery he went out into the London spring.

A ten-minute walk across the park hardly raised his spirits. He avoided the great water-shed of traffic under the quadriga, saw some inappropriately attired equestrians, passed a concourse of scarlet and yellow tulips, left the park under the expanded nostrils of Epstein's liberated elementals, and made his way into Baronsgate.

As he entered that flowing cacophony of changing gears and revving engines, it occurred to him that he himself must now get into bottom gear and stay there until he was parked in some sub-fusc lay-by to await—and here the simile became insufferable—a final towing-off. His predicament was none the better for being commonplace. He walked for a quarter of an hour.

From Baronsgate the western entry into the Capricorns is by an arched passage too low overhead to admit any but pedestrian traffic. It leads into Capricorn Mews and, further along at right angles to the Mews, Capricorn Place. He had passed by it over and over again and would have done so now if it hadn't been for a small, thin cat.

This animal flashed out from under the traffic and shot past him into the passageway. It disappeared at the far end. He heard a scream of tyres and of a living creature.

This sort of thing upset Mr. Whipplestone. He disliked this sort of thing intensely. He would have greatly preferred to remove himself as quickly as possible from the scene and put it out of his mind. What he did, however, was to hurry through the passageway into Capricorn Mews.

The vehicle, a delivery van of sorts, was disappearing into Capricorn Place. A group of three youths outside a garage stared at the cat, which lay like a blot of ink on the pavement.

One of them walked over to it. "Had it," he said.

"Poor pussy!" said one of the others and they laughed objectionably.

The first youth moved his foot as if to turn the cat over. Astonishingly and dreadfully it scrabbled with its hind legs. He exclaimed, stooped down and extended his hand.

It was on its feet. It staggered and then bolted. Towards Mr. Whipplestone, who had come to a halt. He supposed it to be concussed, or driven frantic by pain or fear. In a flash it gave a great spring and was on Mr. Whipplestone's chest, clinging with its small claws and—incredibly—purring. He had been told that a dying cat will sometimes purr. It had blue eyes. The tip of its tail for about two inches was snow white, but the rest of its person was perfectly black. He had no particular antipathy to cats.

He carried an umbrella in his right hand, but with his left arm he performed a startled reflex gesture. He sheltered the cat. It was shockingly thin, but warm and tremulous.

"One of 'er nine lives gawn for a burton," said the youth. He and his friends guffawed themselves into the garage.

"Drat," said Mr. Whipplestone, who long ago had thought it amusing to use spinsterish expletives.

With some difficulty he hooked his umbrella over his left arm and with his right hand inserted his eyeglass and then explored the cat's person. It increased its purrs, interrupting them with a faint mew when he touched its shoulder. What was to be done with it?

Obviously, nothing in particular. It was not badly injured, presumably it lived in the neighborhood, and one had always understood its species to have a phenomenal homing instinct. It thrust its nut-like head under Mr. Whipplestone's jacket and into his waistcoat. It palpated his chest with its paws. He had quite a business detaching it.

He set it down on the pavement. "Go home," he said. It stared up at him and went through the motion of mewing, opening its mouth and showing its pink tongue but giving no sound. "No," he said, "go home!" It was making little preparatory movements of its haunches as if about to spring again.

He turned his back on it and walked quickly down Capricorn Mews. He almost ran.

It is a quiet little street, cobbled and very secluded. It accommodates three garages, a packing agency, two dozen or so small mid-Victorian houses, a minute bistro and four shops. As he approached one of these, a flower shop, he could see reflected in its side windows Capricorn Mews with himself walking towards him. And behind him, trotting in a determined manner, the little cat. It was mewing.

He was extremely put out and had begun to entertain a confused notion of telephoning the R.S.P.C.A. when a van erupted from a garage immediately behind him. It passed him, and when it had gone the cat had disappeared: frightened, Mr. Whipplestone supposed, by the noise.

Beyond the flower shop and on the opposite side of the Mews was the corner of Capricorn Place, leading off to the left. Mr. Whipplestone, deeply ruffled, turned into it.

A pleasing street: narrow, orderly, sunny, with a view, to the left, of tree-tops and the dome of the Baronsgate Basilica. Iron railings and behind them small well-kept Georgian and Victorian houses. Spring flowers in window-boxes. From somewhere or another the smell of freshly brewed coffee.

Cleaning ladies attacked steps and door-knockers. Household ladies were abroad with shopping baskets. A man of Mr. Whipplestone's own age who reeked of the army and was of an empurpled complexion emerged from one of the houses. A perambulator with a self-important baby and an escort of a pedestrian six-year-old, a female propellant and a large dog headed with a purposeful air towards the park. The postman was going his rounds.

In London there are still, however precarious their state, many little streets of the character of the Capricorns. They are upper-middle-class streets and therefore, Mr. Whipplestone had been given to understand, despicable. Being of that class himself, he did not take this view. He found the Capricorns uneventful, certainly, but neither tiresomely quaint nor picturesque nor smug; pleasing, rather, and possessed of a quality which he could only think of as "sparkling." Ahead of him was a pub, the Sun in Splendour. It had an honest untarted look about it and stood at the point where the Place leads into Capricorn Square: the usual railed enclosure of plane trees, grass and a bench or two, well-kept. He turned to the right down one side of it, making for Capricorn Walk.

Moving towards him at a stately pace came a stout, superbly dressed coal-black gentleman leading a white Afghan hound with a scarlet collar and leash.

"My dear Ambassador!" Mr. Whipplestone exclaimed. "How very pleasant!"

"Mr. Whipplestone!" resonated the Ambassador for Ng'ombwana. "I am delighted to see you. You live in these parts?"

"No, no: a morning stroll. I'm — I'm a free man now, Your Excellency."

"Of course. I had heard. You will be greatly missed."

"I doubt it. Your Embassy — I had forgotten for the moment — is quite close by, isn't it?"

"In Palace Park Gardens. I too enjoy a morning stroll with Ahman. We are not, alas, unattended." He waved his gold-mounted stick in the direction of a large person looking anonymously at a plane tree.

"Alas!" Mr. Whipplestone agreed. "The penalty of distinction," he added, neatly, and patted the Afghan.

"You are kind enough to say so."

Mr. Whipplestone's highly specialized work in the Foreign Service had been advanced by a happy manner with foreign — and particularly with African — plenipotentiaries. "I hope I may congratulate Your Excellency," he said and broke into his professional style of verbless exclamation. "The increased rapprochement! The new treaty! Masterly achievements!"

"Achievements – entirely – of our great President, Mr. Whipplestone."

"Indeed, yes. Everyone is delighted about the forthcoming visit. An auspicious occasion."

"As you say. Immensely significant." The Ambassador waited for a moment and then slightly reduced the volume of his superb voice. "Not," he said, "without its anxieties, however. As you know, our great President does not welcome" – he again waved his stick at his bodyguard – "that sort of attention." A sigh escaped him. "He is to stay with us," he said.

"Quite."

"The responsibility!" sighed the Ambassador. He broke off and offered his hand. "You will be at the reception, of course," he said. "We must meet more often! I shall see that something is arranged. Au revoir, Mr. Whipplestone."

They parted. Mr. Whipplestone walked on, passing and, tactfully, ignoring the escort.

Facing him at the point where the Walk becomes the northeast border of the Square was a small house between two large ones. It was painted white with a glossy black front door and consisted of an attic, two floors and a basement. The first-floor windows opened on a pair of miniature balconies, the ground-floor ones were bowed. He was struck by the arrangement of the window-boxes. Instead of the predictable daffodil one saw formal green swags that might have enriched a della Robbia relief. They were growing vines of some sort which swung between the pots where they rooted and were cunningly trimmed so that they swelled at the lowest point of the arc and symmetrically tapered to either end.

Some workmen with ladders were putting up a sign.

He had begun to feel less depressed. Persons who do not live there will talk about "the London feeling." They will tell you that as they walk down a London street they can be abruptly made happy, uplifted in spirit, exhilarated. Mr. Whipplestone had always taken a somewhat incredulous view of these transports but he had to admit that on this occasion he was undoubtedly visited by a liberated sensation. He had a singular notion that the little house had induced this reaction. No. 1, as he now saw, Capricorn Walk.

He approached the house. It was touched on its chimneys and the eastern slope of its roof by sunshine. "Facing the right way," thought Mr. Whipplestone. "In the winter it'll get all the sun there is, I daresay." His own flat faced north.

A postman came whistling down the Walk as Mr. Whipplestone crossed it. He mounted the steps of No. 1, clapped something through the brass flap, and came down so briskly that they nearly collided.

"Woops-a-daisy," said the postman. "Too eager, that's my trouble. Lovely morning, though, innit?"

"Yes," said Mr. Whipplestone, judiciously conceding the point. "It is. Are the present occupants – " He hesitated.

"Gawn. Out last week," said the postman. "But I'm not to know, am I? People ought to make arrangements, din' they sir?" He went off, whistling.

The workmen came down their ladders and prepared to make off. They had erected a sign.

FOR SALE
ALL ENQUIRIES TO
ABLE, VIRTUE & SONS
17, CAPRICORN STREET, S.W.3

II

The Street is the most "important" of the Capricorns. It is wider and busier than the rest. It runs parallel to the Walk and in fact Messrs. Able and Virtue's premises lie exactly back-to-back with the little house at No. 1.

"*Good* morning," said the roundabout lady at the desk on the left-hand side. "*Can* I help you?" she pleaded brightly.

Mr. Whipplestone pulled out the most non-committal stop in his F.O. organ and tempered its chill with a touch of whimsy.

"You may satisfy my idle curiosity if you will be so good," he said. "Ah – concerning No. 1, Capricorn Walk."

"No. 1, the Walk?" repeated the lady. "Yes. Our notice, ackshally, has only just gone up. For sale with stipulations regarding the basement. I'm not quite sure – " She looked across at the young man with a Pre-Raphaelite hair-do behind the right-hand desk. He was contemplating his fingernails and listening to his telephone. "What *is* it about the basement, No. 1, the Walk?" she asked.

He clapped a languid hand over the receiver: "Ay'm coping," he said and unstopped the receiver. "The basement of No. 1," he rattled into it, "is at present occupied as a *pied-à-terre* by the owner. He wishes to retain occupancy. The Suggested Arrangement is that total ownership pass to the purchaser and that he, the vendor, become the tenant of the basement at an agreed rent for a specified period." He listened for a considerable interval. "No," he said, "ay'm afraid it's a firm stipulation. Quate. Quate. Yes. Theng you, madam. Good morning."

"That," said the lady, offering it to Mr. Whipplestone, "is the situation."

Mr. Whipplestone, conscious of a lightness in his head, said: "And the price?" He used the voice in which he had been wont to say: "This should have been dealt with at a lower level."

"Was it thirty-nine?" the lady asked her colleague.

"Thirty-eight."

"Thirty-eight thousand," she relayed to Mr. Whipplestone, who caught back his breath in a civilized little hiss.

"Indeed?" he said. "You amaze me."

"It's a Desirable District," she replied indifferently. "Properties are at a premium in the Capricorns." She picked up a document and glanced at it. Mr. Whipplestone was nettled.

"And the rooms?" he asked sharply. "How many? Excluding, for the moment, the basement."

The lady and the Pre-Raphaelite young gentleman became more attentive. They began to speak in unison and begged each other's pardon.

"Six," gabbled the lady, "in all. Excluding kitchen and Usual Offices. Wall-to-wall carpets and drapes included in purchase price. *And* the Usual Fitments: fridge, range et cetera. Large recep' with adjacent dining-room, ground floor. Master bedroom and bathroom with toilet, first floor. Two rooms with shower and toilet, second floor. Late tenant used these as flat for married couple."

"Oh?" said Mr. Whipplestone, concealing the emotional disturbance that seemed to be lodged under his diaphragm. "A married couple? You mean?"

"Did for him," said the lady.

"I beg your pardon?"

"Serviced him. Cook and houseman. There was an Arrangement by which they also cleaned the basement flat."

The young man threw in: "Which it is hoped will continue. They are Strongly Recommended to purchaser with Arrangement to be arrived at for continued weekly servicing of basement. No obligation, of course."

"Of course not." Mr. Whipplestone gave a small dry cough. "I should like to see it," he said.

"Certainly," said the lady crisply. "When would you — ?"

"Now, if you please."

"I *think* that would suit. If you'll just wait while I — "

She used her telephone. Mr. Whipplestone bumped into a sudden qualm of near-panic. "I am beside myself," he thought.

"It's that wretched cat." He pulled himself together. After all, he was committed to nothing. An impulse, a mere whim, induced he dared say by unaccustomed idleness. What of it?

The lady was looking at him. Perhaps she had spoken to him.

"I beg your pardon," said Mr. Whipplestone.

She decided he was hard-of-hearing. "The house," she articulated pedantically, "is open to view. The late tenants have vacated the premises. The married couple leave at the end of the week. The owner is at home in the basement flat. Mr. Sheridan," she shouted. "That's the vendor's name: Sheridan."

"Thank you."

"Mervyn!" cried the lady, summoning up a wan and uncertain youth from the back office. "No. 1, the Walk. Gentleman to view." She produced keys and smiled definitively upon Mr. Whipplestone. "It's a Quality Residence," she said. "I'm sure you'll think so."

The youth attended him with a defeated air round the corner to No. 1, Capricorn Walk.

"Thirty-eight thousand pounds!" Mr. Whipplestone inwardly expostulated. "Good God, it's outrageous!"

The Walk had turned further into the sun, which now sparkled on No. 1's brass door-knocker and letter-box. Mr. Whipplestone, waiting on the recently scrubbed steps, looked down into the area. It had been really very ingeniously converted, he was obliged to concede, into a ridiculous little garden with everything on a modest scale.

"Pseudo-Japanese," he thought in a panic-stricken attempt to discredit it.

"Who looks after *that*?" he tossed at the youth. "The basement?"

"Yar," said the youth.

("He hasn't the faintest idea," thought Mr. Whipplestone.)

The youth had opened the front door and now stood back for Mr. Whipplestone to enter.

The little hall and stairway were carpeted in cherry red, the glossy walls were an agreeable oyster white. This scheme was continued in a quite sizable drawing-room. The two bow windows curtained in red and white stripes were large and the whole interior remarkably light for a London room. For some twenty years he had vaguely regretted the murkiness of his service flat.

Without warning he was overtaken by an experience that a less sophisticated man might have been tempted to call hallucinatory. He saw, with the utmost clarity, his own possessions occupying this lighthearted room. The Chippendale wall-desk, the crimson sofa with its companion table, the big red glass goblet, the Agatha Troy landscape, the late Georgian bookcase: all were harmoniously accommodated. When the youth opened double doors into a small dining-room, Mr. Whipplestone saw at a glance that his chairs were of precisely the right size and character.

He dismissed these visions. "The partition folds back," he said with a brave show of indifference, "to form one room, I suppose?"

"Yar," said the youth and folded it back. He opened red and white striped curtains in the rear wall and revealed a courtyard and tub garden.

"Lose the sun," Mr. Whipplestone sneered, keeping his head. "Get none in the winter."

It was, however, receiving its full quota now.

"Damp," persisted Mr. Whipplestone defiantly. "Extra expense. Have to be kept up." And he thought: "I'd do better to hold my tongue."

The kitchen was on the left of the dining-room. It was a modernized affair with a service hatch. "Cramped!" Mr. Whipplestone thought of saying, but his heart was not in it.

The stairs were steep, which ought to have been a comfort. Awkward for trays and luggage and suppose one died how would they get one out of it? He said nothing.

The view from the master bedroom through the French windows embraced in its middle distance the Square with the Sun in Splendour on the left and—more distantly on the right—the dome of the Basilica. In the foreground was the Walk with foreshortened views of pedestrians, parked cars and an intermittent passage of traffic. He opened a French window. They were ringing the bells in the Basilica. Twelve o'clock. Some service or another, he supposed. But you couldn't say the house was noisy.

The bells stopped. Somewhere, out of sight, a voice was raised in a reiterated, rhythmical shout. He couldn't distinguish the sense of it but it came nearer. He went out on one of the two little balconies.

"Air-eye-awf," shouted the voice, and round the far corner of the Square came a horse-drawn cart, nodding with tulips and led by a red-faced man. He passed No. 1 and looked up.

"Any time. All fresh," he bawled directly at Mr. Whipplestone, who hastily withdrew.

(His big red glass goblet in the bow window, filled with tulips.)

Mr. Whipplestone was a man who did not indulge in histrionics, but under the lash of whatever madness now possessed him he did, as he made to leave the window, flap the air with two dismissive palms. The gesture brought him face-to-face with a couple, man and woman.

"I beg your pardon," they all said and the small man added: "Sorry, sir. We just heard the window open and thought we'd better see." He glanced at the youth. "Order to view?" he asked.

"Yar."

"You," said Mr. Whipplestone, dead against his will, "must be the—the upstairs—ah—the—"

"That's right, sir," said the man. His wife smiled and made a slight bob. They were rather alike, being round-faced, apple-cheeked and blue-eyed, and were aged, he thought, about fifty-five.

"You are — I understand — ah — still — ah — "

"We've stayed on to set things to rights, sir. Mr. Sheridan's kindly letting us remain until the end of the week. Gives us a chance to find another place, sir, if we're not wanted here."

"I understand you would be — ah — "

"Available, sir?" they both said quickly and the man added, "We'd be glad to stay on if the conditions suited. We've been here with the outgoing tenant six years, sir, and very happy with it. Name of Chubb, sir, references on request and the owner, Mr. Sheridan, below, would speak for us."

"Quite, quite, quite!" said Mr. Whipplestone in a tearing hurry. "I — ah — I've come to no conclusion. On the contrary. Idle curiosity, really. However. In the event — the remote event of my — be very glad — but so far — nothing decided."

"Yes, sir, of course. If you'd care to see upstairs, sir!"

"What!" shouted Mr. Whipplestone as if they'd fired a gun at him. "Oh. Thank you. Might as well, perhaps. Yes."

"Excuse me, sir. I'll just close the window."

Mr. Whipplestone stood aside. The man laid his hand on the French window. It was a brisk movement, but it stopped as abruptly as if a moving film had turned into a still. The hand was motionless, the gaze was fixed, the mouth shut like a trap.

Mr. Whipplestone was startled. He looked down into the street and there, returning from his constitutional and attended by his dog and his bodyguard, was the Ambassador for Ng'ombwana. It was at him that the man Chubb stared. Something impelled Mr. Whipplestone to look at the woman. She had come close and she too, over her husband's shoulder, stared at the Ambassador.

The next moment the figures animated. The window was shut and fastened and Chubb turned to Mr. Whipplestone with a serviceable smile.

"Shall I show the way, sir?" asked Chubb.

The upstairs flat was neat, clean and decent. The little parlour was a perfectly respectable and rather colourless room except perhaps for an enlarged photograph of a round-faced girl of about sixteen which attracted attention through being festooned in black ribbon and flanked on the table beneath it by two vases of dyed immortelles. Some kind of china medallion hung from the bottom edge of the frame. Another enlarged photograph, of Chubb in uniform and Mrs. Chubb in bridal array, hung on the wall.

All the appointments on this floor, it transpired, were the property of the Chubbs. Mr. Whipplestone was conscious that they watched him anxiously. Mrs. Chubb said: "It's home to us. We're settled like. It's such a nice part, the Capricorns." For an unnerving moment he thought she was going to cry.

He left the Chubbs precipitately, followed by the youth. It was a struggle not to re-enter the drawing-room but he triumphed, and shot out of the front door to be immediately involved in another confrontation.

"Good morning," said a man on the area steps. "You've been looking at my house, I think? My name is Sheridan."

There was nothing remarkable about him at first sight unless it was his almost total baldness and his extreme pallor. He was of middle height, unexceptionably dressed and well-spoken. His hair, when he had had it, must have been dark, since his eyes and brows and the wires on the backs of his pale hands were black. Mr. Whipplestone had a faint, fleeting and oddly uneasy impression of having seen him before. He came up the area steps and through the gate and faced Mr. Whipplestone, who in politeness couldn't do anything but stop where he was.

"Good morning," Mr. Whipplestone said. "I just happened to be passing. An impulse."

"One gets them," said Mr. Sheridan, "in the spring." He spoke with a slight lisp.

"So I understand," said Mr. Whipplestone, not stuffily but in a definitive tone. He made a slight move.

"Did you approve?" asked Mr. Sheridan casually.

"Oh charming, charming," Mr. Whipplestone said, lightly dismissing it.

"Good. So glad. Good morning, Chubb, can I have a word with you?" said Mr. Sheridan.

"Certainly, sir," said Chubb.

Mr. Whipplestone escaped. The wan youth followed him to the corner. Mr. Whipplestone was about to dismiss him and continue alone towards Baronsgate. He turned back to thank the youth and there was the house, in full sunlight now with its evergreen swags and its absurd garden. Without a word he wheeled left and left again and reached Able, Virtue & Sons three yards in advance of his escort. He walked straight in and laid his card before the plump lady.

"I should like the first refusal," he said.

From that moment it was a foregone conclusion. He didn't lose his head. He made sensible enquiries and took proper steps about the lease and the plumbing and the state of repair. He consulted his man of business, his bank manager and his solicitor. It is questionable whether if any of these experts had advised against the move he would have paid the smallest attention, but they did not, and to his own continuing astonishment, at the end of a fortnight Mr. Whipplestone moved in.

He wrote cosily to his married sister in Devonshire: "—you may be surprised, to hear of the change. Don't expect anything spectacular, it's a quiet little backwater full of old fogies like me. Nothing in the way of excitement or 'happenings' or violence or beastly demonstrations. It suits me. At my age one prefers the uneventful life and that," he ended, "is what I expect to enjoy at No. 1, Capricorn Walk."

Prophecy was not Mr. Whipplestone's strong point.

III

"That's all jolly fine," said Chief Superintendent Alleyn. "What's the Special Branch think it's doing? Sitting on its fat bottom waving Ng'ombwanan flags?"

"What did he *say*, exactly?" asked Mr. Fox. He referred to their Assistant Commissioner.

"Oh, *you* know!" said Alleyn. "Charm and sweet reason were the wastewords of his ween."

"What's a ween, Mr. Alleyn?"

"I've not the remotest idea. It's a quotation. And don't ask me from where."

"I only wondered," said Mr. Fox mildly.

"I don't even know," Alleyn continued moodily, "how it's spelt. Or what it means, if it comes to that."

"If it's Scotch it'll be with an h, won't it? Meaning: 'few.' Wheen."

"Which doesn't make sense. Or does it? Perhaps it should be 'weird,' but that's something one drees. Now *you're* upsetting me, Br'er Fox."

"To get back to the A.C., then?"

"However reluctantly: to get back to him. It's all about this visit, of course."

"The Ng'ombwanan President?"

"He. The thing is, Br'er Fox, I know him. And the A.C. knows I know him. We were at school together in the same house: Davidson's. Same study, for a year. Nice creature, he was. Not everybody's cup of tea but I liked him. We got on like houses-on-fire."

"Don't tell me," said Fox. "The A.C. wants you to recall old times?"

"I do tell you precisely that. He's dreamed up the idea of a meeting—casual-cum-official. He wants me to put it to the President that unless he conforms to whatever procedure the

Special Branch sees fit to lay on, he may very well get himself bumped off and in any case will cause acute anxiety, embarrassment and trouble at all levels from the Monarch down. And I'm to put this, if you please, tactfully. They don't want umbrage to be taken, followed by a highly publicized flounce-out. He's as touchy as a sea-anemone."

"Is he jibbing, then? About routine precautions?"

"He was always a pig-headed ass. We used to say that if you wanted the old Boomer to do anything you only had to tell him not to. And he's one of those sickening people without fear. And hellish haughty with it. Yes, he's jibbing. He doesn't want protection. He wants to do a Haroun-al-Raschid and bum around London on his own, looking about as inconspicuous as a coal box in paradise."

"Well," said Mr. Fox judiciously, "that's a very silly way to go on. He's a number one assassination risk, that gentleman."

"He's a bloody nuisance. You're right, of course. Ever since he pushed his new industrial legislation through he's been a sitting target for the lunatic right fringe. Damn it all, Br'er Fox, only the other day, when he elected to make a highly publicized call at Martinique, somebody took a pot-shot at him. Missed and shot himself. No arrest. And off goes the Boomer on his merry way, six foot five of him, standing on the seat of his car, all eyes and teeth, with his escort having kittens every inch of the route."

"He sounds a right daisy."

"I believe you."

"I get muddled," Mr. Fox confessed, "over these emergent nations."

"You're not alone, there."

"I mean to say—this Ng'ombwana. What is it? A republic, obviously, but is it a member of the Commonwealth, and if it is why does it have an ambassador instead of a high commissioner?"

"You may well ask. Largely through the manoeuvrings of my old chum the Boomer. They're still a Commonwealth country. More or less. They're having it both ways. All the trappings and complete independence. All the ha'pence and none of the kicks. That's why they insist on calling their man in London an ambassador and setting him up in premises that wouldn't disgrace one of the great powers. Basically it's the Boomer's doing."

"What about his own people? Here? At this Embassy? His Ambassador and all?"

"They're as worried as hell but say that what the President lays down is *it:* the general idea being that they might as well speak to the wind. He's got this notion in his head – it derives from his schooldays and his practising as a barrister in London – that because Great Britain, relatively, has had a non-history of political assassination there won't be any in the present or future. In its maddening way it's rather touching."

"He can't stop the S.B. doing its stuff, though. Not outside the Embassy."

"He can make it hellish awkward for them."

"What's the procedure, then? Do you wait till he comes, Mr. Alleyn, and plead with him at the airport?"

"I do not. I fly to his blasted republic at the crack of dawn tomorrow and you carry on with the Dagenham job on your own."

"Thanks very much. What a treat," said Fox.

"So I'd better go and pack."

"Don't forget the old school tie."

"I do not deign," said Alleyn, "to reply to that silly crack."

He got as far as the door and stopped. "I meant to ask you," he said. "Did you ever come across a man called Samuel Whipplestone? At the F.O.?"

"I don't move in those circles. Why?"

"He was a bit of a specialist on Ng'ombwana. I see he's

lately retired. Nice chap. When I get back I might ask him to dinner."

"Are you wondering if he'd have any influence?"

"We can hardly expect him to crash down on his knees and plead with the old Boomer to use his loaf if he wants to keep it. But I did vaguely wonder. 'Bye, Br'er Fox."

Forty-eight hours later Alleyn, in a tropical suit, got out of a Presidential Rolls that had met him at the main Ng'ombwanan airport. He passed in sweltering heat up a grandiose flight of steps through a lavishly uniformed guard and into the air-conditioned reception hall of the Presidential Palace.

Communication at the top level had taken place and he got the full, instant V.I.P. treatment.

"Mr. Alleyn?" said a young Ng'ombwanan wearing an A.D.C.'s gold knot and tassel. "The President is so happy at your visit. He will see you at once. You had a pleasant flight?"

Alleyn followed the sky-blue tunic down a splendid corridor that gave on an exotic garden.

"Tell me," he asked on the way, "what form of address is the correct one for the President?"

"His Excellency the President," the A.D.C. rolled out, "prefers that form of address."

"Thank you," said Alleyn and followed his guide into an anteroom of impressive proportions. An extremely personable and widely smiling secretary said something in Ng'ombwanan. The A.D.C. translated: "We are to go straight in, if you please." Two dashingly uniformed guards opened double doors and Alleyn was ushered into an enormous room at the far end of which, behind a vast desk, sat his old school chum Bartholomew Opala.

"Superintendent Alleyn, Your Excellency, Mr. President, sir," said the A.D.C. redundantly and withdrew.

The enormous presence was already on its feet and coming, light-footed as a prizefighter, at Alleyn. The huge voice was bellowing: "Rory Alleyn by all that's glorious!" Alleyn's hand was engulfed and his shoulder-blade rhythmically beaten. It was impossible to stand to attention and bow from the neck in what he had supposed to be the required form.

"Mr. President — " he began.

"What? Oh, nonsense, nonsense, nonsense! Balls, my dear man, as we used to say at Davidson's." Davidson's had been their house at the illustrious school they both attended. The Boomer was being too establishment for words. Alleyn noticed that he wore the old school tie and that behind him on the wall hung a framed photograph of Davidson's with the Boomer and himself standing together in the back row. He found this oddly, even painfully touching.

"Come and sit down," the Boomer fussed. "Where, now? Over here! Sit! sit! I couldn't be more delighted."

The steel-wool mat of hair was grey now and stood up high on his head like a toque. The huge frame was richly endowed with flesh and the eyes were very slightly bloodshot, but as if in double exposure Alleyn saw beyond this figure that of one ebony youth eating anchovy toast by a coal fire and saying: "You are my friend: I have had none, here, until now."

"How well you look," the President was saying. "And how little you have changed! You smoke? No? A cigar? A pipe? Yes? Presently, then. You are lunching with us of course. They have told you?"

"This is overwhelming," Alleyn said when he could get a word in. "In a minute I shall be forgetting my protocol."

"Now! Forget it now. We are alone. There is no need."

"My dear — "

"Boomer. Say it. How many years since I heard it!"

"I'm afraid I very nearly said it when I came in. My dear Boomer."

The sudden brilliance of a prodigal smile made its old impression. "That's nice," said the President quietly, and after rather a long silence: "I suppose I must ask you if this is a visit with an object. They were very non-committal at your end, you know. Just a message that you were arriving and would like to see me. Of course I was overjoyed."

Alleyn thought: "This is going to be tricky. One word in the wrong place and I not only boob my mission but very likely destroy a friendship and even set up a politically damaging mistrust."

He said: "I've come to ask you for something and I wish I hadn't got to bother you with it. I won't pretend that my chief didn't know of our past friendship — to me a most valued one. I won't pretend that he didn't imagine this friendship might have some influence. Of course he did. But it's because I think his request is reasonable and because I am very greatly concerned for your safety that I didn't jib at coming."

He had to wait a long time for the reaction. It was as if a blind had been pulled down. For the first time, seeing the slackened jaw and now the hooded, lacklustre eyes, he thought specifically: "I am speaking to a Negro."

"Ah!" said the President at last. "I had forgotten. You are a policeman."

"They say, don't they, if you want to keep a friend, never lend him money. I don't believe a word of it, but if you change the last four words into 'never use your friendship to further your business' I wouldn't quarrel with it. But I'm not doing exactly that. This is more complicated. My end object, believe it or not, sir, is the preservation of your most valuable life."

Another hazardous wait. Alleyn thought: "Yes, and that's exactly how you used to look when you thought somebody had been rude to you. Glazed."

But the glaze melted and the Boomer's nicest look, one of quiet amusement, supervened.

"Now, I understand," he said. "It is your watch-dogs, your Special Branch. 'Please make him see reason, this black man. Please ask him to let us disguise ourselves as waiters and pressmen and men-in-the-street and unimportant guests and be indistinguishable all over the shop.' I am right? That is the big request?"

"I'm afraid, you know, they'll do their thing in that respect as well as they can, however difficult it's made for them."

"Then why all thus fuss-pottery? How stupid!"

"They would all be much happier if you didn't do what you did, for instance, in Martinique."

"And what did I do in Martinique?"

"With the deepest respect: insisted on an extensive reduction of the safety precautions and escaped assassination by the skin of your teeth."

"I am a fatalist," the Boomer suddenly announced, and when Alleyn didn't answer: "My dear Rory, I see I must make myself understood. Myself. What I am. My philosophy. My code. You will listen?"

"Here we go," Alleyn thought. "He's changed less than one would have thought possible." And with profound misgivings he said: "But of course, sir. With all my ears."

As the exposition got under way it turned out to be an extension of the Boomer's schoolboy bloodymindedness seasoned with, and in part justified by, his undoubted genius for winning the trust and understanding of his own people. He enlarged, with intermittent gusts of Homeric laughter, upon the machinations of the Ng'ombwanan extreme right and left who had upon several occasions made determined efforts to secure his death and were, through some mysterious process of reason, thwarted by the Boomer's practice of exposing himself as an easy target. "They see," he explained, "that I am not, as we used to say at Davidson's, standing for their tedious codswallop."

"*Did* we say that at Davidson's?"

"Of course. You must remember. Constantly."

"So be it."

"It was a favourite expression of your own. *Yes,*" shouted the Boomer as Alleyn seemed inclined to demur, "always. We all picked it up from you."

"To return, if we may, to the matter in hand."

"*All* of us," the Boomer continued nostalgically. "You set the tone at Davidson's," and noticing perhaps a fleeting expression of horror on Alleyn's face, he leant forward and patted his knee. "But I digress," he said accurately. "Shall we return to our muttons?"

"Yes," Alleyn agreed with heartfelt relief. "Yes. Let's."

"Your turn," the Boomer generously conceded. "You were saying?"

"Have you thought—but of course you have—what would follow if you *were* knocked off?"

"As you say: of course I have. To quote your favourite dramatist (you see, I remember), 'the filthy clouds of heady murder, spoil and villainy' would follow," said the Boomer with relish. "To say the least of it," he added.

"Yes. Well now: the threat doesn't lie, as the Martinique show must have told you, solely within the boundaries of Ng'ombwana. In the Special Branch they know, and I mean they really *do* know, that there are lunatic fringes in London ready to go to all lengths. Some of them are composed of hangovers from certain disreputable backwaters of colonialism, others have a devouring hatred of your colour. Occasionally they are people with a real and bitter grievance that has grown monstrous in stagnation. You name it. But they're there, in considerable numbers, organized and ready to go."

"I am not alarmed," said the Boomer with maddening complacency. "No, but I mean it. In all truth I do not experience the least sensation of physical fear."

"I don't share your sense of immunity," Alleyn said. "In your boots I'd be in a muck sweat." It occurred to him that he had indeed abandoned the slightest nod in the direction of protocol. "But, all right. Accepting your fearlessness, may we return to the disastrous effect your death would have upon your country? 'The filthy clouds of heady murder' bit. Doesn't that thought at all predispose you to precaution?"

"But my dear fellow, you don't understand. I shall not be killed. I know it. Within myself, I know it. Assassination is not my destiny: it is as simple as that."

Alleyn opened his mouth and shut it again.

"As simple as that," the Boomer repeated. He opened his arms. "You see!" he cried triumphantly.

"Do you mean," Alleyn said very carefully, "that the bullet in Martinique and the spear in a remote village in Ng'ombwana and the one or two other pot-shots that have been loosed off at you from time to time were all predestined to miss?"

"Not only do I believe it but my people—*my people* know it in their souls. It is one of the reasons why I am re-elected unanimously to lead my country."

Alleyn did not ask if it was also one of the reasons why nobody, so far, had had the temerity to oppose him.

The Boomer reached out his great shapely hand and laid it on Alleyn's knee. "You were and you are my good friend," he said. "We were close at Davidson's. We remained close while I read my law and ate my dinners at the Temple. And we are close still. But this thing we discuss now belongs to my colour and my race. My Blackness. Please, do not try to understand: try only, my dear Rory, to accept."

To this large demand Alleyn could only reply: "It's *not* as simple as that."

"No? But why?"

"If I talk about my personal anxiety for you I'll be saying

in effect that I *don't* understand and *can't* accept, which is precisely what you do not want me to say. So I must fall back on my argument as an unwilling policeman with a difficult job. I'm not a member of the Special Branch but my colleagues in that department have asked me to do what I can, which looks a bit like damn-all. I do put it to you that their job, a highly specialized and immensely difficult one, is going to be a hundred percent more tricky if you decline to co-operate. If, for instance, on an impulse you change your route to some reception or walk out of your Embassy without telling anybody and take a constitutional in Kensington Gardens all by yourself. To put it baldly and brutally, if you are killed somebody in the Special Branch is going to be axed, the department's going to fall into general disrepute at the highest and lowest levels, and a centuries-old reputation of immunity from political assassination in England is gone for good. You see, I'm speaking not only for the police."

"The police, as servants of the people," the Boomer began, and then, Alleyn thought, very probably blushed.

"Were you going to say we ought to be kept in our place?" he mildly asked.

The Boomer began to walk about the room. Alleyn stood up.

"You have a talent," the Boomer suddenly complained, "for putting one in the wrong. I remember it of old. At Davidson's."

"What an insufferable boy I must have been," Alleyn remarked. He was getting very bored with Davidson's and really there seemed to be nothing more to say. "I have taken up too much of Your Excellency's time," he said. "Forgive me," and waited to be dismissed.

The Boomer looked mournfully upon him. "But you are lunching," he said. "We have agreed. It is arranged that you shall lunch."

"That's very kind, Your Excellency, but it's only eleven o'clock. Should I make myself scarce in the meantime?"

To his intense dismay he saw that the bloodshot eyes had filled with tears. The Boomer said, with immense dignity: "You have distressed me."

"I'm sorry."

"I was overjoyed at your coming. And now it is all spoilt and you call me Excellency."

Alleyn felt the corners of his mouth twitch and at the same time was moved by a contradictory sense of compassion. This emotion, he realized, was entirely inappropriate. He reminded himself that the President of Ng'ombwana was far from being a sort of inspired innocent. He was an astute, devoted and at times ruthless dictator with, it had to be added, a warm capacity for friendship. He was also extremely observant. "And funny," Alleyn thought, controlling himself. "It's quite maddening of him to be funny as well."

"Ah!" the President suddenly roared out. "You are laughing! My dear Rory, you are laughing," and himself broke into that Homeric gale of mirth. "No, it is too much! Admit! It is too ridiculous! What is it all about? Nothing! Listen, I will be a good boy. I will behave. Tell your solemn friends in your Special Branch that I will not run away when they hide themselves behind inadequate floral decorations and dress themselves up as nonentities with enormous boots. There now! You are pleased? Yes?"

"I'm enchanted," Alleyn said, "if you really mean it."

"But I do. I do. You shall see. I will be decorum itself. Within," he added, "the field of their naïve responsibilities. Within the U.K. in fact. O.K.? Yes?"

"Yes."

"And no more Excellencies. No? Not," the Boomer added without turning a hair, "when we are *tête-à-tête*. As at present."

"As at present," Alleyn agreed, and was instantly reinvolved in an exuberance of hand-shaking.

It was arranged that he would be driven around the city for an hour before joining the President for luncheon. The elegant A.D.C. reappeared. When they walked back along the corridor, Alleyn looked through its French windows into the acid-green garden. It was daubed superbly with flamboyants and veiled by a concourse of fountains. Through the iridescent rise and fall of water there could be perceived, at intervals, motionless figures in uniform.

Alleyn paused. "What a lovely garden," he said.

"Oh, yes?" said the A.D.C., smiling. Reflected colour and reflected lights from the garden glanced across his polished charcoal jaw and cheekbones. "You like it? The President likes it very much."

He made as if to move. "Shall we?" he suggested.

A file of soldiers, armed and splendidly uniformed, crossed the garden left, right, left, right, on the far side of the fountains. Distorted by prismatic cascades, they could dimly be seen to perform a correct routine with the men they had come to replace.

"The changing of the guard," Alleyn said lightly.

"Exactly. They are purely ceremonial troops."

"Yes?"

"As at your Buckingham Palace," explained the A.D.C.

"Quite," said Alleyn.

They passed through the grandiloquent hall and the picturesque guard at the entrance.

"Again," Alleyn ventured, "purely ceremonial?"

"Of course," said the A.D.C.

They were armed, Alleyn noticed, if not to the teeth, at least to the hips, with a useful-looking issue of sophisticated weapons. "Very smartly turned out," he said politely.

"The President will be pleased to know you think so," said

the A.D.C., and they walked into a standing bath of heat and dazzlement.

The Presidential Rolls, heavily garnished with the Ng'ombwanan arms, waited at the foot of the steps. Alleyn was ushered into the back seat while the A.D.C. sat in front. The car was air-conditioned and the windows shut and, thought Alleyn, "if ever I rode in a bullet-proof job, and today wouldn't be the first time, this is it." He wondered if, somewhere in Ng'ombwana security circles there was an influence a great deal more potent than that engendered by the industrious evocation of Davidson's.

They drove under the escort of two ultra-smart, lavishly accoutred motor-cyclists. "Skinheads, bikies, traffic cops, armed escorts," he speculated, "wherever they belch and rev and bound, what gives the species its peculiar air of menacing vulgarity."

The car swept through crowded, mercilessly glaring streets. Alleyn found something to say about huge white monstrosities – a Palace of Culture, a Palace of Justice, a Hall of Civic Authority, a Free Library. The A.D.C. received his civilities with perfect complacency.

"Yes," he agreed. "They are very fine. All new. All since the Presidency. It is very remarkable."

The traffic was heavy, but it was noticeable that it opened before their escort as the Red Sea before Moses. They were stared at, but from a distance. Once, as they made a right-hand turn and were momentarily checked by an oncoming car, the A.D.C., without turning his head, said something to their chauffeur, that made him wince.

When Alleyn, who was married to a painter, looked at the current scene, wherever it might be, he did so with double vision. As a stringently trained policeman, he watched automatically for idiosyncrasies. As a man very sensitively tuned to his wife's way of seeing, he searched for consonancies. As now, when confronted by a concourse of black heads that bobbed, shifted, clustered and dispersed against that inexorable glare, he saw this scene as his wife might like to paint it. He noticed that, in common with many of the older buildings, one in particular was in process of being newly painted. The ghost of a former legend showed faintly through the mask—SANS RIT IMPO T NG TR DI G CO. He saw a shifting, colourful group on the steps of this building and thought how, with simplification, rearrangement and selection, Troy would endow them with rhythmic significance. She would find, he thought, a focal point, some figure to which the others were subservient, a figure of the first importance.

And then, even as this notion visited him, the arrangement occurred. The figures re-formed like fragments in a kaleidoscope and there was the focal point, a solitary man, inescapable because quite still, a grotesquely fat man, with long blond hair, wearing white clothes. A white man.

The white man stared into the car. He was at least fifty yards away, but for Alleyn it might have been so many feet. They looked into each other's faces and the policeman said to himself: "That chap's worth watching. That chap's a villain."

Click, went the kaleidoscope. The fragments slid apart and together. A stream of figures erupted from the interior, poured down the steps and dispersed. When the gap was uncovered the white man had gone.

IV

"It's like this, sir," Chubb had said rapidly. "Seeing that No. 1 isn't a full-time place, being there's the two of us, we been in the habit of helping out on a part-time basis elsewhere in the vicinity. Like, Mrs. Chubb does an hour every other day for Mr. Sheridan in the basement and I go in to the Colonel's – that's Colonel and Mrs. Montfort in the Place – for two hours of a Friday afternoon and every other Sunday evening we baby-sit at 17, the Walk. And – "

"Yes. I see," said Mr. Whipplestone, stemming the tide.

"You won't find anything scamped or overlooked, sir," Mrs. Chubb intervened. "We give satisfaction, sir, in all quarters, really we do. It's just An Arrangement, like."

"And naturally, sir, the wages are adjusted according. We wouldn't expect anything else, sir, would we?"

They had stood side by side with round anxious faces, wide-open eyes and gabbling mouths. Mr. Whipplestone had listened with his built-in air of attentive detachment and had finally agreed to the proposal that the Chubbs were all his for six mornings, breakfast, luncheon and dinner: that provided the house was well kept up they might attend upon Mr. Sheridan or anybody else at their own and his convenience, that on Fridays Mr. Whipplestone would lunch and dine at his club or elsewhere, and that, as the Chubbs put it, the wages were "adjusted according."

"Most of the residents," explained Chubb when they had completed these arrangements and got down to details, "has accounts at the Napoli, sir. You may prefer to deal elsewhere."

"And for butchery," said Mrs. Chubb, "there's – "

They expounded upon the amenities in the Capricorns.

Mr. Whipplestone said: "That all sounds quite satisfactory. Do you know, I think I'll make a tour of inspection." And he did so.

The Napoli is one of the four little shops in Capricorn Mews. It is "shop" reduced to its absolute minimum: a slit of a place where the customers stand in single file and then only eight at a squeeze. The proprietors are an Italian couple, he dark and anxious, she dark and buxom and jolly. Their assistant is a large and facetious Cockney.

It is a nice shop. They cure their own bacon and hams.

Mr. Pirelli makes his own pâté and a particularly good terrine. The cheeses are excellent. Bottles of dry Orvieto are slung overhead and other Italian wines crowd together inside the door. There are numerous exotics in line on the shelves. The Capricornians like to tell each other that the Napoli is "a pocket Fortnum's." Dogs are not allowed, but a row of hooks has been thoughtfully provided in the outside wall and on most mornings there is a convocation of mixed dogs attached to them.

Mr. Whipplestone skirted the dogs, entered the shop and bought a promising piece of Camembert. The empurpled army man, always immaculately dressed and gloved, whom he had seen in the street, was in the shop and was addressed by Mr. Pirelli as "Colonel." (Montfort? wondered Mr. Whipplestone.) The Colonel's lady was with him. An alarming lady, the fastidious Mr. Whipplestone thought, with the face of a dissolute clown and wildly overdressed. They both wore an air of overdone circumspection that Mr. Whipplestone associated with the hazards of a formidable hangover. The lady stood stock-still and bolt upright behind her husband, but as Mr. Whipplestone approached the counter she sidestepped and barged into him, driving her pin heel into his instep.

"I beg your pardon," he cried in pain and lifted his hat.

"Not a bit," she said thickly and gave him what could only be described as a half-awakened leer.

Her husband turned and seemed to sense a nced for conversation. "Not much room for manoeuvrin'," he shouted. "What."

"Quite," said Mr. Whipplestone.

He opened an account, left the shop, and continued his explorations.

He arrived at the scene of his encounter with the little black cat. A large van was backing into the garage. Out of the tail of his eye he thought he saw briefly a darting shadow, and when the van stopped he could have fancied, almost, that he heard a faint, plaintive cry. But there was nothing to support these impressions and he hurried on, oddly perturbed.

At the far end of the Mews, by the entrance to the passageway, is a strange little cavern, once a stable, which has been converted into a shop. Here at this period a baleful fat lady made images of pigs either as doorstops or with roses and daisies on their sides and a hole in their backs for cream or flowers as the fancy might take you. They varied in size but never in design. The kiln was at the back of the cavern, and as Mr. Whipplestone looked in the fat lady stared at him out of her shadows. Across the window was the legend THE PIGGIE POTTERIE, and above the entrance a notice: X. & K. SANSKRIT.

"Commercial candour!" thought Mr. Whipplestone, cracking a little joke for himself. To what nationality, he wondered, could someone called Sanskrit possibly belong? Indian, he supposed. And X? Xavier perhaps. "To make a living," he wondered, "out of the endless reduplication of pottery pigs? And why on earth does this extraordinary name seem to ring a bell?"

Conscious that the fat lady in the shadows still looked at him, he moved on into Capricorn Place and made his way to a rosy brick wall at the far end. Through an opening in this wall one leaves the Capricorns and arrives at a narrow lane passing behind the Basilica precincts and an alleyway ending in the full grandeur of Palace Park Gardens. Here the Ng'ombwana Embassy rears its important front.

Mr. Whipplestone contemplated the pink flag with its insignia of green spear and sun and mentally apostrophized it. "Yes," he thought, "there you are, and for my part, long may you stay there." And he remembered that at some as yet unspecified time but, unless something awful intervened, in the near future, the Ambassador and all his minions would be in no end of a tig getting ready for the state visit of their dynamic President and spotting assassins behind every plane tree. The Special Branch would be raising their punctual plaint and at the F.O., he thought, they'll be dusting down their imperturbability. "I'm out of it all and (I'd better make up my mind to it) delighted to be so. I suppose," he added. Conscious of a slight pang, he made his way home.

II

Lucy Lockett

Mr. Whipplestone had been in residence for over a month. He was thoroughly settled, comfortable and contented and yet by no means lethargically so. On the contrary he had been stimulated by his change of scene and felt lively. Already he was tuned in to life in the Capricorns. "Really," he wrote in his diary, "it's like a little village set down in the middle of London. One runs repeatedly into the same people in the shops. On warm evenings the inhabitants stroll about the streets. One may drop in at the Sun in Splendour, where one finds, I'm happy to say, a very respectable, nay, quite a distinguished white port."

He had been in the habit of keeping a diary for some years. Until now it had confined itself to the dry relation of facts with occasionally a touch of the irony for which he had been slightly famous at the F.O. Now, under the stimulus of his new environment, the journal expanded and became at times almost skittish.

The evening was very warm. His window was open and the curtains, too. An afterglow had suffused the plane trees and kindled the dome of the Basilica but was now faded. There was a smell of freshly watered gardens in the air and the pleasant sound of footfalls mingling with quiet voices drifted in at the open window. The muted roar of Baronsgate seemed distant, a mere background to quietude.

After a time he laid down his pen, let fall his eyeglass, and looked with pleasure at his room. Everything had fitted to a miracle. Under the care of the Chubbs his nice old bits and pieces positively sparkled. The crimson goblet glowed in the window and his Agatha Troy seemed to generate a light of its own.

"How nice everything is," thought Mr. Whipplestone.

It was very quiet in his house. The Chubbs, he fancied, were out for the evening, but they were habitually so unobtrusive in their comings and goings that one was unaware of them. While he was writing, Mr. Whipplestone had been conscious of visitors descending the iron steps into the area. Mr. Sheridan was at home and receiving in the basement flat.

He switched off his desk lamp, got up to stretch his legs, and moved over to the bow window. The only people who were about were a man and a woman coming towards him in the darkening Square. They moved into a pool of light from the open doorway of the Sun in Splendour and momentarily he got a clearer look at them. They were both fat and there was something about the woman that was familiar.

They came on towards him into and out from the shadow of the plane trees. On a ridiculous impulse, as if he had been caught spying, Mr. Whipplestone backed away from his window. The woman seemed to stare into his eyes: an absurd notion since she couldn't possibly see him.

Now he knew who she was: Mrs. or Miss X. Sanskrit. And her companion? Brother or spouse? Brother, almost certainly. The pig-potters.

Now they were out of the shadow and crossed the Walk in full light straight at him. And he saw they were truly awful.

It wasn't that they were lard-fat, both of them, so fat that they might have sat to each other as models for their wares, or that they were outrageously got up. No clothes, it might be argued in these permissive days, could achieve outrageousness. It wasn't that the man wore a bracelet and an anklet and a necklace and earrings or that what hair he had fell like pond-weed from an embroidered head-band. It wasn't even that she (fifty if a day, thought Mr. Whipplestone) wore vast black leather hot-pants, a black fringed tunic and black boots. Monstrous though these grotesqueries undoubtedly were, they were as nothing compared with the eyes and mouths of the Sanskrits, which were, Mr. Whipplestone now saw with something like panic, equally heavily made-up.

"They shouldn't be here," he thought, confusedly protecting the normality of the Capricorns. "People like that. They ought to be in Chelsea. Or somewhere."

They had crossed the Walk. They had approached his house. He backed further away. The area gate clicked and clanged, they descended the iron steps. He heard the basement flat bell. He heard Mr. Sheridan's voice. They had been admitted.

"No, really!" Mr. Whipplestone thought in the language of his youth. "Too much! And he seemed perfectly presentable." He was thinking of his brief encounter with Mr. Sheridan.

He settled down to a book. At least it was not a noisy party down there. One could hear little or nothing. Perhaps, he speculated, the Sanskrits were mediums. Perhaps Mr. Sheridan dabbled in spiritism and belonged to a "circle." They looked like that. Or worse. He dismissed the whole thing and returned to the autobiography of a former chief of his department. It was not absorbing. The blurb made a great fuss about a ten-year interval imposed between the author's death and publication. Why, God knew, thought Mr. Whipplestone, since the crashing old bore could have nothing to disclose that would unsettle the composure of the most susceptible of vestal virgins.

His attention wandered. He became conscious of an uneasiness at the back of his mind: an uneasiness occasioned by a sound, by something he would rather not hear, by something that was connected with anxiety and perturbation. By a cat mewing in the street.

Pah! he thought, as far as one can think "pah." Cats abounded in London streets. He had seen any number of them in the Capricorns, pampered pet-cats. There was an enormous tortoiseshell at the Sun in Splendour and a supercilious white affair at the Napoli. Cats.

It had come a great deal nearer. It was now very close indeed. Just outside, one would suppose, and not moving on. Sitting on the pavement, he dared say, and staring at his house. At him, even. And mewing. Persistently. He made a determined effort to ignore it. He returned to his book. He thought of turning on his radio loud, to drown it. The cries intensified. From being distant and intermittent they were now immediate and persistent.

"I shall not look out of the window," he decided in a fluster. "It would only see me."

"Damnation!" he cried three minutes later. "How dare people lock out their cats! I'll complain to someone."

Another three minutes and he did, against every fibre of disinclination in his body, look out of the window. He saw nothing. The feline lamentations were close enough to drive him dotty. On the steps: that's where they were. On the flight of steps leading up to his front door. "No!" he thought. "No, really this is not good enough. This must be stopped. Before we know where we are—"

Before he knew where he was, he was in his little hall and manipulating his double lock. The chain was disconnected on account of the Chubbs, but he opened the door a mere crack and had no sooner done so than something—a shadow, a meagre atomy—darted across his instep.

Mr. Whipplestone became dramatic. He slammed his door to, leant against it and faced his intruder.

He had known it all along. History, if you could call an incident of not much more than a month ago, history was repeating itself. In the wretched shape of a small black cat: the same cat but now quite dreadfully emaciated, its eyes clouded, its fur staring. It sat before him and again opened its pink mouth in now soundless mews. Mr. Whipplestone could only gaze at it in horror. Its haunches quivered and, as it had done when last they met, it leapt up to his chest.

As his hands closed round it he wondered that it had had the strength to jump. It purred and its heart knocked at his fingers.

"This is too much," he repeated and carried it into his drawing-room. "It will die, I daresay," he said, "and how perfectly beastly that will be."

After some agitated thought he carried it into the kitchen and, still holding it, took milk from the refrigerator, poured some into a saucer, added hot water from the tap, and set it on the floor and the little cat beside it. At first he thought she would pay no attention—he was persuaded the creature was a female—her eyes being half-closed and her chin on the floor. He edged the saucer nearer. Her whiskers trembled. So suddenly that he quite jumped, she was lapping, avidly, frantically as if driven by some desperate little engine. Once she looked up at him.

Twice he replenished the saucer. The second time she did not finish the offering. She raised her milky chin, stared at him, made one or two shaky attempts to wash her face, and suddenly collapsed on his foot and went to sleep.

Some time later there were sounds of departure from the basement flat. Soon after this the Chubbs effected their usual discreet entry. Mr. Whipplestone heard them put up the chain on the front door. The notion came to him that perhaps they had been "doing for" Mr. Sheridan at his party.

"Er – is that you, Chubb?" he called out.

Chubb opened the door and presented himself, apple-cheeked, on the threshold with his wife behind him. It struck Mr. Whipplestone that they seemed uncomfortable.

"Look," he invited, "at this."

Chubb had done so, already. The cat lay like a shadow across Mr. Whipplestone's knees.

"A cat, sir," said Chubb tentatively.

"A stray. I've seen it before."

From behind her husband Mrs. Chubb said: "Nothing of it, sir, is there? It don't look healthy, do it?"

"It was starving."

Mrs. Chubb clicked her tongue.

Chubb said: "Very quiet, sir, isn't it? It hasn't passed away, has it?"

"It's asleep. It's had half a bottle of milk."

"Well, excuse me, sir," Mrs. Chubb said, "but I don't think you ought to handle it. You don't know where it's been, do you, sir?"

"No," said Mr. Whipplestone, and added with a curious inflection in his voice, "I only know where it is."

"Would you like Chubb to dispose of it, sir?"

This suggestion he found perfectly hateful, but he threw out as airily as he could: "Oh, I don't think so. I'll do something about it myself in the morning. Ring up the R.S.P.C.A."

"I daresay if you was to put it out, sir, it'd wander off where it come from."

"Or," suggested Chubb, "I could put it in the garden at the back, sir. For the night, like."

"Yes," Mr. Whipplestone gabbled, "thank you. Never mind. I'll think of something. Thank you."

"Thank you, sir," they said, meaninglessly.

Because they didn't immediately make a move and because he was in a tizzy, Mr. Whipplestone to his own surprise said, "Pleasant evening?"

They didn't answer. He glanced up and found they stared at him.

"Yes, thank you, sir," they said.

"Good!" he cried with a phony heartiness that horrified him. "Good! Good night, Chubb. Good night, Mrs. Chubb."

When they had gone he stroked the cat. She opened her clouded eyes—but weren't they less clouded, now?—gave a faint questioning trill and went to sleep again.

The Chubbs had gone into the kitchen. He felt sure they opened the refrigerator and he distinctly heard them turn on a tap. Washing the saucer, he thought guiltily.

He waited until they had retired upstairs and then himself sneaked into the kitchen with the cat. He had remembered that he had not eaten all the poached scollop Mrs. Chubb gave him for dinner.

The cat woke up and ate quite a lot of scollop.

Entry into his back garden was effected by a door at the end of the passage and down a precipitous flight of steps. It was difficult, holding the cat, and he made rather a noisy descent but was aided by a glow of light from behind the blinds that masked Mr. Sheridan's basement windows. This enabled him to find a patch of unplanted earth against the brick wall at the rear of the garden. He placed the cat upon it.

He had thought she might bolt into the shadows and somehow escape, but no: after a considerable wait she became industrious. Mr. Whipplestone tactfully turned his back.

He was being watched from the basement through an opening between the blind and the window frame.

The shadowy form was almost certainly that of Mr. Sheridan and almost certainly he had hooked himself a peephole and had released it as Mr. Whipplestone turned. The shadowy form retreated.

At the same time a slight noise above his head caused Mr. Whipplestone to look up to the top storey of his house. He was just in time to see the Chubbs' bedroom window being closed. There was, of course, no reason to suppose they also had been watching him.

"I must be getting fanciful," he thought.

A faint rhythmic scuffling redirected his attention to the cat. With her ears laid back and with a zealous concentration that spoke volumes for her recuperative powers, she was tidying up. This exercise was followed by a scrupulous personal toilette, which done she blinked at Mr. Whipplestone and pushed her nut-like head against his ankle.

He picked her up and returned indoors.

II

The fashionable and grossly expensive pet-shop round the corner in Baronsgate had a consulting-room, visited on Wednesday mornings by a veterinary surgeon. Mr. Whipplestone had observed their notice to this effect and the next morning, it being a Wednesday, he took the cat to be vetted. His manner of conveying his intention to the Chubbs was as guarded and non-committal as forty years' experience in diplomacy could make it. Indeed, in a less rarified atmosphere it might almost have been described as furtive.

He gave it out that he was "taking that animal to be attended to." When the Chubbs jumped to the conclusion that this was an euphemism for "put down" he did not correct them. Nor did he think it necessary to mention that the animal had spent the night on his bed. She had roused him at daybreak by touching his face with her paw. When he opened his eyes she had flirted with him, rolling on her side and looking at him from under her arm. And when Chubb came in with his early morning tray, Mr. Whipplestone had contrived to throw his eiderdown over her and later on had treated her to a saucer of milk. He came downstairs with her under the *Times*, chose his moment to let her out by the back door into the garden, and presently called Mrs. Chubb's attention to her. She was demanding vigorously to be let in.

So now he sat on a padded bench in a minute waiting-room, cheek-by-jowl with several Baronsgate ladies, each of whom had a dog in tow. One of them, the one next to Mr. Whipplestone, was the lady who trod on his foot in the Napoli, Mrs. Montfort as he subsequently discovered, the Colonel's lady. They said good-morning to each other when they encountered, and did so now. By and large Mr. Whipplestone thought her pretty awful, though not as awful as the pig-pottery lady of last night. Mrs. Montfort carried on her over-dressed lap a Pekinese, which after a single contemptuous look turned its back on Mr. Whipplestone's cat, who stared through it.

He was acutely conscious that he presented a farcical appearance. The only container that could be found by the Chubbs was a disused birdcage, the home of their parrot, lately deceased. The little cat looked outraged sitting in it, and Mr. Whipplestone looked silly nursing it and wearing his eyeglass. Several of the ladies exchanged amused glances.

"What," asked the ultra-smart surgery attendant, notebook in hand, "is pussy's name?"

He felt that if he said "I don't know" or "It hasn't got one" he would put himself at a disadvantage with these women. "Lucy," he said loudly, and added as an afterthought, "Lockett."

"I see!" she said brightly and noted it down. "You haven't an appointment, have you?"

"I'm afraid not."

"Lucy won't have long to wait," she smiled, and passed on.

A woman with a huge angry short-haired tabby in her arms came through from the surgery.

The newly named Lucy's fur rose. She made a noise that

suggested she had come to the boil. The tabby suddenly let out a yell. Dogs made ambiguous comments in their throats.

"Oh Lor'!" said the newcomer. She grinned at Mr. Whipplestone. "Better make ourselves scarce," she said, and to her indignant cat: "Shut up, Bardolph, don't be an ass."

When they had gone Lucy went to sleep and Mrs. Montfort said: "Is your cat very ill?"

"No!" Mr. Whipplestone quite shouted and then explained that Lucy was a stray starveling.

"Sweet of you," she said, "to care. People are so awful about animals. It makes me quite ill. I'm like that." She turned her gaze upon him. "Chrissy Montfort. My husband's the warrior with the purple face. He's called Colonel Montfort."

Cornered, Mr. Whipplestone murmured his own name.

Mrs. Montfort smelt of very heavy scent and gin. "I know," she said archly. "You're our new boy, aren't you? At No. 1, the Walk? We have a piece of your Chubb on Fridays."

Mr. Whipplestone, whose manners were impeccable, bowed as far as the birdcage would permit.

Mrs. Montfort was smiling into his face. She had laid her gloved hand on the cage. The door behind him had opened. Her smile became fixed as if pinned up at the corners. She withdrew her hand and looked straight in front of her.

From the street there had entered a totally black man in livery with a white Afghan hound on a scarlet leash. The man paused and glanced round. There was an empty place on the other side of Mrs. Montfort. Still looking straight in front of her, she moved far enough along the seat to leave insufficient room on either side of her. Mr. Whipplestone instantly widened the distance between them and with a gesture invited the man to sit down. The man said, "Thank you, sir," and remained where he was, not looking at Mrs. Montfort. The hound advanced his nose towards the cage. Lucy did not wake.

"I wouldn't come too close if I were you, old boy," Mr.

Whipplestone said. The Afghan wagged his tail and Mr. Whipplestone patted him. "I know you," he said, "you're the Embassy dog, aren't you. You're Ahman." He gave the man a pleasant look and the man made a slight bow.

"Lucy Lockett?" said the attendant, brightly emerging. "We're all ready for her."

The consultation was brief but conclusive. Lucy Lockett was about seven months old and her temperature was normal, she was innocent of mange, ringworm or parasites, she was extremely undernourished and therefore in shocking condition. Here the vet hesitated. "There are scars," he said, "and there's been a fractured rib that has looked after itself. She's been badly neglected—I think she may have been actively ill-treated." And catching sight of Mr. Whipplestone's horrified face he added cheerfully: "Nothing that pills and good food won't put right." He said she had been spayed. She was half Siamese and half God knew what, the vet said, turning back her fur and handling her this way and that. He laughed at the white end to her tail and gave her an injection.

She submitted to these indignities with utter detachment, but when at liberty leapt into her protector's embrace and performed her now familiar act of jamming her head under his jacket and lying next his heart.

"Taken to you," said the vet. "They've got a sense of gratitude, cats have. Especially the females."

"I don't know anything about them," said Mr. Whipplestone in a hurry.

Motivated by sales-talk and embarrassment, he bought on his way out a cat bed-basket, a china dish labelled "Kit-bits," a comb and brush and a collar for which he ordered a metal tab with a legend: "Lucy Lockett. 1, Capricorn Walk" and his telephone number. The shop assistant showed him a little red cat-harness for walking out and told him that with patience cats could be induced to co-operate. She put Lucy into it and the result was fetching enough for Mr. Whipplestone to keep it.

He left the parrot cage behind to be called for, and heavily laden, with Lucy again in retreat under his coat, walked quickly home to deploy his diplomatic resources upon the Chubbs, little knowing that he carried his destiny under his jacket.

III

"This is perfectly delightful," said Mr. Whipplestone, turning from his host to his hostess with the slight inclinations of his head and shoulders that had long been occupational mannerisms. "I *am* so enjoying myself."

"Fill up your glass," Alleyn said. "I did warn you that it was an invitation with an ulterior motive, didn't I?"

"I am fully prepared: charmingly so. A superb port."

"I'll leave you with it," Troy suggested.

"No, don't," Alleyn said. "We'll send you packing if anything v.s. and c. crops up. Otherwise it's nice to have you. Isn't it, Whipplestone?"

Mr. Whipplestone embarked upon a speech about his good fortune in being able to contemplate a Troy above his fireplace every evening and now having the pleasure of contemplating the artist herself at her own fireside. He got a little bogged down but fetched up bravely.

"And when," he asked, coming to his own rescue, "are we to embark upon the ulterior motive?"

Alleyn said, "Let's make a move. This is liable to take time."

At Troy's suggestion they carried their port from the house into her detached studio and settled themselves in front of long windows overlooking a twilit London garden.

"I want," Alleyn said, "to pick your brains a little. Aren't you by way of being an expert on Ng'ombwana?"

"Ng'ombwana? I? That's putting it much too high, my dear man. I was there for three years in my youth."

"I thought that quite recently when it was getting its independence – ?"

"They sent me out there, yes. During the exploratory period – mainly because I speak the language, I suppose. Having rather made it my thing in a mild way."

"And you have kept it up?"

"Again, in a mild way: oh, yes. Yes." He looked across the top of his glass at Alleyn. "You haven't gone over to the Special Branch, surely?"

"That's a very crisp bit of instant deduction. No, I haven't. But you may say they've unofficially roped me in for the occasion."

"Of the forthcoming visit?"

"Yes, blast them. Security."

"I see. Difficult. By the way, you must have been the President's contemporary at – " Mr. Whipplestone stopped short. "Is it hoped that you may introduce the personal note?"

"You *are* quick!" Troy said, and he gave a gratified little cackle.

Alleyn said: "I saw him three weeks ago."

"In Ng'ombwana?"

"Yes. Coming the old-boy network like nobody's business."

"Get anywhere?"

"Not so that you'd notice – no, that's not fair. He did undertake not to cut up rough about our precautions but exactly what he meant by that is his secret. I daresay that in the upshot he'll be a bloody nuisance."

"Well?" asked Mr. Whipplestone, leaning back and swinging his eyeglass in what Alleyn felt had been his cross-diplomatic-desk gesture for half a lifetime. "Well, my dear Roderick?"

"Where do you come in?"

"Quite."

"I'd be grateful if you'd—what's the current jargon?—fill me in on the general Ng'ombwanan background. From your own point of view. For instance, how many people would you say have cause to wish the Boomer dead?"

"The Boomer?"

"As he incessantly reminded me, that was His Excellency's schoolboy nickname."

"An appropriate one. In general terms, I should say some two hundred thousand persons, at least."

"Good Lord!" Troy exclaimed.

"Could you," asked her husband, "do a bit of name-dropping?"

"Not really. Not specifically. But again in general terms—well, it's the usual pattern throughout the new African independencies. First of all there are those Ng'ombwanan political opponents whom the President succeeded in breaking, the survivors of whom are either in prison or in this country waiting for his overthrow or assassination."

"The Special Branch flatters itself it's got a pretty comprehensive list in that category."

"I daresay," said Mr. Whipplestone drily. "So did we until one fine day in Martinique a hitherto completely unknown person with a phoney British passport fired a revolver at the President, missed, and was more successful with a second shot at himself. He had no record and his true identity was never established."

"I reminded the Boomer of that incident."

Mr. Whipplestone said archly to Troy: "You know, he's much more fully informed than I am. What's he up to?"

"I can't imagine, but do go on. I, at least, know nothing."

"Well. Among these African enemies, of course, are the extremists who disliked his early moderation and especially his refusal at the outset to sack all his European advisers and officials in one fell swoop. So you get pockets of anti-white terrorists who campaigned for independence but are now prepared to face about and destroy the government they helped to create. Their followers are an unknown quantity but undoubtedly numerous. But you know all this, my dear fellow."

"He's sacking more and more whites now, though, isn't he? However unwillingly?"

"He's been forced to do so by the extreme elements."

"So," Alleyn said, "the familiar, perhaps the inevitable pattern emerges. The nationalization of all foreign enterprise and the appropriation of properties held by European and Asian colonists. Among whom we find the bitterest possible resentment."

"Indeed. And with some reason. Many of them have been ruined. Among the older groups the effect has been completely disastrous. Their entire way of life has disintegrated and they are totally unfitted for any other." Mr. Whipplestone rubbed his nose. "I must say," he added, "however improperly, that some of them are *not* likeable individuals."

Troy asked: "Why's he coming here? The Boomer, I mean?"

"Ostensibly, to discuss with Whitehall his country's needs for development."

"And Whitehall," Alleyn said, "professes its high delight while the Special Branch turns green with forebodings."

"Mr. Whipplestone, you said 'ostensibly,'" Troy pointed out.

"Did I, Mrs. Rory?—Yes. Yes, well it has been rumoured through tolerably reliable sources that the President hopes to negotiate with rival groups to take over the oil and copper resources from the dispossessed, who have, of course, developed them at enormous cost."

"Here we go again!" said Alleyn.

"I don't suggest," Mr. Whipplestone mildly added, "that Lord Karnley or Sir Julian Raphael or any of their associates are likely to instigate a lethal assault upon the President."

"Good!"

"But of course behind those august personages is a host of embittered shareholders, executives and employees."

"Among whom might be found the odd cloak-and-dagger merchant. And apart from all these more or less motivated persons," Alleyn said, "there are the ones policemen like least: the fanatics. The haters of black pigmentation, the lonely woman who dreams about a black rapist, the man who builds Anti-Christ in a black image or who reads a threat to his livelihood in every black neighbour. Or for whom the commonplace phrases – black outlook, black record, as black as it's painted, black villainy, and all the rest of them – have an absolute reference. Black is bad. Finish."

"And the Black Power lot," Troy said, "are doing as much for white, aren't they? The war of the images."

Mr. Whipplestone made a not too uncomfortable little groaning noise and returned to his port.

"I wonder," Alleyn said, "I do wonder how much of that absolute antagonism the old Boomer nurses in his sooty bosom."

"None for you, anyway," Troy said, and when he didn't answer, "surely?"

"My dear Alleyn, I understood he professes the utmost *camaraderie.*"

"Oh, yes! Yes, he does. He lays it on with a trowel. Do you know, I'd be awfully sorry to think the trowel-work overlaid an inimical understructure. Silly, isn't it?"

"It is the greatest mistake," Mr. Whipplestone pronounced, "to make assumptions about relationships that are not clearly defined."

"And what relationship is ever that?"

"Well! Perhaps not. We do what we can with treaties and agreements but perhaps not."

"He did try," Alleyn said. "He did in the first instance try to set up some kind of multi-racial community. He thought it would work."

"Did you discuss that?" Troy asked.

"Not a word. It wouldn't have done. My job was too tricky. Do you know, I got the impression that at least part of his exuberant welcome was inspired by a—well, by a wish to compensate for the ongoings of the new regime."

"It might be so," Mr. Whipplestone conceded. "Who can say?"

Alleyn took a folded paper from his breast pocket. "The Special Branch has given me a list of commercial and professional firms and individuals to be kicked out of Ng'ombwana, with notes on anything in their history that might look at all suspicious." He glanced at the paper. "Does the name Sanskrit mean anything at all to you?" he asked. "X. and K. Sanskrit to be exact. My dear man, what *is* the matter?"

Mr. Whipplestone had shouted inarticulately, laid down his glass, clapped his hands and slapped his forehead.

"Eureka!" he cried stylishly. "I have it! At last. At last!"

"Jolly for you," said Alleyn. "I'm delighted to hear it. What had escaped you?"

"*Sanskrit, Importing and Trading Company, Ng'ombwana.*"

"That's it. Or was it."

"In Edward VIIth Avenue."

"Certainly. I saw it there, only they call it something else now. And Sanskrit has been kicked out. Why are you so excited?"

"Because I saw him last night."

"*You did!*"

"Well, it must have been. They are as like as two disgusting pins."

"They?" Alleyn repeated, gazing at his wife, who briefly crossed her eyes at him.

"How could I have forgotten!" exclaimed Mr. Whipplestone

rhetorically. "I passed those premises every day of my time in Ng'ombwana."

"I clearly see that I mustn't interrupt you."

"My dear Mrs. Roderick, my dear Roderick, do please forgive me," begged Mr. Whipplestone, turning pink. "I must explain myself: too gauche and peculiar. But you see—"

And explain himself he did, pig-pottery and all, with the precision that had eluded him at the first disclosure. "Admit!" he cried when he had finished. "It *is* a singular coincidence, now isn't it?"

"It's all of that," Alleyn said. "Would you like to hear what the Special Branch have got to say about the man—K. Sanskrit?"

"Indeed I would."

"Here goes, then. This information, by the way, is a digest one of Fred Gibson's chaps got from the Criminal Record Office. 'Sanskrit. Kenneth, for Heaven's sake. Age: approx. fifty-eight. Height: five foot ten. Weight: sixteen stone four. Very obese. Blond. Long hair. Dress: eccentric, ultra-modern. Bracelets. Anklet. Necklace. Wears make-up. Probably homosexual. One ring through pierced lobe. Origin: uncertain. Said to be Dutch. Name possibly assumed or corruption of a foreign name. Convicted of fraudulent practices involving the occult, fortune-telling, etc., London, 1940. Served three months sentence for connection with drug traffic, 1942. Since 1950 importer of ceramics, jewellery and fancy goods into Ng'ombwana. Large, profitable concern. Owned blocks of flats and offices now possessed by Ng'ombwanan interests. Strong supporter of apartheid. Known to associate with anti-black and African extremists. Only traceable relative: sister, with whom he is now in partnership, The Piggie Potterie, 12, Capricorn Mews, S.W.3"

"There you are!" said Mr. Whipplestone, spreading out his hands.

"Yes. There we are and not very far on. There's no specific

reason to suppose Sanskrit constitutes a threat to the safety of the President. And that goes for any of the other names on the list. Have a look at it. Does it ring any more bells? Any more coincidences?"

Mr. Whipplestone screwed in his eyeglass and had a look. "Yes, yes, yes," he said drily. "One recognizes the disillusioned African element. *And* the dispossessed. I can add nothing. I'm afraid, my dear fellow, that apart from the odd circumstance of one of your remote possibilities being a neighbour of mine, I am of no use to you. And none in that respect, either, if one comes to think of it. A broken reed," sighed Mr. Whipplestone, "I fear, a broken reed."

"Oh," Alleyn said lightly, "you never know, do you? By the way the Ng'ombwanan Embassy is in your part of the world, isn't it?"

"Yes, indeed. I run into old Karumba sometimes. Their Ambassador. We take our constitutionals at the same hour. Nice old boy."

"Worried?"

"Hideously, I should have thought."

"You'd have been right. He's in a flat spin and treating the S.B. to a hell of a work-out. And what's more he's switched over to me. Never mind about security not being my proper pigeon. He should worry! I know the Boomer and that's enough. He wants me to teach the S.B. its own business. Imagine! If he had his wish there'd be total alarm devices in every ornamental urn and a security man under the Boomer's bed. I must say I don't blame him. He's giving a reception. I suppose you've been invited?"

"I have, yes. And you?"

"In my reluctant role as the Boomer's old school chum. And Troy, of course," Alleyn said, putting his hand briefly on hers.

Then followed rather a long pause.

"Of course," Mr. Whipplestone said, at last, "these things don't happen in England. At receptions and so on. Madmen, at large in kitchens or wherever it was."

"Or at upstairs windows in warehouses?"

"Quite."

The telephone rang and Troy went out of the room to answer it.

"I ought to forbear," Alleyn said, "from offering the maddening observation that there's always a first time."

"Oh nonsense!" flustered Mr. Whipplestone. "Nonsense, my dear fellow! Really! Nonsense! Well," he added uneasily, "one *says* that."

"Let's hope one's right."

Troy came back. "The Ng'ombwanan Ambassador," she said, "would like a word with you, darling."

"God bless his woolly grey head," Alleyn muttered and cast up his eyes. He went to the door but checked. "Another Sanskrit coincidence for you, Sam. I rather think I saw him, too, three weeks ago in Ng'ombwana, outside his erstwhile emporium, complete with anklet and earring. The one and only Sanskrit or I'm a displaced Dutchman with beads and blond curls."

IV

The Chubbs raised no particular objection to Lucy—"so long as it's not unhealthy, sir," Mrs. Chubb said, "I don't mind. Keep the mice out, I daresay."

In a week's time Lucy improved enormously. Her coat became glossy, her eyes bright and her person plumpish. Her attachment to Mr. Whipplestone grew more marked, and he, as he confided in his diary, was in some danger of making an old fool of himself over her. "She is a beguiling little animal," he wrote. "I confess I find myself flattered by her attentions. She has nice ways." The nice ways consisted of keeping a close watch on him, of greeting him on his reappearance after an hour's absence as if he had returned from the North Pole, of tearing about the house with her tail up, affecting astonishment when she encountered him, and of sudden onsets of attachment when she would grip his arm in her forelegs, kick it with her hind legs, pretend to bite him, and then fall into a little frenzy of purrs and licks.

She refused utterly to accommodate to her red harness, but when Mr. Whipplestone took his evening stroll she accompanied him, at first to his consternation. But although she darted ahead and pranced out of hiding places at him, she kept off the street and their joint expeditions became a habit.

Only one circumstance upset them and that was a curious one. Lucy would trot contentedly down Capricorn Mews until they had passed the garage and were within thirty yards of the pottery-pigs establishment. At that point she would go no further. She either bolted home under her own steam or performed her familiar trick of leaping into Mr. Whipplestone's arms. On these occasions he was distressed to feel her trembling. He concluded that she remembered her accident, and yet he was not altogether satisfied with this explanation.

She fought shy of the Napoli because of the dogs tied up outside, but on one visit when there happened to be no customers and no dogs she walked in. Mr. Whipplestone apologized and picked her up. He had become quite friendly with Mr. and Mrs. Pirelli and told them about her. Their response was a little strange. There were ejaculations of "*Poverina!*" and the sorts of noises Italians make to cats. Mrs. Pirelli advanced a finger and crooned. She then noticed the white tip of Lucy's tail and looked very hard at her. She spoke in Italian to her husband, who nodded portentously and said "*Sì*" some ten times in succession.

"Have you recognized the cat?" asked Mr. Whipplestone in alarm. They said they thought they had. Mrs. Pirelli had very little English. She was a large lady and she now made herself a great deal larger in eloquent mime, curving both arms in front of her and blowing out her cheeks. She also jerked her head in the direction of Capricorn Passage. "You mean the pottery person," cried Mr. Whipplestone. "You mean she was that person's cat!"

He realized bemusedly that Mrs. Pirelli had made another gesture, an ancient one. She had crossed herself. She laid her hand on Mr. Whipplestone's arm. "No, no, no. Do not give back. No. *Cattivo. Cattivo,*" said Mrs. Pirelli.

"Cat?"

"No, signor," said Mr. Pirelli. "My wife is saying 'bad man.' They are both bad. Cruel people. Do not return to them your little cat."

"No," said Mr. Whipplestone confusedly. "No, I won't. Thank you. I won't."

And from that day he never took Lucy into the Mews.

Mrs. Chubb, Lucy accepted as a source of food and accordingly performed the obligatory ritual of brushing round her ankles. Chubb, she completely ignored.

She spent a good deal of time in the tub garden at the back of the house making wild balletic passes at imaginary butterflies.

At nine-thirty one morning, a week after his dinner with the Alleyns, Mr. Whipplestone sat in his drawing-room doing the *Times* crossword. Chubb was out shopping and Mrs. Chubb, having finished her housework, was "doing for" Mr. Sheridan in the basement. Mr. Sheridan, who was something in the City, Mr. Whipplestone gathered, was never at home on week-day mornings. At eleven o'clock Mrs. Chubb would return to see about Mr. Whipplestone's luncheon. The arrangement worked admirably.

Held up over a particularly cryptic clue, Mr. Whipplestone's attention was caught by a singular noise, a kind of stifled complaint as if Lucy was mewing with her mouth full. This proved to be the case. She entered the room backwards with sunken head, approached crab-wise and dropped something heavy on his foot. She then sat back and gazed at him with her head on one side and made the enquiring trill that he found particularly fetching.

"What on earth have you got there?" he asked.

He picked it up. It was a ceramic no bigger than a medallion, but it was heavy and must have grievously taxed her delicate little jaws. A pottery fish, painted white on one side and biting its own tail. It was pierced by a hole at the top.

"Where did you get this?" he asked severely.

Lucy lifted a paw, lay down, looked archly at him from under her arm and then incontinently jumped up and left the room.

"Extraordinary little creature," he muttered. "It must belong to the Chubbs."

And when Mrs. Chubb returned from below he called her in and showed it to her. "Is this yours, Mrs. Chubb?" he asked.

She had a technique of not replying immediately to anything that was said to her and she used it now. He held the thing out to her but she didn't take it.

"The cat brought it in," explained Mr. Whipplestone, who always introduced a tone of indifference in mentioning Lucy Lockett to the Chubbs. "Do you know where it came from?"

"I think—it must be—I think it's Mr. Sheridan's, sir," Mrs. Chubb said at last. "One of his ornaments, like. The cat gets through his back window, sir, when it's open for airing. Like when I done it out just now. But I never noticed."

"Does she? Dear me! Most reprehensible! You might put it back, Mrs. Chubb, could you? Too awkward if he should miss it!"

Mrs. Chubb's fingers closed over it. Mr. Whipplestone, looking up at her, saw with suprise that her apple-pink cheeks had blanched. He thought of asking her if she was unwell, but her colour began to reappear unevenly.

"All right, Mrs. Chubb?" he asked.

She seemed to hover on the brink of some reply. Her lips moved and she brushed them with her fingers. At last she said: "I haven't liked to ask, sir, but I hope we give satisfaction, Chubb and me."

"Indeed, you do," he said warmly. "Everything goes very smoothly."

"Thank you, sir," she said and went out. He thought: "That wasn't what she was about to say."

He heard her go upstairs and thought: "I wish she'd return that damned object." But almost immediately she came back. He went through to the dining-room window and watched her descend the outside steps into the back garden and disappear into Mr. Sheridan's flat. Within seconds he heard the door slam and saw her return.

A white pottery fish. Like a medallion. He really must not get into a habit of thinking things had happened before or been heard of or seen before. There were scientific explanations, he believed, for such experiences. One lobe of one's brain working a billionth of a second before the other or something to do with Time Spirals. He wouldn't know. But, of course, in the case of the Sanskrit person it was all perfectly straightforward: he *had* in the past seen the name written up. He had merely forgotten.

Lucy made one of her excitable entrances. She tore into the room as if the devil were after her, stopped short with her ears laid back and affected to see Mr. Whipplestone for the first time: "Heavens! You!"

"Come here," he said sharply.

She pretended not to hear him, strolled absently nearer, and suddenly leapt into his lap and began to knead.

"You are *not,*" he said, checking this painful exercise, "to sneak into other people's flats and steal pottery fish."

And there for the moment the matter rested.

Until five days later when, on a very warm evening, she once more stole the medallion and dumped it at her owner's feet.

Mr. Whipplestone scarcely knew whether he was exasperated or diverted by this repeated misdemeanour. He admonished his cat, who seemed merely to be thinking of something else. He wondered if he could again leave it to Mrs. Chubb to restore the object to its rightful place in the morning and then told himself that really this wouldn't do.

He turned the medallion over in his hand. There was some sort of inscription fired on the reverse side: a wavy X. There was a hole at the top through which, no doubt, a cord could be passed. It was a common little object, entirely without distinction. A keepsake of some sort, he supposed.

Mr. Sheridan was at home. Light from his open kitchen window illuminated the back regions and streaked through gaps in his sitting-room curtains.

"You're an unconscionable nuisance," Mr. Whipplestone said to Lucy Lockett.

He put the medallion in his jacket pocket, let himself out at his front door, took some six paces along the pavement and passed through the iron gate and down the short flight of steps to Mr. Sheridan's door. Lucy, anticipating an evening stroll, was too quick for him. She shot over his feet and down the steps and hid behind a dwarfed yew tree.

He rang the doorbell.

It was answered by Mr. Sheridan. The light in his little entrance lobby was behind him, so that his face was in shadow. He had left the door into his sitting-room open and Mr. Whipplestone saw that he had company. Two armchairs in view had their backs towards him, but the tops of their occupants' heads showed above them.

"I do apologize," said Mr. Whipplestone, "not only for disturbing you but for—" He dipped into his pocket and then held out the medallion. "This," he said.

Mr. Sheridan's behaviour oddly repeated that of Mrs. Chubb. He stood stock-still. Perhaps no more than a couple of seconds passed in absolute silence, but it seemed much longer before he said: "I don't understand. Are you—?"

"I must explain," Mr. Whipplestone said, and did.

While he was explaining, the occupant of one of the chairs turned and looked over the back. He could see only the top of the head, the forehead and the eyes, but there was no mistaking Mrs. Montfort. Their eyes met and she ducked out of sight.

Sheridan remained perfectly silent until the end of the recital and even then said nothing. He had made no move to recover his property, but on Mr. Whipplestone's again offering it, extended his hand.

"I'm afraid the wretched little beast has taken to following Mrs. Chubb into your flat. Through your kitchen window, I imagine. I am so very sorry," said Mr. Whipplestone.

Sheridan suddenly became effusive. "Not another syllable," he lisped. "Don't give it another thought. It's of no value, as you can see. I shall put it out of reach. Thank you so much. Yes."

"Good night," said Mr. Whipplestone.

"Good night, good night. Warm for the time of year, isn't it? Good night. Yes."

Certainly, the door was not shut in his face, but the moment he turned his back it was shut very quickly.

As he reached the top of the iron steps he was treated to yet another repetitive occurrence. The Sanskrits, brother and sister, were crossing the street towards him. At the same moment his cat, who had come out of hiding, barged against his leg and bolted like black lightning down the street.

The second or two that elapsed while he let himself out by

the area gate brought the Sanskrits quite close. Obviously they were again visiting down below. They waited for him to come out. He smelt them and was instantly back in Ng'ombwana. What was it? Sandarac? They made incense of it and burnt it in the markets. The man was as outlandish as ever. Even fatter. And painted. Bedizened. And as Mr. Whipplestone turned quickly away, what *had* he seen, dangling from that unspeakable neck? A medallion? A white fish? He was further disturbed by the disappearance so precipitately of Lucy, and greatly dismayed by the notion that she might get lost. He was in two minds whether to go after her or call to her and make a fool of himself in so doing.

While he still hesitated he saw a small shadow moving towards him. He did call, and suddenly she came tearing back and, in her familiar fashion, launched herself at him. He carried her up his own steps.

"That's right," he said. "You come indoors. Come straight indoors. Where we both belong."

But when they had reached their haven, Mr. Whipplestone gave himself a drink. He had been disturbed by too many almost simultaneous occurrences, the most troublesome of which was his brief exchange with Mr. Sheridan. "I've seen him before," he said to himself, "and I don't mean here, when I took the house. I mean in the past. Somewhere. Somewhere. And the impression is not agreeable."

But his memory was disobliging, and after teasing himself with unprofitable speculation he finished his drink and in a state of well-disciplined excitement telephoned his friend Superintendent Alleyn.

III

Catastrophe

The Ng'ombwanan Embassy had been built for a Georgian merchant prince and was really far too grand, Alleyn saw, for an emergent African republic. It had come upon the market at the expiration of a long lease and had been snatched up by the Boomer's representatives in London. It would not have ill become a major power.

He saw a splendid house, beautifully proportioned and conveying by its very moderation a sense of calm and spaciousness. The reception rooms, covering almost the whole of the ground floor, gave at the rear on to an extensive garden with, among other felicities, a small lake. This garden had fallen into disrepair but had been most elegantly restored by Vistas of Baronsgate. Their associated firm, Décor and Design, also of Baronsgate, had been responsible for the interior.

"They must have got more than they bargained for," Alleyn said, "when the occupants brought in their bits and pieces."

He was casing the premises in the company, and at the invitation, of his opposite number in the Special Branch, Superintendent Fred Gibson, a vast, pale, muted man, who was careful to point out that they were there at the express invitation of the Ng'ombwanan Ambassador and were, virtually, on Ng'ombwanan soil.

"We're here on sufferance if you like," Gibson said in his paddy voice. "Of course they're still a Commonwealth nation of sorts, but I reckon they could say 'Thanks a lot, goodbye for now' any time they fancied."

"I believe they could, Fred."

"Not that I want the job. Gawd, no! But as soon as His Nibs pokes his nose out-of-doors he's our bit of trouble and no mistake."

"Tricky for you," said Alleyn. He and Gibson had been associates in their early days and knew each other pretty well.

They were at one end of a reception saloon or ballroom to which they had been shown by an enormous African flunkey who had then withdrawn to the opposite end, where he waited, motionless.

Alleyn was looking at a shallow recess which occupied almost the whole of their end. It was lined with a crimson and gold paper on which had been hung Ng'ombwanan artifacts – shields, masks, cloaks, spears – so assembled as to form a sort of giant African Trophy flanked with Heraldic Achievements. At the base of this display was a ceremonial drum. A spotlight had been set to cover the area. It was an impressive arrangement and in effect harked back to the days when the house was built and Nubian statues and little black turbaned pages were the rage in London. The Boomer, Alleyn thought, would not be displeased.

A minstrels' gallery ran round three sides of the saloon, and Gibson explained that four of his men as well as the orchestra would be stationed up there.

Six pairs of French windows opened on the garden. Vistas had achieved a false perspective by planting on either side of the long pond – yew trees, tall in the foreground, diminishing in size until they ended in miniatures. The pond itself had been correspondingly shaped. It was wide where the trees were tall and narrowed throughout its length. The *trompe l'oeil* was startling. Alleyn had read somewhere or another of Henry Irving's production of *The Corsican Brothers* with six-foot guardsmen nearest the audience and midgets in the background. The effect here, he thought, would be the reverse of Irving's, for at the far end of the little lake a pavilion had been set up where the Boomer, the Ambassador and a small assortment of distinguished guests would assemble for an *al fresco* entertainment. From the saloon they would look like Gullivers in Lilliput. Which again, Alleyn reflected, would not displease the Boomer.

He and Gibson spoke in undertones because of the flunkey.

"You see how the land lies," said Gibson. "I'll show you the plan in a sec. The whole show—this evening party—takes place on the ground floor. And later in the bloody garden. Nobody goes upstairs except the regular house staff and we look after that one. Someone at every stairhead, don't you worry. Now. As you see, the entrance hall's behind us at a lower level and the garden through the windows in front. On your left are the other reception rooms: a smaller drawing-room, the dining-room—you could call it a banqueting hall without going too far—and the kitchens and offices. On our right, opening off the entrance hall behind us, is a sort of ladies' sitting-room, and off that, on the other side of the alcove with all the hardware," said Gibson, indicating the Ng'ombwanan trophies, "is the ladies' cloakroom. Very choice. You know. Ankle-deep carpets. Armchairs, dressing-tables. Face-stuff provided and two attendants. The W.C.'s themselves, four of them, have louvre windows opening on the garden. You could barely get a fair shot at the pavilion through any of them because of intervening trees. Still. We're putting in a reliable female sergeant."

"Tarted up as an attendant?"

"Naturally."

"Fair enough. Where's the men's cloakroom?"

"On the other side of the entrance hall. It opens off a sort of smoking-room or what-have-you that's going to be set up with a bar. The lavatory windows in their case would give a better line on the pavilion and we're making arrangements accordingly."

"What about the grounds?"

"The grounds are one hell of a problem. Greenery all over the shop," grumbled Mr. Gibson.

"High brick wall, though?"

"Oh, yes. And iron spikes, but what of that? We'll do a complete final search – number one job – at the last moment. House, garden, the lot. And a complete muster of personnel. The catering's being handled by Costard et Cie of Mayfair. Very high class. Hand-picked staff. All their people are what they call maximum-trusted, long-service employees."

"They take on extra labour for these sorts of jobs though, don't they?"

"I know, but they say, nobody they can't vouch for."

"What about – " Alleyn moved his head very slightly in the direction of the man in livery, who was gazing out of the window.

"The Ng'ombwanan lot? Well. The household's run by one of them. Educated in England trained at a first-class hotel in Paris. Top credentials. The Embassy staff was hand-picked in Ng'ombwana, they tell me. I don't know what that's worth, the way things are in those countries. All told, there are thirty of them, but some of the President's household are coming over for the event. The Ng'ombwanans, far as I can make out, will more or less stand round looking pretty. That chap there." Mr. Gibson continued, slurring his words and talking out of the corner of his mouth, "is sort of special: you might say a ceremonial bodyguard to the President. He hangs round on formal occasions dressed up like a cannibal and carrying a dirty big symbolic spear. Like a mace-bearer, sort of, or a sword-of-state. You name it. He came in advance with several of the President's personal staff. The Presidential plane, as you probably know, touches down at eleven tomorrow morning."

"How's the Ambassador shaping up?"

"Having kittens."

"Poor man."

"One moment all worked up about the party and the next in a muck sweat over security. It was at his urgent invitation we came in."

"He rings me up incessantly on the strength of my knowing the great panjandrum."

"Well," Gibson said, "that's why *I've* roped you in, isn't it? And seeing you're going to be here as a guest – excuse me if my manner's too familiar – the situation becomes what you might call provocative. Don't misunderstand me."

"What do you want me to do, for pity's sake? Fling myself in a protective frenzy on the Boomer's bosom every time down in the shrubbery something stirs?"

"Not," said Gibson pursuing his own line of thought, "that I think we're going to have real trouble. Not really. Not at this reception affair. It's his comings and goings that are the real headache. D'you reckon he's going to co-operate? You know. Keep to his undertaking with you and not go drifting off on unscheduled jaunts?"

"One can but hope. What's the order of events? At the reception?"

"For a kick-off, he stands in the entrance hall on the short flight of steps leading up to this room, with this spear-carrying character behind him and the Ambassador on his right. His aides will be back a few paces on his left. His personal bodyguard will form a lane from the entrance right up to him. They carry sidearms as part of their full-dress issue. I've got eight chaps outside covering the walk from the cars to the entrance and a dozen more in and about the hall. They're in livery. Good men. I've fixed it with the Costard people that they'll give them enough to do, handing champagne round and that, to keep them in the picture."

"What's the drill, then?"

"As the guests arrive from nine-thirty onwards, they get their names bawled out by the major-domo at the entrance. They walk up the lane between the guards, the Ambassador presents them to the President, and they shake hands and pass in here. There's a band (Louis Francini's lot, I've checked them) up in the minstrels' gallery and chairs for the official party on the dais in front of the hardware. Other chairs round the walls."

"And we all mill about in here for a spell, do we?"

"That's right. Quaffing your bubbly," said Gibson tonelessly. "Until ten o'clock, when the French windows will all be opened and the staff, including my lot, will set about asking you to move into the garden."

"And that's when your headache really sets in, is it, Fred?"

"My oath! Well, take a look at it."

They moved out through the French windows into the garden. A narrow terrace separated the house from the wide end of the pond, which was flanked on each converging side by paved walks. And there, at the narrow end, was the pavilion: an elegant affair of striped material caught up by giant spears topped with plumes. Chairs for the guests were set out on each side of that end of the lake, and the whole assembly was backed by Mr. Gibson's hated trees.

"Of course," he said gloomily, "there will be all these perishing fairy-lights. You notice even they get smaller as they go back. To carry out the effect, like. You've got to hand it to them, they've been thorough."

"At least they'll shed a bit of light on the scene."

"Not for long, don't you worry. There are going to be musical items and a film. Screen wheeled out against the house here, and the projector on a perch at the far end. And while that's on, out go the lights except in the pavilion, if you please, where they're putting an ornamental godalmighty lamp which will show His Nibs up like a sitting duck."

"How long does that last?"

"Twenty minutes all told. There's some kind of dance. Followed by a native turn-out with drums and one or two other items including a singer. The whole thing covers about an hour. At the expiration of which you all come back for supper in the banqueting room. And then, please God, you all go home."

"You couldn't persuade them to modify their plans at all?"

"Not a chance. It's been laid on by headquarters."

"Do you mean in Ng'ombwana, Fred?"

"That's right. Two chaps from Vistas and Decór and Design were flown out with plans and photographs of this pad at which the President took a long hard look and then dreamt up the whole treatment. He sent one of his henchmen over to see it was laid on according to specifications. I reckon it's as much as the Ambassador's job's worth to change it. And how do you like this?" Gibson asked with a poignant note of outrage in his normally colourless voice. "The Ambassador's given us definite instructions to keep well away from this bloody pavilion. President's orders and no excuse-me's about it."

"He's a darling man is the Boomer!"

"He's making a monkey out of us. I set up a security measure only to be told the President won't stand for it. Look—I'd turn the whole exercise in if I could get someone to listen to me. Pavilion and all."

"What if it rains?"

"The whole shooting match moves indoors and why the hell do I say 'shooting match'?" asked Mr. Gibson moodily.

"So we pray for a wet night?"

"Say that again."

"Let's take a look indoors."

They explored the magnificence of the upper floors, still attended by the Ng'ombwanan spear-carrier, who always removed himself to the greatest possible distance but never left them completely alone. Alleyn tried a remark or two, but the man seemed to have little or no English. His manner was stately and utterly inexpressive.

Gibson re-rehearsed his plan of action for the morrow and Alleyn could find no fault in it. The Special Branch is a bit of a loner in the Service. It does not gossip about its proceedings, and except when they overlap those of another arm, nobody asks it anything. Alleyn, however, was on such terms with Gibson and the circumstances were so unusual as to allow them to relax these austerities. They retired to their car and lit their pipes. Gibson began to talk about subversive elements from emergent independencies known to be based on London and with what he called "violence in their CRO."

"Some are all on their own," he said, "and some kind of coagulate like blood. Small-time secret societies. Mostly they don't get anywhere but there are what you might call malignant areas. And of course you can't discount the pro."

"The professional gun?"

"They're still available. There's Hinny Packmann. He's out after doing bird in a Swedish stir. He'd be available if the money was right. He doesn't operate under three thousand."

"Hinny's in Denmark."

"That's right, according to Interpol. But he could be imported. I don't know anything about the political angle," Gibson said. "Not my scene. Who'd take over if this man was knocked off?"

"I'm told there'd be a revolution of sorts, that mercenaries would be sent in, a puppet government set up, and that in the upshot the big interests would return and take over."

"Yes. Well, there's that aspect and then again you might get the solitary fanatic. He's the type I really do *not* like," Gibson said, indignantly drawing a nice distinction between potential assassins. "No record, as likely as not. You don't know where to look for him."

"You've got the guest list of course."

"Of course. I'll show it to you. Wait a sec."

He fished it out of an inner pocket and they conned it over. Gibson had put a tick beside some five dozen names.

"They've all been on the Ng'ombwanan scene in one capacity or another," he said. "From the oil barons at the top to ex-business men at the bottom, and nearly all of them have been or are in process of being kicked out. The big idea behind this reception seems to be a sort of 'nothing personal intended' slant. 'Everybody loves everybody' and please come to my party!"

"It hurts me more than it does you?"

"That's right. And they've all accepted, what's more."

"Hullo!" Alleyn exclaimed, pointing to the list. "They've asked *him!*"

"Which is that? Ah. Yes. Him. Now, he *has* got a record."

"See the list your people kindly supplied to me," Alleyn said, and produced it.

"That's right. Not for violence, of course, but a murky background and no error. Nasty bit of work. I don't much fancy *him.*"

"His sister makes pottery pigs about one minute away from the Embassy," said Alleyn.

"I know that. Very umpty little dump. You'd wonder why, wouldn't you, with all the money he must have made in Ng'ombwana."

"Has he still got it, though? Mightn't he be broke?"

"Hard to say. Question of whether he laid off his bets before the troubles began."

"Do you know about this one?" Alleyn asked, pointing to the name Whipplestone on the guest list.

Gibson instantly reeled off a thumbnail sketch of Mr. Whipplestone.

"That's the man," Alleyn said. "Well now, Fred, this may be a matter of no importance, but you may as well lay back your ears and listen." And he related Mr. Whipplestone's story of his cat and the pottery fish. "Whipplestone's a bit perturbed about it," he said in the end, "but it may be entirely beside the point as far as we're concerned. This man in the basement, Sheridan, and the odious Sanskrit may simply meet to play bridge. Or they might belong to some potty little esoteric circle: fortune-telling or spiritism or what have you."

"That's what Sanskrit first got borrowed for. Fortune-telling and false pretences. He did his bird for drugs. It was after he came out of stir that he set himself up as a merchant in Ng'ombwana. He's one of the dispossessed," said Gibson.

"I know."

"You do?"

"I think I saw him outside his erstwhile premises when I was there three weeks ago."

"Fancy that."

"About the ones that get together to belly-ache in exile — you don't, I suppose, know of a fish medallion lot?"

"Nah!" said Gibson disgustedly.

"And Mr. Sheridan doesn't appear on the guest list. What about a Colonel and Mrs. Montfort? They were in Sheridan's flat that evening."

"Here. Let's see."

"No," Alleyn said, consulting the list. "No Montforts under the M's."

"Wait a sec. I knew there was something. Look here. Under C. 'Lt. Col. Cock-burn-Montfort, Barset Light Infantry (retd).' What a name. Cock-burn."

"Isn't it usually pronounced Coburn?" Alleyn mildly suggested. "Anything about him?"

" 'Info.' Here we are. 'Organized Ng'ombwanan army. Stationed there from 1960 until Independence in 1971 when present government assumed complete control!' "

"Well," Alleyn said after a longish pause, "it still doesn't have to amount to anything. No doubt ex-Ng'ombwanan colonials tend to flock together like ex-Anglo-Indians. There may be a little clutch of them in the Capricorns all belly-aching cosily together. What about the staff? The non-Ng'ombwanans, I mean."

"We're nothing if not thorough. Every last one's been accounted for. Want to look?"

He produced a second list. "It shows the Costard employees together. Regulars first, extras afterwards. Clean as whistles, the lot of them."

"This one?"

Gibson followed Alleyn's long index finger and read under his breath, " 'Employed by Costards as extra waiter over period of ten years. In regular employment as domestic servant. Recent position: eight years. Excellent references. Present employment—' Hullo, 'ullo."

"Yes?"

" 'Present employment at 1, Capricorn Walk, S.W.3.' "

"We seem," Alleyn said, "to be amassing quite a little clutch of coincidences, don't we?"

II

"It's not often," Alleyn said to his wife, "that we set ourselves up in this rig, is it?"

"You look as if you did it as a matter of course every night. Like the jokes about Empire builders in the jungle. When there was an Empire. Orders and decorations to boot."

"What does one mean exactly, by 'to boot'?"

"You tell me, darling, you're the purist."

"I was when I courted my wife."

Troy, in her green gown, sat on her bed and pulled on her long gloves. "It's worked out all right," she said. "Us. Wouldn't you say?"

"I would say."

"What a bit of luck for us."

"All of that."

He buttoned up her gloves for her. "You look marvellous," he said. "Shall we go?"

"Is our svelte hired limousine at the door?"

"It is."

"Whoops, then, hark chivvy away."

Palace Park Gardens had been closed to general traffic by the police, so the usual crowd of onlookers was not outside the Ng'ombwanan Embassy. The steps were red-carpeted, a flood of light and strains of blameless and dated melodies streamed through the great open doorway. A galaxy of liveried men, black and white, opened car doors and slammed them again.

"Oh Lord, I've forgotten the damn' card!" Troy exclaimed.

"I've got it. Here we go."

The cards, Alleyn saw, were being given a pretty hard look by the men who received them and were handed on to other men seated unobtrusively at tables. He was amused to see, hovering in the background, Superintendent Gibson in tails and a white tie looking a little as if he might be an Old Dominion Plenipotentiary.

Those guests wishing for the cloakrooms turned off to the right and left and on re-entering the hall were martialled back to the end of the double file of Ng'ombwanan guards, where they gave their names to a superb black major-domo who roared them out with all the resonant assurance of a war drum.

Troy and Alleyn had no trappings to shed and passed directly into the channel of approach.

And there, at the far end on the flight of steps leading to the great saloon, was the Boomer himself in state, backed by his spear-carrier and wearing a uniform that might have been inspired by the Napoleonic Old Guard upon whom had been lightly laid the restraining hand of Sandhurst.

Troy muttered: "He's wonderful. Gosh, he's glorious!"

"She'd like to paint him," thought Alleyn.

The patently anxious Ambassador, similarly if less gorgeously uniformed, was stationed on the Boomer's right. Their personal staff stood about in magnificent attitudes behind them.

"Mis-tar and Mrs. Roderick Alleyn."

That huge and beguiling smile opened and illuminated the Boomer's face. He said loudly, "No need for an introduction here," and took Alleyn's hands in both his gloved ones.

"And this is the famous wife!" he resonantly proclaimed. "I am so glad. We meet later. I have a favour to ask. Yes?"

The Alleyns moved on, conscious of being the object of a certain amount of covert attention.

"Rory?"

"Yes, I know. Extra special, isn't he?"

"Whew!"

"What?"

" 'Whew.' Incredulous whistle."

"Difficult, in competition with Gilbert and Sullivan."

They had passed into the great saloon. In the minstrels' gallery instrumentalists, inconspicuously augmented by a clutch of Gibson's silent henchmen, were discussing *The Gondoliers. "When everyone is somebodee, then no-one's anybody!"* they brightly and almost inaudibly chirped.

Trays with champagne were circulated. Jokes about constabular boots and ill-fitting liveries were not appropriate. Among the white servants it was impossible to single out Fred Gibson's men.

How to diagnose the smell of a grand assembly? Beyond

the luxurious complexity of cosmetics, scent, flowers, hairdressers' lotions, remote foods and alcohol, was there something else, something peculiar to this particular occasion? Somewhere in these rooms were they burning that stuff—what was it?—sandarac? That was it. Alleyn had last smelt it in the Presidential Palace in Ng'ombwana. That and the indefinably alien scent of persons of a different colour. The curtains were drawn across the French windows, but the great room was not overheated as yet. People moved about it like well-directed extras in the central scene of some feature film.

They encountered acquaintances: the subject of a portrait Troy had painted some years ago for the Royal Commonwealth Society, Alleyn's great white chief and his wife. Someone he knew in the Foreign Office and, unexpectedly, his brother, Sir George Alleyn: tall, handsome, ambassadorial and entirely predictable. Troy didn't really mind her brother-in-law but Alleyn always found him a bit of an ass.

"Good Lord!" said Sir George. "Rory!"

"George."

"And Troy, my dear. Looking too lovely. Charming! Charming! And what, may one ask, are you doing, Rory, in this galère?"

"They got me in to watch the tea-spoons, George."

"Jolly good, ha-ha. Matter of fact," said Sir George, bending archly down to Troy, "between you and me and the gatepost I've no idea why I'm here myself. Except that we've all been asked."

"Do you mean your entire family, George?" enquired his brother. "Twins and all?"

"So amusing. I mean," he told Troy, "the *corps diplomatique* or at least those of us who've had the honour to represent Her Majesty's Government in 'furrin parts,'" said Sir George, again becoming playful. "Here we all are! *Why*, we don't quite know!" he gaily concluded.

"To raise the general tone, I expect," said Alleyn gravely. "Look, Troy, there's Sam Whipplestone. Shall we have a word with him?"

"Do let's."

"See you later, perhaps, George."

"I understand there's to be some sort of *fête champêtre*."

"That's right. Mind you don't fall in the pond."

Troy said when they were at a safe remove, "If I were George I'd thump you."

Mr. Whipplestone was standing near the dais in front of the Ng'ombwanan display of arms. His faded hair was beautifully groomed and his rather withdrawn face wore a gently attentive air. His eyeglass was at the alert. When he caught sight of the Alleyns he smiled delightedly, made a little bow, and edged towards them.

"What a *very* grand party," he said.

"Disproportionate, would you say?" Alleyn hinted.

"Well, coming it rather strong, perhaps. I keep thinking of *Martin Chuzzlewit.*"

" 'Todgers were going it'?"

"Yes." Mr. Whipplestone looked very directly at Alleyn. "All going well in your part of the picture?" he asked.

"Not *mine,* you know."

"But you've been consulted."

"Oh," said Alleyn, "that! Vaguely. Quite unofficial. I was invited to view. Brother Gibson's laid on a maximum job."

"Good."

"By the way, did you know your man was on the strength tonight? Chubb?"

"Oh, yes. He and Mrs. Chubb have been on the caterer's supplementary list for many years, he tells me. They're often called upon."

"Yes."

"Another of our coincidences, did you think?"

"Well — hardly that, perhaps."

"How's Lucy Lockett?" Troy asked.

Mr. Whipplestone made the little grimace that allowed his glass to dangle. "Behaving herself with decorum," he said, primly.

"No more thieving sorties?"

"Thank God, no," he said with some fervour. "You must meet her, both of you," he added, "and try Mrs. Chubb's cooking. Do say you will."

"We'd like that very much," said Troy warmly.

"I'll telephone tomorrow and we'll arrange a time."

"By the way," Alleyn said, "talking of Lucy Lockett reminds me of your Mr. Sheridan. Have you any idea what he does?"

"Something in the City, I think. Why?"

"It's just that the link with the Sanskrit couple gives him a certain interest. There's no connection with Ng'ombwana?"

"Not that I know."

"He's not here tonight," Alleyn said.

One of the A.D.C.'s was making his way through the thickening crowd. Alleyn recognized him as his escort in Ng'ombwana. He saw Alleyn and came straight to him, all eyes and teeth.

"Mr. Alleyn, His Excellency the Ambassador wishes me to say that the President will be very pleased if you and Mrs. Alleyn will join the official party for the entertainment in the garden. I will escort you when the time comes. Perhaps we could meet here."

"That's very kind," Alleyn said. "We shall be honoured."

"Dear me," said Mr. Whipplestone when the A.D.C. had gone, "Todgers *are* going it and no mistake."

"It's the Boomer at it again. I wish he wouldn't."

Troy said: "What do you suppose he meant when he said he had a favour to ask."

"He said it to you, darling. Not me."

"I've got one I'd like to ask him, all right."

"No prize offered for guessing the answer. She wants," Alleyn explained to Mr. Whipplestone, "to paint him."

"Surely," he rejoined with his little bow, "that wish has only to be made known — Good God!"

He had broken off to stare at the entrance into the saloon where the last arrivals were coming in. Among them, larger, taller, immeasurably more conspicuous than anyone else in their neighbourhood, were Mr. Whipplestone's bugbears: the Sanskrits, brother and sister.

They were, by and large, appropriately attired. That is to say, they wore full evening dress. The man's shirt, to Mr. Whipplestone's utterly conventional taste, was unspeakable, being heavily frilled and lacy with a sequin or two winking in its depths. He wore many rings on his dimpled fingers. His fair hair was cut in a fringe and concealed his ears. He was skilfully but unmistakably *en maquillage,* as Mr. Whipplestone shudderingly put it to himself. The sister, vast in green fringed satin, also wore her hair, which was purple, in a fringe and side-pieces. These in effect squared her enormous face. They moved slowly, like two huge vessels shoved from behind by tugs.

"I thought you'd be surprised," Alleyn said. He bent his head and shoulders, being so tall, in order that he and Mr. Whipplestone could converse without shouting. The conglomerate roar of voices now almost drowned the orchestra, which pursuing its course through the century had now reached the heyday of Cochran's Revues.

"You knew they were invited?" Mr. Whipplestone said, referring to the Sanskrits. "Well, *really!*"

"Not very delicious, I agree. By the way, somewhere here there's another brace of birds from your Capricorn preserves."

"Not — "

"The Montforts."

"That is less upsetting."

"The Colonel had a big hand, it appears, in setting up their army."

Mr. Whipplestone looked steadily at him. "Are you talking about Cockburn-Montfort?" he said at last.

"That's right."

"Then why the devil couldn't his wife say so," he crossly exclaimed. "Silly creature! Why leave out the Cockburn? Too tiresome. Yes, well, naturally *he'd* be asked. I never met him. He hadn't appeared on the scene in my early days and he'd gone when I returned." He thought for a moment. "Sadly run to seed," he said. "And his wife, too, I'm afraid."

"The bottle?"

"I should imagine the bottle. I did tell you, didn't I, that they were there in Sheridan's basement that evening when I called. And that she dodged down?"

"You did, indeed."

"And that she had – um – ?"

"Accosted you in the pet-shop? Yes."

"Quite so."

"Well, I daresay she'll have another fling if she spots you tonight. You might introduce us, if she does."

"Really?"

"Yes, really."

And after about ten minutes Mr. Whipplestone said that there the Cockburn-Montforts, in fact, were, some thirty feet away and drifting in their direction. Alleyn suggested that they move casually towards them.

"Well, my dear fellow, if you insist."

So it was done. Mrs. Cockburn-Montfort spotted Mr. Whipplestone and bowed. They saw her speak to her husband, obviously suggesting they should effect an encounter.

"Good evening!" she cried as they approached. "What odd places we meet in, don't we? Animal shops and embassies." And when they were actually face-to-face: "I've told my husband about you and your piteous little pusscat. Darling, this is Mr. Whipplestone, our new boy at No. 1, the Walk. Remember?"

"Hiyar," said Colonel Cockburn-Montfort.

Mr. Whipplestone, following what he conceived to be Alleyn's wishes, modestly deployed his social expertise. "How do you do," he said, and to the lady: "Do you know, I feel quite ashamed of myself. I didn't realize, when we encountered, that your husband was *the* Cockburn-Montfort. Of Ng'ombwana," he added, seeing that she looked nonplussed.

"Oh. Didn't you? We rather tend to let people forget the Cockburn half. So often and so shy-makingly mispronounced," said Mrs. Cockburn-Montfort, gazing up first at Alleyn and then at Mr. Whipplestone, who thought, "At least they both seem to be sober," and he reflected that very likely they were never entirely drunk. He introduced Alleyn, and at once she switched all her attention to him, occasionally throwing a haggard, comradely glance at Troy, upon whom, after a long, glazed look, the Colonel settled his attention.

In comparison with the Sanskrits they were, Mr. Whipplestone thought, really not so awful, or perhaps more accurately, they were awful in a more acceptable way. The Colonel, whose voice was hoarse, told Troy that he and his wife had been hard on the Alleyns' heels when they were greeted by the President. He was evidently curious about the cordiality of their reception and began, without much subtlety, to fish. Had she been to Ng'ombwana? If so, why had they never met? He would certainly have not forgotten if they had, he added, and performed the gesture of brushing up his moustache at the corners while allowing his eyes to goggle slightly. He became quite persistent in his gallantries, and Troy thought the best way to cut them short was to say that her husband had been at school with the President.

"Ah!" said the Colonel. "Really? That explains it." It would have been hard to say why she found the remark offensive.

A hush fell on the assembly and the band in the gallery became audible. It had approached the contemporary period and was discussing *My Fair Lady* when the President and his entourage entered the salon. They made a scarcely less than royal progress to the dais under the trophies. At the same time, Alleyn noticed, Fred Gibson turned up in the darkest part of the gallery and stood looking down at the crowd. "With a Little Bit of Luck," played the band, and really, Alleyn thought, it might have been Fred's signature-tune. The players faded out obsequiously as the Boomer reached the dais.

The ceremonial spear-carrier had arrived and stood, motionless and magnificent, in a panoply of feathers, armlets, anklets, necklets and lion-skins against the central barbaric trophy. The Boomer seated himself. The Ambassador advanced to the edge of the dais. The conductor drew an admonitory flourish from his players.

"Your Excellency, Mr. President, sir. My Lords, Ladies and Gentlemen," said the Ambassador, and went on to welcome his President, his guests and, in general terms, the excellent rapprochement that obtained between his government and that of the United Kingdom, a rapprochement that encouraged the promotion of an ever-developing – his theme became a little foggy round the edges, but he brought it to a sonorous conclusion and evoked a round of discreet applause.

The Boomer then rose. Troy thought to herself: "I'm going to remember this. Sharply. Accurately. Everything. That great hussar's busby of grey hair. Those reflected lights in the hollows of temple and cheek. The swelling blue tunic, white paws and glittering hardware. And the background, for Heaven's sake! No, but I've got to. I've got to."

She looked at her husband, who raised one eyebrow and muttered: "I'll ask."

She squeezed his hand violently.

The Boomer spoke briefly. Such was the magnificence of his voice that the effect was less of a human instrument than of some enormous double-bass. He spoke predictably of enduring bonds of fellowship in the Commonwealth and less formally of the joys of revisiting the haunts of his youth. Pursuing this theme, to Alleyn's deep misgiving, he dwelt on his school-days and of strongly cemented, never to be broken friendships. At which point, having obviously searched the audience and spotted his quarry, he flashed one of his startling grins straight at the Alleyns. A general murmur was induced and Mr. Whipplestone, highly diverted, muttered something about "the cynosure of all eyes." A few sonorous generalities rounded off the little speech. When the applause had subsided the Ambassador announced a removal to the gardens, and simultaneously the curtains were drawn back and the six pairs of French windows flung open. An enchanting prospect was revealed. Golden lights, star-shaped and diminishing in size, receded into the distance and were reflected in the small lake, itself subscribing to the false perspective that culminated, at the far end, in the brilliantly lit scarlet and white pavilion. Vistas of Baronsgate had done themselves proud.

"The stage-management, as one feels inclined to call it," said Mr. Whipplestone, "is superb. I look forward excitedly to seeing you both in the pavilion."

"You've had too much champagne," Alleyn said, and Mr. Whipplestone made a little crowing noise.

The official party passed into the garden and the guests followed in their wake. Alleyn and Troy were duly collected by the A.D.C. and led to the pavilion. Here they were enthusiastically greeted by the Boomer and introduced to ten distinguished guests, among whom Alleyn was amused to find his brother George, whose progress as a career-diplomat had hoisted him into more than one ambassadorial post. The other guests consisted of the last of the British governors in Ng'ombwana and representatives of associated African independencies.

It would be incorrect to say that the Boomer was enthroned in his pavilion. His chair was not raised above the others, but it was isolated and behind it stood the ceremonial spear-bearer. The guests, in arrow formation, flanked the President. From the house and to the guests seated on either side of the lake they must present, Alleyn thought, a remarkable picture.

The musicians had descended from their gallery into the garden and were grouped, modestly, near the house, among trees that partly concealed the lavatorial louvre windows Gibson had pointed out to Alleyn.

When the company was settled, a large screen was wheeled in front of the French windows facing down the lake towards the pavilion. A scene in the Ng'ombwanan wild-lands was now projected on this screen. A group of live Ng'ombwanan drummers then appeared before it, the garden lights were dimmed, and the drummers performed. The drums throbbed and swelled, pulsed and thudded, disturbing in their monotony, unseemly in their context: a most unsettling noise. It grew to a climax. A company of warriors, painted and armed, erupted from the dark and danced. Their feet thumped down on the mown turf. From the shadows, people, Ng'ombwanans presumably, began to clap the rhythm. More and more of the guests, encouraged perhaps by champagne and the anonymity of the shadows, joined in this somewhat inelegant response. The performance crashed to a formidable conclusion.

The Boomer threw out a few explanatory observations. Champagne was again in circulation.

Apart from the President himself, Ng'ombwana had produced one other celebrity: a singer, by definition a bass but with the astonishing vocal range of just over four octaves, an attribute that he exploited without the least suggestion of break or transition. His native name, unpronounceable by Europeans, had been simplified as Karbo and he was world-famous.

He was now to appear.

He came from the darkened ballroom and was picked up in front of the screen by a strong spotlight: a black man in conventional evening dress, with a quite extraordinary air of distinction.

All the golden stars and all the lights in the house were out. The orchestra lamps were masked. Only the single lamp by the President, complained of by Gibson, remained alight, so that the President and the singer, at opposite ends of the lake, were the only persons to be seen in the benighted garden.

The orchestra played an introductory phrase.

A single deep sustained note of extraordinary strength and beauty floated from the singer.

While it still hung on the air a sound like that of a whip-lash cracked out, and somewhere in the house a woman screamed and screamed and screamed.

The light in the pavilion went out.

What followed was like the outbreak of a violent storm: a confusion of voices, of isolated screams, less insistent than the continuous one, of shouted orders, of chairs overturned, of something or someone falling into the water. Of Alleyn's hand on Troy's shoulder. Then of his voice: "Don't move, Troy. Stay there." And then, unmistakably, the Boomer's great voice roaring out something in his own tongue and Alleyn saying: "No, you don't. No!" Of a short guttural cry near at hand and a thud. And then from many voices like the king and courtiers in the play: "Lights! Lights! Lights!"

They came up, first in the ballroom and then overhead in the garden. They revealed some of the guests still seated on either side of the lake but many on their feet talking confusedly. They revealed also the great singer, motionless, still in his spotlight, and a number of men who emerged purposefully from several directions, some striding up to the pavilion and some into the house.

And in the pavilion itself men with their backs to Troy shutting her in, crowding together and hiding her husband from her. Women making intermittent exclamations in the background.

She heard her brother-in-law's voice raised in conventional admonition—"Don't panic, anybody. Keep calm. No need to panic"—and even in her confusion thought that however admirable the advice, he did unfortunately sound ridiculous.

His instructions were in effect repeated, not at all ridiculously, by a large, powerful man who had appeared beside the singer.

"Keep quiet and stay where you are, ladies and gentlemen, if you please," said this person, and Troy at once recognized the Yard manner.

The screaming woman had moved away somewhere inside the house. Her cries had broken down into hysterical and incomprehensible speech. They became more distant and were finally subdued.

And now the large purposeful man came into the pavilion. The men who had blocked Troy's view backed away, and she saw what they had all been looking at.

A prone figure, face down, arms spread, dressed in a flamboyant uniform, split down the back by a plumed spear. The sky-blue tunic had a glistening patch round the place of entry. The plume, where it touched the split, was red.

Alleyn was kneeling by the figure.

The large purposeful man moved in front of her and shut off this picture. She heard Alleyn's voice: "Better clear the place." After a moment he was beside her, holding her arm and turning her away. "All right?" he said. "Yes?" She nodded and found herself being shepherded out of the pavilion with the other guests.

When they had gone Alleyn returned to the spiked figure and again knelt beside it. He looked up at his colleague and slightly shook his head.

Superintendent Gibson muttered, "They've done it!"

"Not precisely," Alleyn said. He stood up and at once the group of men moved further back. And there was the Boomer, bolt upright in the chair that was not quite a throne, breathing deeply and looking straight before him.

"It's the Ambassador," Alleyn said.

IV

Aftermath

The handling of the affair at the Ng'ombwanan Embassy was to become a classic in the annals of police procedure. Gibson, under the hard drive of a muffled fury, and with Alleyn's co-operation, had within minutes transformed the scene into one that resembled a sort of high-toned drafting-yard. The speed with which this was accomplished was remarkable.

The guests, marshalled into the ballroom, were, as Gibson afterwards put it, "processed" through the dining-room. There they were shepherded up to a trestle table upon which the elaborate confections of Costard et Cie had been shoved aside to make room for six officers summoned from Scotland Yard. These men sat with copies of the guest list before them and with regulation tact checked off names and addresses.

Most of the guests were then encouraged to leave by a side door, a general signal having been sent out for their transport. A small group were asked, very civilly, to remain.

As Troy approached the table she saw that among the Yard officers Inspector Fox, Alleyn's constant associate, sat at the end of the row, his left ear intermittently tickled by the tail of an elaborately presented cold pheasant. When he looked over the top of his elderly spectacles and saw her, he was momentarily transfixed. She leant down. "Yes, Br'er Fox, me," she murmured. "Mrs. R. Alleyn, 48 Regency Close, S.W.3."

"Fancy!" said Mr. Fox to his list. "What about getting home?" he mumbled. "All right?"

"Perfectly. Hired car. Someone's ringing them. Rory's fixed it."

Mr. Fox ticked off the name, "Thank you, madam," he said aloud. "We won't keep you"; and so Troy went home, and not until she got there was she to realize how very churned up she had become.

The curtained pavilion had been closed and police constables posted outside. It was lit inside and glowed like some scarlet and white striped bauble in the dark garden. Distorted shadows moved, swelled and vanished across its walls. Specialists were busy within.

In a small room normally used by the controller of the household as an office, Alleyn and Gibson attempted to get some sort of sense out of Mrs. Cockburn-Montfort.

She had left off screaming but had the air of being liable to start up again at the least provocation. Her face was streaked with mascara, her mouth hung open, and she pulled incessantly at her lower lip. Beside her stood her husband, the Colonel, holding, incongruously, a bottle of smelling-salts.

Three women in lavender dresses with caps and stylish aprons sat in a row against the wall as if waiting to make an entrance in unison for some soubrettish turn. The largest of them was a police sergeant.

Behind the desk a male uniform sergeant took notes and upon it sat Alleyn, facing Mrs. Cockburn-Montfort. Gibson stood to one side, holding on to the lower half of his face as if it were his temper and had to be stifled.

Alleyn said: "Mrs. Cockburn-Montfort, we are all very sorry indeed to badger you like this, but it really is a most urgent matter. Now. I'm going to repeat, as well as I can, what I *think* you have been telling us, and if I go wrong please, *please* stop me and say so. Will you?"

"Come on, Chrissy old girl," urged her husband. "Stiff upper lip. It's all over now. Here!" He offered the smelling-salts but was flapped away.

"You," Alleyn said, "were in the ladies' cloakroom. You had gone there during the general exodus of the guests from the ballroom and were to rejoin your husband for the concert in the garden. There were no other guests in the cloakroom, but these ladies, the cloakroom attendants, were there? Right? Good. Now. You had had occasion to use one of the four lavatories, the second from the left. You were still there when the lights went out. So far, then, have we got it right?"

She nodded, rolling her gaze from Alleyn to her husband. "Now the next bit. As clearly as you can, won't you? What happened immediately after the lights went out?"

"I couldn't think what had happened. I mean *why*? I've told you. I really do think," said Mrs. Cockburn-Montfort, squeezing out her voice like toothpaste, "that I might be let off. I've been *hideously* shocked, I thought I was going to be killed. Truly. Hughie—?"

"Pull yourself together, Chrissy, for God's sake. Nobody's killed you. Get on with it. Sooner said, sooner we'll be shot of it."

"You're so *hard*," she whimpered. And to Alleyn: "Isn't he? Isn't he hard?"

But after a little further persuasion she did get on with it.

"I was still *there*," she said. "In the loo. Honestly!—Too awkward. And all the lights had gone out but there was a kind of glow outside those slatted sort of windows. And I suppose it was something to do with the performance. You know. That drumming and some sort of dance. I knew you'd be cross, Hughie, waiting for me out there and the concert started and all that, but one can't help these things, can one?"

"All right. We all know something had upset you."

"Yes, well they finished—the dancing and drums had finished — and — and so had I and I was nearly going when the door burst open and hit me. Hard. On — on the back. And he took hold of me. By the arm. Brutally. And threw me out. I'm bruised and shaken and suffering from shock and you keep me here. He threw me so violently that I fell. In the cloakroom. It was much darker there than in the loo. Almost pitch dark. And I lay there. And outside I could hear clapping and after that there was music and a voice. I suppose it was wonderful, but to me, lying there hurt and shocked, it was like a lost soul."

"Go on, please."

"And then there was that ghastly shot. Close. Shattering, in the loo. And the next thing — straight after that — he burst out and kicked me."

"Kicked you. You mean deliberately — ?"

"He fell over me," said Mrs. Cockburn-Montfort. "Almost fell, and in so doing kicked me. And I thought now he's going to shoot me. So of course I screamed. And screamed."

"Yes?"

"And he bolted."

"And then?"

"Well, then there were those three." She indicated the attendants. "Milling about in the dark and kicking me too. By accident, of course."

The three ladies stirred in their seats.

"Where had they come from?"

"How should I know! Well, anyway, I *do* know because I heard the doors bang. They'd been in the other three loos."

"All of them?" Alleyn looked at the sergeant. She stood up. "Well?" he asked.

"To try and see Karbo, sir," she said, scarlet-faced. "He was just outside. Singing."

"Standing on the seats, I suppose, the lot of you."

"Sir."

"I'll see you later," Gibson threatened. "Sit down."

"Sir."

"Now, Mrs. Cockburn-Montfort," Alleyn said. "What happened next?"

Someone, it appeared, had a torch, and by its light they had hauled Mrs. Cockburn-Montfort to her feet.

"Was this you?" Alleyn asked the sergeant, who said it was. Mrs. Cockburn-Montfort had continued to yell. There was a great commotion going on in the garden and other parts of the house. And then all the lights went on. "And that girl," she said, pointing at the sergeant, "that one. There. *Do you know what she did!*"

"Slapped your face, perhaps, to stop you screaming?"

"How she *dared!* After all that. And shouting questions at me. And then she had the impertinence to say she couldn't hang round there and left me to the other two. I must say, they had the decency to give me aspirins."

"I'm so glad," said Alleyn politely. "Now, will you please answer the next one very carefully. Did you get any impression at all of what this man was like? There was a certain amount of reflected light from the louvres. Did you get anything like a look at him, however momentary?"

"Oh, yes," she said quite calmly. "Yes, indeed I did. He was black."

An appreciable silence followed this statement. Gibson cleared his throat.

"Are you sure of that? Really sure?" Alleyn asked.

"Oh, perfectly. I saw his head against the window."

"It couldn't, for instance, have been a white person with a black stocking over his head?"

"Oh, no. I think he *had* a stocking over his head but I could tell." She glanced at her husband and lowered her voice. "Besides," she said, "I smelt him. If you've lived out there as we did, you can't mistake it."

Her husband made a sort of corroborative noise.

"Yes?" Alleyn said. "I understand they notice the same phenomenon in us. An African friend of mine told me that it took him almost a year before he left off feeling faint in lifts during the London rush hours."

And before anyone could remark upon this, he said: "Well, and then one of our people took over and I think from this point we can depend upon his report." He looked at Gibson. "Unless you — ?"

"No," Gibson said. "Thanks. Nothing. We'll have a type-written transcript of this little chat, madam, and we'll ask you to look it over and sign it if it seems O.K. Sorry to have troubled you." And he added the predictable coda. "You've been very helpful," he said. Alleyn wondered how much these routine civilities cost him.

The Colonel, ignoring Mr. Gibson, barked at Alleyn. "I take it I may remove my wife. She ought to see her doctor."

"Of course. Do. Who is your doctor, Mrs. Cockburn-Montfort? Can we ring him up and ask him to meet you at your house?"

She opened her mouth and shut it again when the Colonel said: "We won't trouble you, thank you, good evening to you."

They had got as far as the door before Alleyn said: "Oh, by the way! Did you by any chance get the impression that the man was in some kind of uniform? Or livery?"

There was a long pause before Mrs. Cockburn-Montfort said: "I'm afraid not. No. I've no idea."

"No? By the way, Colonel, are those your smelling-salts?"

The Colonel stared at him as if he were mad and then, vacantly, at the bottle in his hand.

"Mine!" he said. "Why the devil should they be mine?"

"They are mine," said his wife, grandly. "Anyone would suppose we'd been shop-lifting. Honestly!"

She put her arm in her husband's and, clinging to him, gazed resentfully at Alleyn.

"When that peculiar little Whipple-whatever-it-is introduced you, he might have told us you were a policeman. Come on, Hughie darling," said Mrs. Cockburn-Montfort, and achieved quite a magnificent exit.

II

It had taken all of Alleyn's tact, patience and sheer authority to get the Boomer stowed away in the library, a smallish room on the first floor. When he had recovered from the effects of shock, which must surely, Alleyn thought, have been more severe than he permitted himself to show, he developed a strong inclination to conduct enquiries on his own account.

This was extremely tricky. At the Embassy they were technically on Ng'ombwanan soil. Gibson and his Special Branch were there specifically at the invitation of the Ng'ombwanan Ambassador, and how far their authority extended in the somewhat rococo circumstance of that Ambassador having been murdered on the premises was a bit of a poser.

So, in a different key, Alleyn felt, was his own presence on the scene. The Special Branch very much likes to keep itself to itself. Fred Gibson's frame of mind, at the moment, was one of rigidly suppressed professional chagrin and personal mortification. His initial approach would never have been made under ordinary circumstances, and now Alleyn's presence on, as it were, the S.B.'s pitch, gave an almost grotesque twist to an already extremely delicate situation. Particularly since, with the occurrence of a homicide, the focus of responsibility might now be said to have shifted to Alleyn, in whose division the crime had taken place.

Gibson had cut through this dilemma by ringing up his

principals and getting authority for himself and Alleyn with the consent of the Embassy to handle the case together. But Alleyn knew the situation could well become a very tricky one.

"Apparently," Gibson said, "we carry on until somebody stops us. Those are my instructions, anyway. Yours, too, on three counts: your A.C., your division, and the personal request of the President."

"Who at the moment wants to summon the entire household including the spear-carrier and harangue them in their own language."

"Bloody farce," Gibson mumbled.

"Yes, but if he insists – Look," Alleyn said, "it mightn't be such a bad idea for them to go ahead if we could understand what they were talking about."

"Well – "

"Fred, suppose we put out a personal call for Mr. Samuel Whipplestone to come at once – you know: 'be kind enough' and all that. Not sound as if we're breathing down his neck."

"What about it – ?" asked Gibson unenthusiastically.

"He speaks Ng'ombwanan. He lives five minutes away and will be home by now. No. 1, Capricorn Walk. We can ring up. Not in the book yet, I daresay, but get through," said Alleyn to an attendant sergeant and as he went to the telephone, "Samuel Whipplestone. Send a car round. I'll speak to him."

"The idea being?" Mr. Gibson asked woodenly.

"We let the President address the troops – indeed, come to that, we can't stop him, but at least we'll know what's being said."

"Where is he, for God's sake? *You* put him somewhere," Mr. Gibson said, as if the President were a mislaid household utensil.

"In the library. He's undertaken to stay there until I go

back. We've got coppers keeping obbo in the passage."

"I should hope so. If this was a case of the wrong victim, chummy may well be gunning for the right one."

The sergeant was speaking on the telephone. "Superintendent Alleyn would like a word with you, sir."

Alleyn detected in Mr. Whipplestone's voice an overtone of occupational cool. "My dear Alleyn," he said, "this is a most disturbing occurrence. I understand the Ambassador has been — assassinated."

"Yes."

"How very dreadful. Nothing could have been worse."

"Except the intended target taking the knock."

"Oh — I see. The President."

"Listen," Alleyn said and made his request.

"Dear me," said Mr. Whipplestone.

"I know it's asking a lot. Damn cheek in fact. But it would take us some time to raise a neutral interpreter. It wouldn't do for one of the Ng'ombwanans."

"No, no, no, no, quite. Be quiet, Lucy. Yes. Very well, I'll come."

"I'm uncommonly grateful. You'll find a car at your door. 'Bye."

"Coming?" Gibson said.

"Yes. Sergeant, go and ask Mr. Fox to meet him and bring him here, will you? Pale. About sixty. Eyeglass. V.I.P. treatment."

"Sir."

And in a few minutes Mr. Whipplestone, stepping discreetly and having exchanged his tailcoat for a well-used smoking jacket, was shown into the room by Inspector Fox, whom Alleyn motioned to stay.

Gibson made a morose fuss of Mr. Whipplestone.

"You'll appreciate how it is, sir. The President insists on addressing his household staff and — "

"Yes, yes. I quite understand, Mr. Gibson. Difficult for you. I wonder, could I know what happened? It doesn't really affect the interpreter's role, of course, but—briefly?"

"Of course you could," Alleyn said. "Briefly then: Somebody fired a shot that you must have heard, apparently taking aim from the ladies' loo. It hit nobody, but when the lights went up the Ambassador was lying dead in the pavilion, spitted by the ceremonial Ng'ombwanan spear that was borne behind the President. The spear-carrier was crouched a few paces back, and as far as we can make out—he speaks no English—maintains that in the dark, when everybody was milling about in a hell of a stink over the shot, he was given a chop on the neck and his spear snatched from him."

"Do you believe this?"

"I don't know. I was there, in the pavilion, with Troy. She was sitting next to the President and I was beside her. When the shot rang out I told her to stay put and at the same time saw the shape of the Boomer half rise and make as if to go. His figure was momentarily silhouetted against Karbo's spotlight on the screen at the other end of the lake. I shoved him back in his chair, told him to pipe down, and moved in front of him. A split second later something crashed down at my feet. Some ass called out that the President had been shot. The Boomer and a number of others yelled for lights. They came up and—there was the Ambassador, literally pinned to the ground."

"A mistake then?"

"That seems to be the general idea—a mistake. They were of almost equal height and similar build. Their uniforms, in silhouette, would look alike. He was speared from behind and, from behind, would show up against the spotlit screen. There's one other point. My colleague here tells me he had two security men posted near the rear entrance to the pavilion. After the shot they say the black waiter came plunging out. They grabbed him but say he appeared to be just plain scared. That's right, isn't it, Fred?"

"That's the case," Gibson said. "The point being that while they were finding out what they'd caught, you've got to admit that it's just possible in that bloody blackout, if you'll excuse me, sir, somebody might have slipped into the pavilion."

"Somebody?" said Mr. Whipplestone.

"Well, anybody," Alleyn said. "Guest, waiter, what-have-you. It's unlikely but it's just possible."

"And got away again? After the – event?"

"Again – just remotely possible. And now, Sam, if you don't mind – "

"Of course."

"Where do they hold this tribal gathering, Fred? The President said the ballroom. O.K.?"

"O.K."

"Could you check with him and lay that on – I'll see how things are going in the pavilion and then join you. All right? Would that suit you?"

"Fair enough."

"Fox, will you come with me?"

On the way he gave Fox a succinct account of Mrs. Cockburn-Montfort's story and of the pistol shot, if pistol shot it was, in its relation to the climactic scene in the garden.

"Quite a little puzzle," said Fox cosily.

In the pavilion they found two uniform policemen, a photographic and a fingerprint expert – Detective Sergeants Thompson and Bailey – together with Sir James Curtis, never mentioned by the press without the additional gloss of "the celebrated pathologist." Sir James had completed his superficial examination. The spear, horridly incongruous, still stuck up at an angle from its quarry and was being photographed in close-up by Thompson. Not far from the body lay an overturned chair.

"This is a pretty kettle of fish you've got here, Rory," said Sir James.

"Is it through the heart?"

"Plumb through and well into the turf underneath, I think we'll find. Otherwise it wouldn't be so rigid. It looks as though the assailant followed through the initial thrust and, with a forward lunge, literally pinned him down."

"Ferocious."

"Very."

"Finished?" Alleyn asked Thompson as he straightened up. "Complete coverage? All angles? The lot?"

"Yes, Mr. Alleyn."

"Bailey? What about dabs?"

Bailey, a mulishly inclined officer, said he'd gone over the spear and could find evidence of only one set of prints and that they were smeared. He added that the camera might bring up something latent but he didn't hold out many hopes. The angle of the spear to the body had been measured. Sir James said it had been a downward thrust. "Which would indicate a tall man," he said.

"Or a middle-sized man on a chair?" Alleyn suggested.

"Yes. A possibility."

"All right," Alleyn said. "We'd better withdraw that thing."

"You'll have a job," Sir James offered.

They did have a job and the process was unpleasant. In the end the body had to be held down and the spear extracted by a violent jerk, producing a sickening noise and an extrusion of blood.

"Turn him over," Alleyn said.

The eyes were open and the jaw collapsed, turning the Ambassador's face into a grotesque mask of astonishment. The wound of entry was larger than that of exit. The closely cropped turf was wet.

"Horrible," Alleyn said shortly.

"I suppose we can take him away?" Sir James suggested. "I'll do the P.M. at once."

"I'm not so sure about that. We're on Ng'ombwanan ground. We're on sufferance. The mortuary van's outside all right, but I don't think we can do anything about the body unless they say so."

"Good Lord!"

"There may be all sorts of taboos, observances and what-have-you."

"Well," said Sir James, not best pleased, "in that case I'll take myself off. You might let me know if I'm wanted."

"Of course. We're all walking about like a gaggle of Agags, it's so tricky. Here's Fred Gibson."

He had come to say that the President wished the body to be conveyed to the ballroom.

"What for?" Alleyn demanded.

"This assembly or what-have-you. Then it's to be put upstairs. He wants it flown back to Ng'ombwana."

"Good evening to you," said Sir James and left.

Alleyn nodded to one of the constables, who fetched two men, a stretcher and a canvas. And so his country's representative re-entered his Embassy, finally relieved of the responsibility that had lain so heavily on his mind.

Alleyn said to the constables: "We'll keep this tent exactly as it is. One of you remains on guard." And to Fox: "D'you get the picture, Br'er Fox? Here we all were, a round dozen of us, including, you'll be surprised to hear, my brother."

"Is that so, Mr. Alleyn? Quite a coincidence."

"If you don't mind, Br'er Fox, we won't use that word. It's cropped up with monotonous regularity ever since I took my jaunt to Ng'ombwana."

"Sorry, I'm sure."

"Not at all. To continue. Here we were, in arrowhead formation with the President's chair at the apex. There's his chair and that's Troy beside it. On his other side was the Ambassador. The spear-carrier, who is at present under surveillance in the gents' cloaks, stood behind his master's chair. At the rear are those trestle tables used for drinks, and a bit further forward an overturned, pretty solid wooden chair, the purpose of which escapes me. The entrance into the tent at the back was used by the servants. There were two of them, the larger being one of the household henchmen and the other a fresh-faced, chunky specimen in Costard's livery. Both of them were in evidence when the lights went out."

"And so," said Fox, who liked to sort things out, "as soon as this Karbo artist appears, his spotlight picks him up and makes a splash on the screen behind him. And from the back of the tent where this spear expert is stationed, anybody who stands up between him and the light shows up like somebody coming in late at the cinema."

"That's it."

"And after the shot was fired you stopped the President from standing up, but the Ambassador *did* stand up and Bob, in a manner of speaking, was your uncle."

"In a manner of speaking, he was."

"Now then," Fox continued in his stately manner. "Yes. This shot. Fired, we're told by the lady you mentioned, from the window of the female conveniences. No weapon's been recovered, I take it?"

"Give us a chance."

"And nobody's corroborated the lady's story about this dirty big black man who kicked her?"

"No."

"And this chap hasn't been picked up?"

"He is like an insubstantial pageant faded."

"Just so. And do we assume, then, that having fired his shot and missed his man, an accomplice, spear-carrier or what have you, did the job for him?"

"That may be what we're supposed to think. To my mind it stinks. Not to high Heaven, but slightly."

"Then what – ?"

"Don't ask me, Br'er Fox. But designedly or not, the shot created a diversion."

"And when the lights came on?"

"The President was in his chair where I'd shoved him and Troy was in hers. The other two ladies were in theirs. The body was three feet to the President's left. The guests were milling about all over the shop. My big brother was ordering them in a shaky voice not to panic. The spear-carrier was on his knees nursing his carotid artery. The chair was overturned. No servants."

"I get the picture."

"Good, come on, then. The corroboree, pow-wow, conventicle or coven, call it what you will, is now in congress and we are stayed for." He turned to Bailey and Thompson. "Not much joy for you chaps at present, but if you can pick up something that looks too big for a female print in the second on the left of the ladies' loos it will be as balm in Gilead. Away we go, Fox."

But as they approached the house they were met by Gibson, looking perturbed, with Mr. Whipplestone in polite attendance.

"What's up, Fred?" Alleyn asked. "Have your race relations fractured?"

"You could put it like that," Mr. Gibson conceded. "He's making things difficult."

"The President?"

"That's right. He won't collaborate with anyone but you."

"Silly old chump."

"He won't come out of his library until you've gone in."

"What's bitten him, for the love of Mike?"

"I doubt if he knows."

"Perhaps," Mr. Whipplestone ventured, "he doesn't like the introduction of me into the proceedings?"

"I wouldn't say that, sir," said Gibson unhappily.

"What a nuisance he contrives to be," Alleyn said. "I'll talk to him. Are the hosts of Ng'ombwana mustered in the ballroom?"

"Yes. Waiting for Master," said Gibson.

"Any developments, Fred?"

"Nothing to rave about. I've had a piece of that sergeant in the cloakroom. It seems she acted promptly enough after she left her grandstand seat and attended to Mrs. C.-M. She located the nearest of my men and gave him the info. A search for chummy was set up with no results and I was informed. The men on duty outside the house say nobody left it. If they say so, nobody did," said Gibson, sticking his jaw out. "We've begun to search for the gun or whatever it was."

"It sounded to me like a pistol," said Alleyn. "I'd better beard the lion in his library, I suppose. We'll meet here. I'm damned sorry to victimize you like this, Sam."

"My dear fellow, you needn't be. I'm afraid I'm rather enjoying myself," said Mr. Whipplestone.

III

Alleyn scarcely knew what sort of reception he expected to get from the Boomer or what sort of tactics he himself should deploy to meet it.

In the event, the Boomer behaved pretty much according to pattern. He strode down upon Alleyn and seized his hands. "Ah!" he roared, "you are here at last. I am glad. Now we shall get this affair settled."

"I'm afraid it's far from being settled at the moment."

"Because of all these pettifogging coppers. And believe me, I do not include you in that category, my dear Rory."

"Very good of you, sir."

" 'Sir. Sir. Sir'—what tommy-rot. Never mind. We shall not waste time over details. I have come to a decision and you shall be the first to hear what it is."

"Thank you, I'll be glad to know."

"Good. Then listen. I understand perfectly that your funny colleague—what is his name?"

"Gibson?" Alleyn ventured.

"Gibson, Gibson. I understand perfectly that the well-meaning Gibson and his band of bodyguards and so on were here at the invitation of my Ambassador. I am correct?"

"Yes."

"Again, good. But my Ambassador has, as we used to say at Davidson's, kicked over the bucket, and in any case the supreme authority is mine. Yes?"

"Of course it is."

"Of course it is," the Boomer repeated with immense satisfaction. "It is mine and I propose to exercise it. An attempt has been made upon my life. It has failed as all such attempts are bound to fail. That I made clear to you on the happy occasion of your visit."

"So you did."

"Nevertheless, an attempt has been made," the Boomer repeated. "My Ambassador has been killed and the matter must be cleared up."

"I couldn't agree more."

"I therefore have called together the people of his household and will question them in accordance with our historically established democratic practice. In Ng'ombwana."

As Alleyn was by no means certain what this practice might turn out to be he said, cautiously, "Do you feel that somebody in the household may be responsible?"

"One may find that this is not so. In which case—" The great voice rumbled into silence.

"In which case?" Alleyn hinted.

"My dear man, in which case I hope for your and the well-meaning Gibson's collaboration."

So he'd got it all tidied up, Alleyn thought. The Boomer would handle the black elements and he and the C.I.D. could make what they liked of the white. Really, it began to look like a sort of inverted form of apartheid.

"I don't have to tell you," he said, "that authorities at every level will be most deeply concerned that this should have happened. The Special Branch, in particular, is in a great taking-on about it."

"Hah! So much," said the Boomer with relish, "for all the large men in the shrubberies. What?"

"All right. *Touché.*"

"All the same, my dear Rory, if it is true that I was the intended victim, it might well be said that I owe my life to you."

"Rot."

"Not rot. It would follow logically. You pushed me down in my chair, and there was this unhappy Ambassador waving his arms about and looking like me. So—blam! Yes, yes, yes. In that case, I would owe you my life. It is a debt I would not willingly incur with anyone but you—with you I would willingly acknowledge it."

"Not a bit," Alleyn said, in acute embarrassment. "It may turn out that my intervention was merely a piece of unnecessary bloody cheek—" He hesitated and was inspired to add, "as we used to say at Davidson's." And since this did the trick, he hurried on. "Following that line of thought," he said, "you might equally say that I was responsible for the Ambassador's death."

"That," said the Boomer grandly, "is another pair of boots."

"Tell me," Alleyn asked, "have you any theories about the pistol shot?"

"Ah!" he said quickly. "Pistol! So you have found the weapon?"

"No. I call it a pistol shot provisionally. Gun. Revolver. Automatic. What you will. With your permission, we'll search."

"Where?"

"Well—in the garden. And the pond, for instance."

"The pond?"

Alleyn gave him a digest of Mrs. Cockburn-Montfort's narrative. The Boomer, it appeared, knew the Cockburn-Montforts quite well and indeed had actually been associated with the Colonel during the period when he helped organize the modern Ng'ombwanan army. "He was efficient," said the Boomer, "but unfortunately he took to the bottle. His wife is, as we used to say, hairy round the hocks."

"She says the man in the lavatory was black."

There followed a longish pause. "If that is correct, I shall find him," he said at last.

"He certainly didn't leave these premises. All the exits have been closely watched."

If the Boomer was tempted to be rude once more about Mr. Gibson's methods he restrained himself. "What is the truth," he asked, "about this marksman? Did he, in fact, fire at me and miss me? Is that proved?"

"Nothing is proved. Tell me, do you trust—absolutely—the spear-carrier?"

"Absolutely. But I shall question him as if I do not."

"Will you—and I'm diffident about asking this—will you allow me to be there? At the assembly?"

For a moment he fancied he saw signs of withdrawal, but if so they vanished at once. The Boomer waved his paw.

"Of course. Of course. But my dear Rory, you will not understand a word of it."

"Do you know Sam Whipplestone? Of the F.O. and lately retired?"

"I know *of* him. Of course. He has had many connections with my country. We have not met until tonight. He was a guest. And he is present now with your Gibson. I couldn't understand why."

"I asked him to come. He speaks your language fluently and he's my personal friend. Would you allow him to sit in with me? I'd be very grateful."

And now, Alleyn thought, he really was in for a rebuff—but no, after a disconcerting interval the Boomer said: "This is a little difficult. An enquiry of this nature is never open to persons who have no official standing. Our proceedings are never made public."

"I give you my firm undertaking that they wouldn't be in this instance. Whipplestone is the soul of discretion. I can vouch for him."

"You can?"

"I can and I do."

"Very well," said the Boomer. "But no Gibsons."

"All right. But why have you taken against poor Gibson?"

"Why? I cannot say why. Perhaps because he is so large." The enormous Boomer pondered for a moment. "And so pale," he finally brought out. "He is very, very pale."

Alleyn said he believed the entire household was now assembled in the ballroom and the Boomer said that he would go there. Something in his manner made Alleyn think of a star actor preparing for his entrance.

"It is perhaps a little awkward," the Boomer reflected. "On such an occasion I should be attended by my Ambassador and my personal *mlinzi*—my guard. But since the one is dead and the other possibly his murderer, it is not feasible."

"Tiresome for you."

"Shall we go?"

They left, passing one of Gibson's men in Costard's livery.

In the hall they found Mr. Whipplestone, patient in a high-backed chair. The Boomer, evidently minded to do his thing properly, was extremely gracious. Mr. Whipplestone offered perfectly phrased regrets for the Ambassador's demise and the Boomer told him that the Ambassador had spoken warmly of him and had talked of asking him to tea.

Gibson was nowhere to be seen, but another of his men quietly passed Alleyn a folded paper. While Mr. Whipplestone and the Boomer were still exchanging compliments, he had a quick look at it.

"Found the gun," it read. "See you, after."

IV

The ballroom was shut up. Heavy curtains were drawn across the French windows. The chandeliers sparkled, the flowers were brilliant. Only a faint reek of champagne, sandarac and cigarette smoke suggested the aftermath of festivities. The ballroom had become Ng'ombwana.

A crowd of Ng'ombwanans waited at the end of the great saloon where the red alcove displayed its warlike trophies.

It was a larger assembly than Alleyn had expected: men in full evening dress whom he supposed to be authoritative persons in the household, a controller, a secretary, under-secretaries. There were some dozen men in livery and as many women with white head-scarves and dresses, and there was a knot of under-servants in white jackets clustered at the rear of the assembly. Clearly they were all grouped in conformance with the domestic hierarchy. The President's aides-de-camp waited at the back of the dais. And ranked on each side of it, armed and immovable, was his guard in full ceremonial kit: scarlet tunics, white kilts, immaculate leggings, glistening accoutrements.

And on the floor in front of the dais was a massive table, bearing under a lion's hide the unmistakable shape of the shrouded dead.

Alleyn and Mr. Whipplestone entered in the wake of the Boomer. The guard came to attention, the crowd became very still. The Boomer walked slowly and superbly to his dais. He gave an order and two chairs were placed on the floor not far from the bier. He motioned Alleyn and Mr. Whipplestone to take them. Alleyn would have greatly preferred an inconspicuous stand at the rear, but there was no help for it and they took their places.

"I daren't write, dare I?" Mr. Whipplestone muttered, "and nor dare I talk."

"You'll have to remember."

"All jolly fine."

The Boomer, seated in his great chair, his hands on the arms, his body upright, his chin raised, his knees and feet planted together, looked like an effigy of himself. His eyes, as always a little bloodshot, rolled and flashed, his teeth gleamed, and he spoke in a language which seemed to be composed entirely of vowels, gutturals and clicks. His voice was so huge that Mr. Whipplestone, trying to speak like a ventriloquist, ventured two words.

"Describing incident," he said.

The speech seemed to grow in urgency. He brought both palms down sharply on the arms of his chair. Alleyn wondered if he only imagined that a heightened tension invested the audience. A pause and then, unmistakably, an order.

"Spear, chap," ventriloquized Mr. Whipplestone. "Fetch."

Two of the guards came smartly to attention, marched to meet each other, faced front, saluted, about-turned and marched out. Absolute stillness followed this proceeding. Sounds from outside could be heard. Gibson's men in the garden, no doubt, and once, almost certainly, Gibson's voice.

When the silence had become very trying indeed, the soldiers returned with the spear-carrier between them.

He was still dressed in his ceremonial garments. His anklets and armbands shone in the lamplight and so did his burnished body and limbs. But he's not really *black,* Alleyn thought. "If Troy painted him he would be anything but black – blue, mole, purple, even red where his body reflects the carpet and walls." He was glossy. His close-cropped head sat above its tier of throat-rings like a huge ebony marble. He wore his lion's skin like a lion. Alleyn noticed that his right arm was hooked under it as if in a sling.

He walked between his guards to the bier. They left him there, isolated before his late Ambassador and his President and close enough to Alleyn and Mr. Whipplestone for them to smell the sweet oil with which he had polished himself.

The examination began. It was impossible most of the time for Alleyn to guess what was being said. Both men kept very still. Their teeth and eyes flashed from time to time, but their big voices were level and they used no gesture until suddenly the spearman slapped the base of his own neck.

"Chop," breathed Mr. Whipplestone. "Karate. Sort of."

Soon after this there was a break and neither man spoke for perhaps eight seconds; then, to Alleyn's surprise and discomfiture, the Boomer began to talk, still in the Ng'ombwanan tongue, to him. It was a shortish observation. At the end of it the Boomer nodded to Mr. Whipplestone, who cleared his throat.

"The President," he said, "directs me to ask you if you will give an account of what you yourself witnessed in the pavilion. He also directs me to translate what you say, as he wishes the proceedings to be conducted throughout in the Ng'ombwanan language."

They stood up. Alleyn gave his account, to which the Boomer reacted as if he didn't understand a word. Mr. Whipplestone translated.

Maintaining this laborious procedure, Alleyn was asked if after the death had been discovered he had formed any opinion as to whether the spearman was, in fact, injured.

Looking at the superb being standing there like a rock, it was difficult to imagine that a blow on the carotid nerve or anywhere else for that matter could cause him the smallest discomfiture. Alleyn said: "He was kneeling, with his right hand in the position he has just shown. His head was bent, his left hand clenched and his shoulders hunched. He appeared to be in pain."

"And then," translated Mr. Whipplestone, "what happened?"

Alleyn repressed an insane desire to remind the Boomer that he was there at the time and invite him to come off it and talk English.

He said: "There was a certain amount of confusion. This was checked by — " he looked straight at the Boomer — "the President, who spoke in Ng'ombwanan to the spearman, who appeared to offer some kind of statement or denial. Subsequently five men on duty from the Special Branch of the C.I.D. arrived with two of the President's guard who had been stationed outside the pavilion. The spearman was removed to the house."

Away went Mr. Whipplestone again.

The Boomer next wished to know if the police had obtained any evidence from the spear itself. Alleyn replied that no report had been released under that heading.

This, apparently, ended his examination, if such it could be called. He sat down.

After a further silence, and it occurred to Alleyn that the Ng'ombwanans were adepts in non-communication, the Boomer rose.

It would have been impossible to say why the atmosphere, already far from relaxed, now became taut to twanging point. What happened was that the President pointed, with enormous authority, at the improvised bier and unmistakably pronounced a command.

The spearman, giving no sign of agitation, at once extended his left hand — the right was still concealed in his bosom — and drew down the covering. And there was the Ambassador, open-mouthed, goggle-eyed, making some sort of indecipherable declaration.

The spearman, laying his hand upon the body, spoke boldly and briefly. The President replied even more briefly. The lion-skin mantle was replaced, and the ceremony — assembly, trial, whatever it might be — was at an end. At no time during the final proceedings had the Boomer so much as glanced at Alleyn.

He now briefly harangued his hearers. Mr. Whipplestone muttered that he ordered any of them who had any information, however trivial, bearing however slightly on the case, to speak immediately. This met with an absolute silence. His peroration was to the effect that he himself was in command of affairs at the Embassy. He then left. His A.D.C.'s followed, and the one with whom Alleyn was acquainted paused by him to say the President requested his presence in the library.

"I will come," Alleyn said, "in ten minutes. My compliments to the President, if you please."

The A.D.C. rolled his eyes, said, "But — ", changed his mind and followed his master.

"That," said Mr. Whipplestone, "was remarkably crisp."

"If he doesn't like it he can lump it. I want a word with Gibson. Come on."

Gibson, looking sulky, and Fox were waiting for them at their temporary quarters in the controller's office. On the desk, lying on a damp unfolded handkerchief, was a revolver. Thompson and Bailey stood nearby with their tools of trade.

"Where?" said Alleyn.

"In the pond. We picked it up with a search-lamp. Lying

on the blue tiled bottom at the corner opposite the conveniences and three feet in from the margin."

"Easy chucking distance from the loo window."

"That's correct."

"Anything?" Alleyn asked Bailey.

"No joy, Mr. Alleyn. Gloves, I reckon."

"It's a Luger," Alleyn said.

"They are not hard to come by," Mr. Whipplestone said, "in Ng'ombwana."

"You know," Alleyn said, "almost immediately after the shot, I heard something fall into the pond. It was in the split second before the rumpus broke out."

"Well, well," said Fox. "Not," he reasoned, "a very sensible way for him to carry on. However you look at it. Still," he said heavily, "that's how they do tend to behave."

"Who do, Br'er Fox?"

"Political assassins, the non-professionals. They're a funny mob, by all accounts."

"You're dead right there, Teddy," said Mr. Gibson. "I suppose," he added, appealing to Alleyn, "we retain possession of this Luger, do we?"

"Under the circumstances we'll be lucky if we retain possession of our wits. I'm damned if I know. The whole thing gets more and more like a revival of the Goon Show."

"The A.C., your department, rang."

"What's *he* want?"

"To say the Deputy Commissioner will be calling in to offer condolences or what have you to the President. And no doubt," said Gibson savagely, "to offer me his advice and congratulations on a successful operation. *Christ!*" he said, and turned his back on his colleagues.

Alleyn and Fox exchanged a look.

"You couldn't have done more," Alleyn said after a moment. "Take the whole lay-out, you couldn't have given any better coverage."

"That bloody sergeant in the bog."

"All right. But if Mrs. Cockburn-Montfort's got it straight, the sergeant wouldn't have stopped him in the dark, wherever she was."

"I told them. I told these bastards they shouldn't have the blackout."

"But," said Fox, in his reasonable way, "the gun-man didn't do the job anyway. There's that aspect, Mr. Gibson, isn't there?"

Gibson didn't answer this. He turned round and said to Alleyn: "We've got to find out if the President's available to see the D.C."

"When?"

"He's on his way in from Kent. Within the hour."

"I'll find out." Alleyn turned to Mr. Whipplestone. "I can't tell you, Sam, how much obliged to you I am," he said. "If it's not asking too much, could you bear to write out an account of that black – in both senses – charade in there while it's still fresh in your mind? I'm having another go at the great panjandrum in the library."

"Yes, of course," said Mr. Whipplestone. "I'd like to."

So he was settled down with writing materials and immediately took on the air of being at his own desk in his own rather rarified office with a secretary in deferential attendance.

"What's horrible for us, Fred?" Alleyn asked. It was a regulation enquiry for which he was known at the Yard.

"We've got that lot from the tent party still waiting. Except the ones who obviously hadn't a clue about anything. And," Gibson added a little awkwardly, "Mrs. Alleyn. She's gone, of course."

"I can always put her through the hoops at home."

"And – er," said Gibson still more awkwardly, "there is – er – your brother."

"*What!*" Alleyn shouted. "George! You don't tell me you've

got George sitting on his fat bottom waiting for the brutal police bit?"

"Well – "

"Mrs. Alleyn *and* Sir George," said Fox demurely. "And we're not allowed to mention coincidence."

"Old George," Alleyn pondered, "what a lark! Fox, you might press on with statements from that little lot. Including George. While I have another go at the Boomer. What about you, Fred?"

"Get on with the bloody routine, I suppose. Could you lend me these two," he indicated Bailey and Thompson, "for the ladies' conveniences? Not that there's much chance of anything turning up there. Still, we've got this Luger-merchant roaming round somewhere in the establishment. We're searching for the bullet, of course, and that's no piece of cake. Seeing you," he said morosely, and walked out.

"You'd better get on with the loo," Alleyn said to Bailey and Thompson, and himself returned to the library.

V

"Look," Alleyn said, "it's this way. You – Your Excellency – can, as of course you know, order us off whenever you feel like it. As far as enquiries inside the Embassy are concerned, we can become *persona non grata* at the drop of a hat and as such would have to limit our activities, of which you've no doubt formed an extremely poor opinion, to looking after your security whenever you leave these premises. We will also follow up any lines of enquiry that present themselves outside the Embassy. Quite simply it's a matter of whether or not you wish us to carry on as we are or make ourselves scarce. Colonel Sinclaire, the Deputy Commissioner of the Metropolitan Police, is on his way. He hopes he may be allowed to wait upon you.

No doubt he will express his deep regrets and put the situation before you in more or less the same terms I have used."

For the first time since they had renewed their acquaintance, Alleyn found a kind of hesitancy in the Boomer's manner. He made as if to speak, checked himself, looked hard at Alleyn for a moment, and then began to pace up and down the library with the magnificent action that really did recall clichés about caged panthers.

At last he stopped in front of Alleyn and abruptly took him by the arms. "What," he demanded, "did you think of our enquiry? Tell me."

"It was immensely impressive," Alleyn said at once.

"Yes? You found it so? But you think it strange, don't you, that I, who have eaten my dinners and practised my profession as a barrister, should subscribe to such a performance. After all, it was not much like the proceedings of the British coroner's inquest?"

"Not conspicuously like. No."

"No. And yet, my dear Rory, it told me a great deal more than would have been elicited by that highly respectable court."

"Yes?" Alleyn said politely. And with a half-smile: "Am I to know what it told Your Excellency?"

"It told My Excellency that my *nkuki mtu mwenye* – my *mlinzi*, my man with the spear – spoke the truth."

"I see."

"You are non-committal. You want to know how I know?"

"If it suits you to tell me."

"I am," announced the Boomer, "the son of a paramount chief. My father and his and his, back into the dawn, were paramount chiefs. If this man, under oath to protect me, had been guilty of murdering my innocent and loyal servant he could not have uncovered the body before me and declared his innocence. Which is what he did. It would not be possible."

"I see."

"And you would reply that such evidence is not admissible in a British court of law."

"It would be *admissible,* I daresay. It could be eloquently pleaded by able counsel. It wouldn't be accepted, *ipso facto,* as proof of innocence. But you know that as well as I do."

"Tell me this. It is important for me. Do you believe what I have said?"

"I think I do," Alleyn said slowly. "You know your people. You tell me it is so. Yes. I'm not sure but I am inclined to believe you are right."

"Ah!" said the Boomer. "So now we are upon our old footing. That is good."

"But I must make it clear to you. Whatever I may or may not think has no bearing on the way I'll conduct this investigation: either inside the Embassy, if you'll have us here, or outside it. If there turns out to be cogent evidence, in our book, against this man, we'll follow it up."

"In any case, the event having taken place in this Embassy, on his own soil, he could not be tried in England," said the Boomer.

"No. Whatever we find, in that sense, is academic. He would be repatriated."

"And this person who fires off German weapons in ladies' lavatories. You say he also is black."

"Mrs. Cockburn-Montfort says so."

"A stupid woman."

"Tolerably so, I'd have thought."

"It would be better if her husband beat her occasionally and left her at home," said the Boomer with one of his gusts of laughter.

"I should like to know, if it isn't too distressing for you to speak of him, something of the Ambassador himself. Did you like him very much? Was he close to you? Those sorts of questions?"

The Boomer dragged his great hand across his mouth, made a long rumbling sound in his chest, and sat down.

"I find it difficult," he said at last, "to answer your question. What sort of man was he? A fuddy-duddy, as we used to say. He has come up, in the English sense, through the ranks. The peasant class. At one time he was a nuisance. He saw himself staging some kind of *coup*. It was all rather ridiculous. He had certain administrative abilities but no real authority. That sort of person."

Disregarding this example of Ng'ombwanan snob-thinking, Alleyn remarked that the Ambassador must have been possessed of considerable ability to have got where he did. The Boomer waved a concessionary hand and said that the trend of development had favoured his advancement.

"Had he enemies?"

"My dear Rory, in an emergent nation like my own every man of authority has or has had enemies. I know of no specific persons."

"He was in a considerable taking-on about security during your visit," Alleyn ventured, to which the Boomer vaguely replied: "Oh. Did you think so?"

"He telephoned Gibson and me on an average twice a day."

"Boring for you," said the Boomer in his best public school manner.

"He was particularly agitated about the concert in the garden and the blackout. So were we for that matter."

"He was a fuss-pot," said the Boomer.

"Well, damn it all, he had some cause, as it turns out."

The Boomer pursed up his generous mouth into a double mulberry and raised his brows. "If you put it like that."

"After all, he is dead."

"True," the Boomer admitted.

Nobody can look quite so eloquently bored as a Negro. The eyes are almost closed, showing a lower rim of white, the mouth droops, the head tilts. The whole man suddenly seems to wilt. The Boomer now exhibited all these signals of ennui and Alleyn, remembering them of old, said: "Never mind. I mustn't keep you any longer. Could we, do you think, just settle these two points: First, will you receive the Deputy Commissioner when he comes?"

"Of course," drawled the Boomer without opening his eyes.

"Second. Do you wish the C.I.D. to carry on inside the Embassy or would you prefer us to clear out? The decision is Your Excellency's, of course, but we would be grateful for a definite ruling."

The Boomer opened his slightly bloodshot eyes. He looked full at Alleyn. "Stay," he said.

There was a tap at the door and Gibson, large, pale and apologetic, came in.

"I'm sure I beg your pardon, sir," he said to the President. "Colonel Sinclaire, the Deputy Commissioner, has arrived and hopes to see you."

The Boomer, without looking at Gibson, said: "Ask my equerry to bring him in."

Alleyn walked to the door. He had caught a signal of urgency from his colleague.

"Don't you go, Rory," said the Boomer.

"I'm afraid I must," said Alleyn.

Outside, in the passage, he found Mr. Whipplestone fingering his tie and looking deeply perturbed. Alleyn said: "What's up?"

"It may not be anything," Gibson answered. "It's just that we've been talking to the Costard man who was detailed to serve in the tent."

"Stocky, well set-up, fair-haired?"

"That's him. Name of Chubb," said Gibson.

"Alas," said Mr. Whipplestone.

V

Small Hours

Chubb stood more or less to attention, looking straight before him with his arms at his sides. He cut quite a pleasing figure in Costard et Cie's discreet livery: midnight blue shell-jacket and trousers with gold endorsements. His faded blond hair was short and well brushed, his fresh West Country complexion and blue eyes deceptively gave him the air of an outdoor man. He still wore his white gloves.

Alleyn had agreed with Mr. Whipplestone that it would be best if the latter were not present at the interview. "Though," Alleyn said, "there's no reason at all to suppose that Chubb, any more than my silly old brother George, had anything to do with the event."

"I know, I know," Mr. Whipplestone had returned. "Of course. It's just that, however illogically and stupidly, I would prefer Chubb *not* to have been on duty in that wretched pavilion. Just as I would prefer him *not* to have odd-time jobs with Sheridan and those beastly Montforts. And it *would* be rather odd for me to be there, wouldn't it? Very foolish of me, no doubt. Let it go at that."

So Alleyn and an anonymous sergeant had Chubb to themselves in the controller's office.

Alleyn said: "I want to be quite sure I've got this right. You were in and out of the pavilion with champagne which you fetched from an icebox that had been set up outside the pavilion. You did this in conjunction with one of the Embassy servants. He waited on the President and the people immediately surrounding him, didn't he? I remember that he came to my wife and me soon after we had settled there."

"Sir," said Chubb.

"And you looked after the rest of the party."

"Sir."

"Yes. Well now, Chubb, we've kept you hanging about all this time in the hope that you can give us some help about what happened in the pavilion."

"Not much chance of that, sir. I never noticed anything, sir."

"That makes two of us, I'm afraid," Alleyn said. "It happened like a bolt from the blue, didn't it? Were you actually in the pavilion? When the lights went out?"

Yes, it appeared. At the back. He had put his tray down on a trestle table in preparation for the near blackout, about which the servants had all been warned. He had remained there through the first item.

"And were you still there when the singer, Karbo, appeared?" Yes, he said. Still there. He had had an uninterrupted view of Karbo, standing in his spotlight with his shadow thrown up behind him on the white screen.

"Did you notice where the guard with the spear was standing?" Yes. At the rear. Behind the President's chair.

"On your left, would that be?"

"Yes, sir."

"And your fellow waiter?"

"The nigger?" said Chubb, and after a glance at Alleyn, "Beg pardon, sir. The native."

"The African, yes."

"He was somewhere there. At the rear. I never took no notice," said Chubb stonily.

"You didn't speak to either of them, at all?"

"No thanks. I wouldn't think they knew how."

"You don't like black people?" Alleyn said lightly.

"No, sir."

"Well. To come to the moment when the shot was fired. I'm getting as many accounts as possible from the people who were in the pavilion, and I'd like yours too, if you will. You remember that the performer had given out one note, if that's the way to put it. A long-drawn-out sound. And then – as you recall it – what?"

"The shot, sir."

"Did you get an impression about where the sound came from?"

"The house, sir."

"Yes. Well, now, Chubb. Could you just, as best as you are able, tell me your own impressions of what followed the shot. In the pavilion, I mean."

Nothing clear-cut emerged. People had stood up. A lady had screamed. A gentleman had shouted out not to panic. ("George," Alleyn thought.)

"Yes. But as far as what you actually *saw*. From where you were, at the back of the pavilion?"

Hard to say, exactly, Chubb said in his wooden voice. People moving about a bit but not much. Alleyn said that they had appeared, hadn't they? "Like black silhouettes against the spotlit screen." Chubb agreed.

"The guard – the man with the spear? He was on your left. Quite close to you. Wasn't he?"

"At the start, sir, he was. Before the pavilion lights went out."

"And afterwards?"

There was a considerable pause: "I couldn't say, exactly, sir. Not straightaway, like."

"How do you mean?"

Chubb suddenly erupted. "I was grabbed," he said. "He sprung it on me. *Me!* From behind. *Me!*"

"Grabbed? Do you mean by the spearman?"

"Not him. The other black bastard."

"The waiter?"

"Yes. Sprung it on me. From behind. *Me!*"

"What did he spring on you? A half-Nelson?"

"Head-lock! I couldn't speak. *And* he put in the knee."

"How did you know it was the waiter?"

"I knew all right. I knew and no error."

"But *how?*"

"Bare arm for one thing. And the smell: like salad oil or something. I knew."

"How long did this last?"

"Long enough," said Chubb, fingering his neck. "Long enough for his mate to put in the spear, I reckon."

"Did he hold you until the lights went up?"

"No, sir. Only while it was being done. So I couldn't see it. The stabbing. I was doubled up. *Me!*" Chubb reiterated with, if possible, an access of venom. "But I heard. The sound. You can't miss it. And the fall."

The sergeant cleared his throat.

Alleyn said: "This is enormously important, Chubb. I'm sure you realize that, don't you? You're saying that the Ng'ombwanan waiter attacked and restrained you while the guard speared the Ambassador."

"Sir."

"All right. Why, do you suppose? I mean, why you, in particular?"

"I was nearest, sir, wasn't I? I might of got in the way or done something quick, mightn't I?"

"Was a small hard chair overturned during this attack?"

"It might of been," Chubb said after a pause.

"How old are you, Chubb?"

"Me, sir? Fifty-two, sir."

"What did you do in World War II?"

"Commando, sir."

"Ah!" Alleyn said, quietly. "I see."

"They wouldn't of sprung it across me in those days, sir."

"I'm sure they wouldn't. One more thing. After the shot and before you were attacked and doubled up, you saw the Ambassador, did you, on his feet? Silhouetted against the screen?"

"Sir."

"Did you recognize him?"

Chubb was silent.

"Well — did you?"

"I — can't say I did. Not exactly."

"How do you mean — not exactly?"

"It all happened so quick, didn't it? I — I reckon I thought he was the other one. The President."

"Why?"

"Well. Because. Well, because, you know, he was near where the President sat, like. He must of moved away from his own chair, sir, mustn't he? And standing up like he was in command, as you might say. And the President had roared out something in their lingo, hadn't he?"

"So, you'd say, would you, Chubb, that the Ambassador was killed in mistake for the President?"

"I couldn't say that, sir, could I? Not for certain. But I'd say he might of been. He might easy of been."

"You didn't see anybody attack the spearman?"

"*Him!* He couldn't of been attacked, could he? I was the one that got clobbered, sir, wasn't I? Not him: he did the big job, didn't he?"

"He maintains that he was given a chop and his spear was snatched out of his grasp by the man who attacked him. He says that he didn't see who this man was. You may remember that when the lights came up and the Ambassador's body was seen, the spearman was crouched on the ground up near the back of the pavilion."

Through this speech of Alleyn's, such animation as Chubb

had displayed deserted him. He reverted to his former manner, staring straight in front of him with such a wooden air that the ebb of colour from his face and its dark, uneven return seemed to bear no relation to any emotional experience.

When he spoke it was to revert to his favourite observation. "I wouldn't know about any of that," he said. "I never took any notice to that."

"Didn't you? But you were quite close to the spearman. You were standing by him. I happen to remember seeing you there."

"I was a bit shook up. After what the other one done to me."

"So it would seem. When the lights came on, was the waiter who attacked you, as you maintain, still there?"

"Him? He'd scarpered."

"Have you seen him since then?"

Chubb said he hadn't, but added that he couldn't tell one of the black bastards from another. The conventional mannerisms of the servant together with his careful grammar had almost disappeared. He sounded venomous. Alleyn then asked him why he hadn't reported the attack on himself immediately to the police, and Chubb became injured and exasperated. What chance had there been for that, he complained, with them all being shoved about into queues and drafted into groups and told to behave quiet and act co-operative and stay put and questions and statements would come later.

He began to sweat and put his hands behind his back. He said he didn't feel too good. Alleyn told him that the sergeant would make a typescript of his statement and he would be asked to read and sign it if he found it correct.

"In the meantime," he said, "we'll let you go home to Mr. Whipplestone."

Chubb, reverting to his earlier style, said anxiously: "Beg pardon, sir, but I didn't know you knew—"

"I know Mr. Whipplestone very well. He told me about you."

"Yes, sir. Will that be all, then, sir?"

"I think so, for the present. Good night to you, Chubb."

"Thank you, sir. Good night, sir."

He left the room with his hands clenched.

"Commando, eh?" said the sergeant to his notes.

II

Mr. Fox was doing his competent best with the group of five persons who sat wearily about the apartment that had been used as a sort of bar-cum-smoking-room for male guests at the party. It smelt of stale smoke, the dregs of alcohol, heavy upholstery and, persistently, of the all-pervading sandarac. It wore an air of exhausted raffishness.

The party of five being interviewed by Mr. Fox and noted down by a sergeant consisted of a black plenipotentiary and his wife; the last of the governors of British Ng'ombwana and *his* wife, and Sir George Alleyn, Bart. They were the only members of the original party of twelve guests who had remembered anything that might conceivably have a bearing upon events in the pavilion, and they remained after a painstaking winnowing had disposed of their companions.

The ex-governor, who was called Sir John Smythe, remembered that immediately after the shot was fired everybody moved to the front of the pavilion. He was contradicted by Lady Smythe, who said that for her part she had remained rivetted in her chair. The plenipotentiary's wife, whose understanding of English appeared to be rudimentary, conveyed through her husband that she, also, had remained seated. Mr. Fox reminded himself that Mrs. Alleyn, instructed by her husband, had not risen. The plenipotentiary recalled that the chairs had been set out in an inverted V shape with the President and his Ambassador at the apex and the guests forming the two wide-angled wings.

"Is that the case, sir?" said Fox comfortably. "I see. So that when you gentlemen stood up you'd all automatically be forward of the President? Nearer to the opening of the pavilion than he was? Would that be correct?"

"Quite right, Mr. Fox. Quite right," said Sir George, who had adopted a sort of uneasy reciprocal attitude towards Fox and had, at the outset, assured him jovially that he'd heard a great deal about him, to which Fox replied: "Is that the case, sir? If I might just have your name."

It was Sir George who remembered the actual order in which the guests had sat, and although Fox had already obtained this information from Alleyn, he gravely noted it down. On the President's left had been the Ambassador, Sir John and Lady Smythe, the plenipotentiary's wife, the plenipotentiary, a guest who had now gone home, and Sir George himself. "In starvation corner, what?" said Sir George lightly to the Smythes, who made little deprecatory noises.

"Yes, I see, thank you, sir," said Fox. "And on the President's right hand, sir?"

"Oh!" said Sir George waving his hand. "My brother. My brother and his wife. Yes. 'Strordinary coincidence." Apparently feeling the need for some sort of endorsement, he turned to his fellow guests. "My brother, the bobby," he explained. "Ridiculous, what?"

"A very distinguished bobby," Sir John Smythe murmured, to which Sir George returned: "Oh, quite! Quite! Not for me to say but—he'll do." He laughed and made a jovial little grimace.

"Yes," said Fox to his notes. "And four other guests who have now left. Thank you, sir." He looked over the top of his spectacles at his hearers. "We come to the incident itself. There's this report: pistol shot or whatever it was. The lights in the pavilion are out. Everybody except the ladies and the President gets to his feet. Doing what?"

"How d'you mean, doing what?" Sir John Smythe asked.

"Well, sir, did everybody face out into the garden trying to see what was going on — apart from the concert item, which I understand stopped short when the report was heard."

"Speaking for myself," said Sir George, "I stayed where I was. There were signs of — ah — agitation and — ah — movement. Sort of thing that needs to be nipped in the bud if you don't want a panic on your hands."

"And you nipped it, sir?" Fox asked.

"Well — I wouldn't go so far — one does one's best. I mean to say — I said something. Quietly."

"If there had been any signs of panic," said Sir John Smythe drily, "they did not develop."

"— 'did not develop,'" Mr. Fox repeated. "And in issuing your warning, sir, did you face inwards? With your back to the garden?"

"Yes. Yes, I did," said Sir George.

"And did you notice anything at all out of the way, sir?"

"I couldn't see anything, my dear man. One was blinded by having looked at the brilliant light on the screen and the performer."

"There wasn't any reflected light in the pavilion?"

"No," said Sir George crossly. "There wasn't. Nothing of the kind. It was too far away."

"I see, sir," said Fox placidly.

Lady Smythe suddenly remarked that the light on the screen was reflected in the lake. "The whole thing," she said, "was dazzling and rather confusing." There was a general murmur of agreement.

Mr. Fox asked if during the dark interval anybody else had turned his or her back on the garden and peered into the interior. This produced a confused and doubtful response, from which it emerged that the piercing screams of Mrs. Cockburn-

Montfort within the house had had a more marked effect than the actual report. The Smythes had both heard Alleyn telling the President to sit down. After the report everybody had heard the President shout out something in his own language. The plenipotentiary said it was an order. He shouted for lights. And immediately before or after that, Sir John Smythe said, he had been aware of something falling at his feet.

And then the lights had gone up.

"And I can only add, Inspector," said Sir John, "that I really have nothing else to say that can have the slightest bearing on this tragic business. The ladies have been greatly shocked and I must beg you to release them from any further ordeal."

There was a general and heartfelt chorus of agreement. Sir George said, "Hear, hear," very loudly.

Fox said this request was very reasonable he was sure, and he was sorry to have put them all to so much trouble and he could assure the ladies that he wouldn't be keeping them much longer. There were no two ways about it, he added, this was quite a serious affair, wasn't it?

"Well, then — " said Sir John, and there was a general stir.

At this juncture Alleyn came in. In some curious and indefinable fashion he brought a feeling of refreshment with him rather like that achieved by a star whose delayed entry, however quietly executed, lifts the scene and quickens the attention of his audience.

"We are so sorry," he said, "to have kept you waiting like this. I'm sure Mr. Fox will have explained. This is a very muddling, tragic and strange affair, and it isn't made any simpler for me, at any rate, by finding myself an unsatisfactory witness and an investigating copper at one and the same time."

He gave Lady Smythe an apologetic grin and she said — and may have been astonished to hear herself — "You poor man."

"Well, there it is, and I can only hope one of you has come

up with something more useful than anything I've been able to produce."

His brother said: "Done our best. What!"

"Good for you," Alleyn said. He was reading the sergeant's notes.

"We're hoping," said Sir John, "to be released. The ladies – "

"Yes, of course. It's been a beastly experience and you must all be exhausted."

"What about yourself?" asked Lady Smythe. She appeared to be a lady of spirit.

Alleyn looked up from the notes. "Oh," he said. "You can't slap me back. These notes seem splendidly exhaustive and there's only one question I'd like to put to you. I know the whole incident was extremely confused, but I would like to learn if you all, for whatever reason or for no reason, are persuaded of the identity of the killer?"

"Good God!" Sir George shouted. "Really, my dear Rory! Who else could it be but the man your fellows marched off. And I must compliment you on their promptitude, by the way."

"You mean – ?"

"Good God, I mean the great hulking brute with the spear. I beg your pardon," he said to the black plenipotentiary and himself turned scarlet. "Afraid I spoke out of turn. Sure you understand."

"George," said his brother with exquisite courtesy, "would you like to go home?"

"I? We all would. Mustn't desert the post, though. No preferential treatment.'

"Not a morsel, I assure you. I take it, then," Alleyn said, turning to the others, "that you all believe the spear-carrier was the assailant?"

"Well – yes," said Sir John Smythe. "I mean – there he was. Who else? And my God, there was the spear!"

The black plenipotentiary's wife said something rather loudly in their native tongue.

Alleyn looked a question at her husband, who cleared his throat. "My wife," he said, "has made an observation."

"Yes?"

"My wife has said that because the victim fell beside her, she heard."

"Yes? She heard?"

"The sound of the strike and the death noise," he held a brief consultation with his wife. "Also a word. In Ng'ombwanan. Spoken very low by a man. By the Ambassador himself, she thinks."

"And the word – in English?"

"'*Traitor,*'" said the plenipotentiary. After a brief pause he added: "My wife would like to go now. There is blood on her dress."

III

The Boomer had changed into a dressing-gown and looked like Othello in the last act. It was a black and gold gown, and underneath it crimson pyjamas could be detected. He had left orders that if Alleyn wished to see him he was to be roused, and he now received Alleyn, Fox, and an attenuated but still alert Mr. Whipplestone in the library. For a moment or two Alleyn thought he was going to jib at Mr. Whipplestone's presence. He fetched up short when he saw him, seemed about to say something, but instead decided to be gracious. Mr. Whipplestone, after all, managed well with the Boomer. His diplomacy was of an acceptable tinge: deferential without being fulsome, composed but not consequential.

When Alleyn said he would like to talk to the Ng'ombwanan servant who waited on them in the pavilion, the Boomer made no comment but spoke briefly on the house-telephone.

"I wouldn't have troubled you with this," Alleyn said, "but I couldn't find anybody who was prepared to accept the responsibility of producing the man without your authority."

"They are all in a silly state," generalized the Boomer. "Why do you want this fellow?"

"The English waiter in the pavilion will have it that the man attacked him."

The Boomer lowered his eyelids. "How very rococo," he said, and there was no need for him to add "as we used to say at Davidson's." It had been a catch phrase in their last term and worn to death in the usage. With startling precision it again returned Alleyn to that dark room smelling of anchovy toast and a coal fire, and to the group mannerisms of his and the Boomer's circle so many years ago.

When the man appeared he cut an unimpressive figure, being attired in white trousers, a singlet and a wrongly buttoned tunic. He appeared to be in a state of perturbation and in deep awe of his President.

"I will speak to him," the Boomer announced.

He did so, and judging by the tone of his voice, pretty sharply. The man, fixing his white-eyeballed gaze on the far wall of the library, answered with, or so it seemed to Alleyn, the clockwork precision of a soldier on parade.

"He says no," said the Boomer.

"Could you press a little?"

"It will make no difference. But I will press."

This time the reply was lengthier. "He says he ran into someone in the dark and stumbled and for a moment clung to this person. It is ridiculous, he says, to speak of it as an attack. He had forgotten the incident. Perhaps it was this servant."

"Where did he go after this encounter?"

Out of the pavilion, it appeared, finding himself near the rear door and frightened by the general rumpus. He had been rounded up by security men and drafted with the rest of the household staff to one end of the ballroom.

"Do you believe him?"

"He would not dare to lie," said the Boomer calmly.

"In that case I suppose we let him go back to bed, don't we?"

This move having been effected, the Boomer rose and so, of course, did Alleyn, Mr. Whipplestone and Fox.

"My dear Rory," said the Boomer, "there is a matter which should be settled at once. The body. It will be returned to our country and buried according to our custom."

"I can promise you that every assistance will be offered. Perhaps the Deputy Commissioner has already given you that assurance."

"Oh, yes. He was very forthcoming. A nice chap. I hear your pathologist spoke of an autopsy. There can be no autopsy."

"I see."

"A thorough enquiry will be held in Ng'ombwana."

"Good."

"And I think, since you have completed your investigations, have you not, it would be as well to find out if the good Gibson is in a similar case. If so I would suggest that the police, after leaving and at their convenience, kindly let me have a comprehensive report of their findings. In the meantime I shall set my house in order."

As this was in effect an order to quit, Alleyn gave his assurance that there would be a complete withdrawal of the Yard forces. The Boomer expressed his appreciation of the trouble that had been taken and said, very blandly, that if the guilty person was discovered to be a member of his own household, Alleyn, as a matter of courtesy, would be informed. On the other hand the police would no doubt pursue their security precautions outside the Embassy. These pronouncements made such sweeping assumptions that there was nothing more to be said. Alleyn had begun to take his leave when the Boomer interrupted him.

He said: "There is one other matter I would like to settle."

"Yes?"

"About the remainder of my stay in England. It is a little difficult to decide."

"Does he," Alleyn asked himself, "does the Boomer, by any blissful chance, consider taking himself back to Ng'ombwana? Almost at once? With the corpse, perhaps? What paeans of thanksgiving would spring from Gibson's lips if it were so."

" — the Buck House dinner party, of course, stands," the Boomer continued. "Perhaps a quieter affair will be envisaged. It is not for me to say," he conceded.

"When is that?"

"Tomorrow night. No. Tonight. Dear me, it is almost two in the morning!"

"Your other engagements?" Alleyn hinted.

"I shall cancel the tree-planting affair and of course I shall not attend the race-meeting. That would not look at all the thing," he said rather wistfully, "would it?"

"Certainly not."

"And then there's the Chequers visit. I hardly know what to say." And with his very best top-drawer manner to the fore, the Boomer turned graciously to Mr. Whipplestone. "So difficult," he said, "isn't it? Now, tell me. What would you advise?"

This, Alleyn felt, was a question to try Mr. Whipplestone's diplomatic resources to their limit. He rose splendidly to his ordeal.

"I'm quite sure," he said, "that the Prime Minister and, indeed, all the organizations and hosts who had hoped to entertain Your Excellency will perfectly understand that this appalling affair puts anything of the sort out of the question."

"Oh," said the Boomer.

"Your Excellency need have no misgivings under that heading, at least," Mr. Whipplestone gracefully concluded.

"Good," said the Boomer, a trifle dismally, Alleyn thought.

"We mustn't keep you up any longer," Alleyn said, "but before we take ourselves off I would like, if I may, to ask one final rather unorthodox question."

"What is that?"

"You are, I know, persuaded that neither the Ng'ombwanan waiter nor the guard—the *mlinzi,* is it?—is a guilty man."

"I am sure of it."

"And you believe, don't you, that Mrs. Cockburn-Montfort was mistaken in thinking her assailant was an African?"

"She is a very stupid, hysterical woman. I place no value on anything she says."

"Have they—the Cockburn-Montforts—any reason to harbour resentment against you or the Ambassador?"

"Oh, yes," he said promptly. "They had reason and I've no doubt they still do. It is well known that the Colonel, having had a hand in the formation of our armed forces, expected to be retained and promoted. I believe he actually saw himself in a very exalted role. But, as you know, my policy has been to place my own people in all key positions. I believe the Colonel went into unwilling retirement, breathing fire. In any case," the Boomer added as an afterthought, "he had become alcoholic and no longer responsible."

"But they were asked to the reception?"

"Oh, yes! It was a suitable gesture. One could not ignore him. And now—what is this unorthodox question, my dear Rory?"

"Simply this. Do you suspect anyone—specifically—of the murder of your Ambassador?"

Again that well-remembered hooded look with the half-closed eyes. After a very long pause, the Boomer said: "I have no idea, beyond my absolute certainty of the innocence of the *mlinzi.*"

"One of your guests in the pavilion?"

"Certainly not."

"I'm glad about that, at least," said Alleyn drily.

"My dear boy!" For a moment Alleyn thought they were to be treated to one of those bursts of Homeric laughter, but instead his friend touched him gently on the shoulder and gave him a look of such anxiety and affection that he found himself oddly moved.

"Of course it was not a guest. Beyond that," the Boomer said, "I have nothing to say."

"Well, then — " Alleyn glanced at Fox and Mr. Whipplestone, who once more made appropriate motions for departure.

"I too have a question," said the Boomer, and they checked. "My government wishes for a portrait to be hung in our Assembly. I would like, formally, to ask if your wife will accept this commission."

"I'll deliver the message," said Alleyn, concealing his astonishment.

At the door he muttered to the others: "I'll join you in a moment," and when they had gone he said: "I've got to say this. You will look after yourself, won't you?"

"Of course."

"After all — "

"You need have no qualms. I shall sleep very soundly with my *mlinzi* outside my door."

"You don't mean — ?"

"Certainly. It is his treasured privilege."

"For God's sake!"

"I shall also lock my door."

Alleyn left on a gale of laughter.

They went in silence to their extemporized office. When they got there Mr. Whipplestone passed his thin hand over his thinner hair, dropped into a chair and said, "He was lying."

"The President, sir?" asked Fox in his best scandalized voice. "About the spearman?"

"No, no, no, no! It was when he said he didn't suspect anybody — specifically — of the crime."

"Come on," Alleyn said. "Tell us. Why?"

"For a reason that you will find perfectly inadmissible. His manner. I did, at one time, know these people as well, perhaps, as a white person can. I like them. They are not ready liars. But my dear Alleyn, you yourself know the President very well indeed. Did you have the same reaction?"

Alleyn said: "He is an honourable person and a very loyal friend. I believe it'd go deeply against the grain for him to lie to me. Yes, I did think he was uncomfortable. I think he may suspect somebody. I think he is withholding something."

"Have you any idea what?"

Alleyn shoved his hands down in his trouser pockets and walked about the room. In his white tie and tails, with miniatures on his coat and with his general air of uncontrived elegance, he presented an odd contrast to Mr. Fox in his work-a-day suit, to the sergeant in uniform, and even to Mr. Whipplestone in his elderly smoking-jacket and scarf.

"I've nothing," he said at last, "that will bear the light of day. Let's leave it for the moment and stick to facts, shall we? Sam, could you, before we go, give us a résumé of what was said at that showdown in the ballroom? I know you've written a report and I'm damn' grateful and will go over every word of it very carefully indeed. But just to go on with. And also exactly what the waiter said, which sounds like a sequel to What the Butler Saw, doesn't it? When he came into the library?"

"I'll try," said Mr. Whipplestone. "Very well. The waiter. At the outset the President told him to give an account of himself during the crucial minutes before and after the murder took place. His reply as far as I can translate it literally was, 'I will say what I must say.'"

"Meaning, in effect, 'I must speak the truth'?"

"Precisely. But he could equally have meant: 'I will say what I am forced to say.'"

"Suggesting that he had been intimidated?"

"Perhaps. I don't know. He then said that he'd collided with the other waiter in the dark."

"Chubb?"

"Quite so," said Mr. Whipplestone uneasily.

"And Chubb says the man attacked him."

"Exactly. So you have told me."

"Do you think the man was lying?"

"I think he might have merely left out mention of the attack."

"Yes, I see. And the man himself: the spearman—*mlinzi* or whatever? Was he at all equivocal?"

Mr. Whipplestone hesitated. "No," he said at last. "No, with him it was different. He said—and I think I remember it exactly—that he had taken a terrible—in the sense of awe-inspiring, terrifying if you like—oath of loyalty to the President and therefore could never, if he were guilty, declare his innocence to the President on the body of his victim."

"That's almost exactly how the President translated him to me."

"Yes. And I think it is a true statement. But—well, my dear Alleyn, I hope you won't think I've got an awful cheek if I suggest to you that the President is on the whole a naïve person and that he is not going to heed, not even perhaps notice, any vague ambiguities that might cast doubt upon his men. But of course you know him very well and I don't."

"Do I?" said Alleyn. "Perhaps. There are times when I wonder. It's not a simple story: I can assure you of that."

"There's something very likeable about him. You were quite close friends, I think you said, at school."

"He's always roaring out that I was his best friend. He was certainly one of mine. He's got a very good brain, you know. He sailed through his law like nobody's business. But you're right," Alleyn said thoughtfully, "he cuts dead anything he doesn't want to believe."

"And of course he doesn't want to believe that one of his own people committed a crime?" Mr. Whipplestone urged.

Fox made a noise of agreement.

Alleyn said: "No. Perhaps he doesn't—*want* to," and vexedly rubbed his nose. "All the same," he said, "I think we may be fishing in the wrong pond. In very muddy waters, at all events."

"Do you mind," Mr. Whipplestone asked, "if I put a very direct question to you?"

"How can I tell till I hear it?"

"Quite. Here goes then. Do you think an attempt was made upon the President?"

"Yes."

"And do you think it will be repeated?"

"I think it's only too likely that something else may be tried. Only too likely," said Alleyn.

There was a long silence.

"What happens now, Mr. Alleyn?" asked Fox, at last.

"I'm damned if I know. Call it a night, I suppose. We've been given our marching orders and no mistake. Come on. We'd better tell Fred Gibson, hadn't we?"

Mr. Gibson was not sorry to get the sack from the Embassy. It relieved him of an untenable and undefinable task and left him free to supervise the orthodox business of mounting security measures outside the premises and wherever the President might take it into his head to go during the remainder of his visit. He expressed muffled but profound satisfaction when Alleyn pointed out that the public appearances would probably be curtailed when not cancelled.

"You could say," he mumbled presently, "that after a fashion we've picked up a bit of joy in this show." And he divulged that they had found the shell of the shot fired from the Luger. It was on the ground outside the lavatory window. They'd had no luck with a bullet.

"But," said Gibson with a kind of huffy satisfaction, "I don't reckon we need to shed tears over that one. Take a look at this."

He opened his large pale hand. Alleyn and Fox bent over it.

"Wad?" Fox said. "Here! Wait a sec. I wonder now."

"Yes," Alleyn said. "Fred. I wonder if you've drawn a blank."

They left the Embassy.

Troy was awake when Alleyn got home. She called out to him to save him the trouble of trying not to disturb her. When he came in she was sitting up in bed with her arms round her knees.

"Not a nice party, after all," he said. "I'm sorry, my darling."

"Have you — ?"

"No. Troy, I had to let you go off without a word. I couldn't look after you. Were you very much shocked?"

"I didn't really see. Well — yes — I did see but in a funny sort of way it didn't look — real. And it was only for a flash — not more than a second or two. In a way, I didn't believe it."

"Good."

"Everybody sort of milling around."

"That's right."

"And you got us all out of the way so very expeditiously."

"Did I?"

"Yes. But — " she bit her lip and said very quickly — "it was the spear, wasn't it? He was speared?"

He nodded, and put her irregular dark locks of hair out of her eyes.

"Then," Troy said, "haven't you arrested that superb-looking being?"

"The Boomer says the superb-looking being didn't do it. And anyway we haven't the authority inside the Embassy. It's a rum go and no mistake. Do you want to hear?"

"Not now. You'd better get some sleep."

"Same to you. I shall have a bath. Good morning, my love. Oh — I forgot. I have a present for you from the Boomer!"

"For me? What can you mean?"

"He wants you to paint him. His suggestion, not mine."

Troy was immovable for several seconds. She then gave Alleyn a quick exultant look and suddenly burrowed into her pillow.

He stared down at her and reflected on things one was supposed to remember about the artistic temperament. He touched her hair and went off to his bath with the dawn light paling the window.

VI

Afternoon in the Capricorns

When, in response to a telephone call taken by Troy, Alleyn called on the following afternoon at No. 1, Capricorn Walk, he was received on the front steps by Lucy Lockett, the cat. She sat with a proprietory air on the top step and had a good look at him.

"I know who *you* are," said Alleyn. "Good afternoon, my dear." He extended his forefinger. Lucy rose, stretched elaborately, yawned, and advanced her whiskers to within an inch of the fingertip. Mr. Whipplestone looked out of his open bow window.

"There you are," he said. "I won't be a second."

Lucy sprang adroitly from the steps to the window-sill and thence into the bosom of her master, who presently opened the front door, still carrying her.

"Come in, do, do," he said. "We've been expecting you."

"What a nice house you've got."

"Do you think so? I must say I like it."

"You hadn't far to walk last night—or this morning."

"No. Do you know, Alleyn, when I was coming home at whatever eldrich hour, I caught myself wondering—well, *al-*

most wondering – if the whole affair could have been some sort of hallucination. Rather like that dodging-about-in-time nonsense they do in science fiction plays, as if it had happened off the normal temporal plane. The whole thing so very – ah – off-beat. Wasn't it?"

"Was and is," Alleyn agreed.

He found Mr. Whipplestone himself rather off-beat as he sat primly on his desk chair in his perfectly tailored suit, with his Trumper-style hair-cut, his discreet necktie, his elegant cuff-links, his eyeglass and, pounding away at his impeccable waistcoat, his little black cat.

"About Chubb," he said anxiously. "I'm awfully *bothered* about Chubb. You see, I don't know – and he hasn't said anything – and I must say Mrs. Chubb looks too ghastly for words."

"He hasn't told you the black waiter attacked him?"

"He hasn't told me anything. I felt it was not advisable for me to make any approach."

"What's your opinion of Chubb? What sort of impression have you formed, by and large, since the Chubbs have been looking after you?"

Mr. Whipplestone had some difficulty in expressing himself, but it emerged that from his point of view the Chubbs were as near perfection as made no difference. In fact, Mr. Whipplestone said wistfully, one had thought they no longer existed except perhaps in the employment of millionaires.

"I've sometimes wondered if they were too good to be true. Ominous foreboding!" he said.

"Didn't you say Chubb seemed to have taken a scunner on blacks?"

"Well, yes. I rather fancied so. It was when I looked over this house. We were in the room upstairs and – oh, Lord, it was the poor old boy himself – the Ambassador – walked down the street. The Chubbs were near the window and saw him.

It was nothing, really. They stared. My dear Alleyn, you won't take from this any grotesque suggestion that Chubb – well, no, of course you won't."

"I only thought a prejudice of that sort might colour any statement he offered. He certainly made no bones about his dislike when we talked to him."

"Not surprising when you tell me one of them had half-strangled him!"

"*He* told me that."

"Don't you believe him?"

"I don't know," Alleyn said with an odd twist in his voice. "Perhaps. But with misgivings."

"Surely," Mr. Whipplestone said, "it can be a very straightforward affair, after all. For whatever motive, the Ng'ombwanan guard and the waiter conspire to murder either the Ambassador or the President. At the crucial moment the servant finds Chubb in the way and doubles him up, leaving the guard free to commit the crime. The guard kills the Ambassador. To the President he professes himself to be what my poor Chubb calls clobbered."

"Yes," Alleyn said. "As neat as a new pin – almost."

"So you see – you see!" cried Mr. Whipplestone, stroking the cat.

"And the pistol shot?"

"Part of the conspiracy – I don't know – yes. That awful lady says it was a black person, doesn't she? Well, then!"

"Whoever it was probably fired a blank."

"Indeed? There you are, then. A diversion. A red-herring calculated to attract the attention of all of you away from the pavilion and to bring the President to his feet."

"As I said," Alleyn conceded. "New pins aren't in it."

"Then – *why* – ?"

"My dear man, I don't know. I promise you, I don't know. It's by the pricking of my thumbs or some other intimation not admissible in the police manuals. It just all seems to me to be a bit too much of a good thing. Like those fish in aspic that ocean-going cruisers display in the tropics and never serve."

"Oh, come!"

"Still, there are more tenable queries to be raised. Item. Mrs. C.-M.'s black thug with a stocking over his head. Seen dimly against the loo window, unseen during the assault in the dressing-room. Rushed out of the ladies' into the entrance hall — there's no other exit — where there were four of Gibson's men, one of them hard-by the door. They all had torches. None of them got any impression of anybody emerging precipitately into the hall. Incidentally, there was another S.B. man near the master-switch in the rear passage who killed the blackout about ten seconds after he heard the pistol shot. In those ten seconds the murder was done."

"Well?"

"Well, our girlfriend has it that after the shot her assailant, having chucked her out of the loo, emerged still in the blackout, kicked her about a bit and then bolted, leaving her prone and in the dark. And then, she says, the loo-ladies, including your blushing sergeant, emerged and fell about all over her. Still in the dark. The loo-ladies, on the other hand, maintain they erupted into the anteroom immediately after the shot."

"They were confused, no doubt."

"The sergeant wasn't."

"Drat!" said Mr. Whipplestone. "What's all this got to do with my wretched Chubb?"

"I've not the remotest idea. But it tempts me to suspect that when it comes to equivocation your black candidates have nothing on Mrs. Cockburn-Montfort."

Mr. Whipplestone thought this over. Lucy tapped his chin with her paw and then fell asleep.

"Do I take it," he asked at last, "that you think Mrs. C.-M. lied extensively about the black man with the stocking over his head?"

"I think she invented him."

"Then who the devil fired the shot?"

"Oh," Alleyn said. "No difficulty with that one, I fancy. She did."

II

Mr. Whipplestone was much taken aback by this pronouncement. He gave himself time to digest its implications. He detached his cat and placed her on the floor, where with an affronted and ostentatious air she set about cleaning herself. He brushed his waistcoat, crossed his legs, joined his fingertips and finally said: "How very intriguing." After a further pause he asked Alleyn if he had any more specific material to support his startling view of Mrs. Cockburn-Montfort's activities.

Not specific, perhaps, Alleyn conceded. But he pointed out that a black male person planning to fire the pistol, whether or not it was loaded with a blank, would have been much better advised to do so from the men's lavatory, where his presence would not be noticed, than from the women's, where it extravagantly would. In the men's he would be taken for an attendant if he was in livery and for a guest if he was not.

"Really," Alleyn said, "it would be the height of dottiness for him to muscle in to the female offices, where he might—as indeed according to Mrs. C.-M. he *did*—disturb a lady already *in situ*."

"True," said Mr. Whipplestone moodily. "True. True. True."

"Moreover," Alleyn continued, "the sergeant, who, however naughty her lapse, displayed a certain expertise in the sequel, is persuaded that no rumpus beyond the shot and subsequent screams of Mrs. C.-M. disturbed the seclusion of those premises."

"I see."

"As for the weapon, an examination of the barrel, made by

an expert this morning, confirms that the solitary round was probably a blank. There are no finger-prints. This is negative evidence except that the sergeant, supported by the two orthodox attendants, says that Mrs. C.-M. was wearing shoulder-length gloves. The normal practice under these circumstances is for such gloves to be peeled off the hand from the wrist. The glove is then tucked back into the arm-piece, which remains undisturbed. But the lady was fully gloved and buttoned, and according to her own account certainly had no chance to effect this readjustment. She would hardly sit on the floor putting on gloves and yelling pen-and-ink."

"All very plausible," said Mr. Whipplestone. Alleyn thought that he was hurriedly rearranging his thoughts to accommodate this new development.

"I fancy," Alleyn said, "it's a bit better than that. I can't for the life of me think of any other explanation that will accommodate all the discrepancies in the lady's tarradiddle. And what's more she was taking dirty great sniffs at her own smelling salts to make herself cry. At any rate I'm going to call upon her."

"When!" quite shouted Mr. Whipplestone.

"When I leave you. Why? What's up?"

"Nothing," he said in a hurry, "nothing really. Except that you'll probably be admitted by Chubb."

"By *Chubb!*"

"He – ah – he 'does for' the Cockburn-Montforts on Friday afternoons. There's nothing in that, you know, Alleyn. The Chubbs have one or two, as it were, casual jobs about the neighbourhood. They baby-sit every other Sunday at No. 17, for instance. It's an arrangement."

"And Mrs. Chubb obliges your tenant in the basement, doesn't she?"

"An hour every other day. She will give us tea, by the way." He glanced at the clock. "Any second now. I asked for it very early, hoping you would join me. Mrs. Alleyn said something about your not having had time for luncheon."

"How very kind, I shall enjoy it."

Lucy, after some preparatory clawing at the foot of the door into the hall, succeeded in opening it wide enough to make an exit, which she effected with her tail up and an ambiguous remark.

"Sometimes," said Mr. Whipplestone, "I've felt almost inclined to pump the Chubbs."

"About Sheridan and the Cockburn-Montforts?"

"Discreetly. Yes. But of course one doesn't do that sort of thing. Or," Mr. Whipplestone said with a self-deprecatory lift of his hand, "I don't."

"No," Alleyn said, "I don't suppose you do. Do you mind, though, if I have a word with Mrs. Chubb?"

"Here? Now?" he said, evidently dismayed by the suggestion.

"Well – later if you'd rather."

"She's awfully upset. About Chubb being man-handled by that black waiter and interviewed afterwards."

"I'll try not to add to her woes. It really is just routine, Sam, as far as I know."

"Well, I do hope it doesn't turn out to be – anything else. Sh!"

He held up his finger. From somewhere outside the room came a series of intermittent bumps or taps. They grew louder.

Alleyn went to the door left ajar by Lucy Lockett and looked out.

To see Lucy herself backing down the stairs crab-wise and dragging some small object by a chain. It bumped from step to wooden step. When she arrived at the bottom she contrived with some difficulty to take the object up in her mouth. Giving out distorted mews, she passed Alleyn, re-entered the drawing-room, and dropped her trophy at Mr. Whipplestone's feet.

"Oh no, oh no!" he cried out. "Not again. For pity's sake, not again!"

But it was, in fact, a white pottery fish.

While he still gazed at it with the liveliest dismay, a clink of china sounded in the passage. With extraordinary swiftness Alleyn scooped up the fish and dropped it in his pocket.

"Not a word," he said.

Mrs. Chubb came in with a tea-tray.

Alleyn gave her good-afternoon and brought forward a small table to Mr. Whipplestone's chair. "Is this the right drill?" he asked, and she thanked him nervously and set down her tray. When she had left and he had heard her go upstairs he said: "It's not Sheridan's fish. She brought it from above."

Mr. Whipplestone's jaw dropped. He stared at Alleyn as if he had never seen him before. "Show me," he said at last.

Alleyn produced the object and dangled it by its chain in front of Mr. Whipplestone, who said: "Yes. It is. I've remembered."

"What have you remembered?"

"I think I told you. The first time she stole it. Or rather one like it. From down below. I had the curious feeling I'd seen it before. And then again, that evening when I returned it to Sheridan. Round that ghastly fellow Sanskrit's fat neck. The same feeling. Now I've remembered: it was on the day I inspected the premises. The fish was in the Chubbs' room upstairs. Hanging from a photograph of a girl with black ribbon attached to the frame. Rather morbid. And this," said Mr. Whipplestone, ramming home his point, "is it." He actually covered his face with his hands. "And that," he said, "is *very* uncomfortable news."

"It may turn out to be of no great matter after all. I wouldn't get too up-tight about it, if I were you. This may simply be the outward and visible sign of some harmlessly potty little cult they all belong to."

"Yes, but *Chubb?* And those dubious — those more than dubious Cockburn-Montforts and those frankly appalling Sanskrits. No, I don't like it," said Mr. Whipplestone. "I don't like it at all." His distracted gaze fell upon Lucy, who was posed tidily *couchant* with her paws tucked under her chest. "And the cat!" he remembered. "The cat, of whose reprehensible habits I say nothing, took fright at the very sight of that ghastly pair. She bolted. And the Pirellis at the Napoli think she belonged to the Sanskrit woman. And she had been ill-treated."

"I don't quite see . . ."

"Very well. Very well. Let it pass. Have some tea," Mr. Whipplestone distractedly invited, "and tell me what you propose to do about that thing: that medallion, that — fish."

Alleyn took it from his pocket and turned it over in his hand. A trademark like a wavy X had been fired into the reverse side.

"Roughish little job," he said. "Lucky she didn't break it. If you don't mind, I think I'll go upstairs and return it to its owner. It gives me the entrée, doesn't it?"

"I suppose so. Yes. Well. If you must."

"It'll save you a rather tricky confrontation, Sam."

"Yes. Thank you. Very good. Yes."

"I'll nip up before she has time to return to her kitchen. Which is their sitting-room?"

"First door on the landing."

"Right."

He left Mr. Whipplestone moodily pouring tea, climbed the stairs, and tapped at the door.

After a pause it was opened by Mrs. Chubb, who stared at him with something like terror in her eyes. He asked her if he might come in for a moment, and for a split second wondered if she was going to say no and shut the door in his face. But she stood aside with her fingers at her lips and he went in.

He saw, at once, the photograph on the wall. A girl of about sixteen with a nice, round, fresh-looking face very like Mrs. Chubb's. The black ribbons had been made into rosettes and fastened to the top corners of the frame. On the photograph itself, neatly written, was a legend: April 4, 1953—May 1, 1969.

Alleyn took the medallion from his pocket. Mrs. Chubb made a strange little falsetto noise in her throat.

He said: "I'm afraid Lucy has been up to her tricks again. Mr. Whipplestone tells me she's done this sort of thing before. Extraordinary animals, cats, aren't they? Once they get a notion into their heads, there's no stopping them. It belongs here, doesn't it?"

She made no move to take it. A drawing-pin lay on the table under the photograph. Alleyn pushed it back into its hole and looped the chain over it. "The cat must have pulled it out," he said, and then: "Mrs. Chubb, you're feeling poorly, aren't you? I'm so sorry. Sit down, won't you, and let me see if I can do something about it? Would you like a drink of water? No. Then, do sit down."

He put his hand under her arm. She was standing in front of a chair and dropped into it as if she couldn't help herself. She was as white as a sheet and trembling.

Alleyn drew up another chair for himself.

"Mr. Whipplestone told me you'd been very much upset by what happened last night and now I'm afraid I've gone and made matters worse," he said.

Still she didn't speak, and he went on: "I don't expect you know who I am. It was I who interviewed your husband last night. I'm an old friend of Mr. Whipplestone's and I know how greatly he values your service."

Mrs. Chubb whispered: "The police?"

"Yes, but there's no need to worry about that. Really."

"He set on 'im," she said. "That—" she shut her eyes for a second—"*black* man. Set on 'im."

"I know. He told me."

"It's the truth." And with startling force she repeated this, loudly. "It's the truth. Sir. Do you believe that, sir? Do you believe it's the truth?"

Alleyn thought: " 'Do I believe this, do I believe the other thing?' Everybody asking what one believes. The word becomes meaningless. It's what one knows that matters in this muddle." He waited for a moment and then said: "A policeman may only believe what he finds out for himself, without any possible doubt, to be true. If your husband was attacked, as he says he was, we shall find out."

"Thank Gawd," she whispered. And then: "I'm sorry, I'm sure, to give way like this. I can't think what's come over me."

"Never mind."

He got up and moved towards the photograph. Mrs. Chubb blew her nose.

"That's an attractive face," Alleyn said. "Is it your daughter?"

"That's right," she said. "Was."

"I'm sorry. Long ago?"

"Six years."

"An illness?"

"An accident." She made as if to speak, pressed her lips together and then shot out, as if defiantly: "She was the only one, our Glynis was."

"I can see the likeness."

"That's right."

"Was the medallion special to her, perhaps?"

She didn't answer. He turned round and found her staring at the photograph and wetting her lips. Her hands were clasped.

"If it was," he said, "of course you'd be very upset when you thought you'd lost it."

"It wasn't hers."

"No?"

"I hadn't noticed it wasn't there. It gave me a turn, like. When you – you held it out."

"I'm sorry," Alleyn repeated.

"It doesn't matter."

"Was it in London – the accident?"

"Yes," she said, and shut her mouth like a trap.

Alleyn said lightly: "It's a rather unusual-looking medallion, isn't it? An order or a badge or something of that sort perhaps?"

She pulled her hands apart as if the gesture needed force to accomplish it.

"It's my husband's," she said. "It's Chubb's."

"A club badge, perhaps?"

"You could call it that, I suppose."

She had her back to the door. It opened and her husband stood on the threshold.

"I don't know anything about it," she said loudly. "It's got nothing to do with anything. Nothing."

Chubb said: "You're wanted downstairs."

She got up and left the room without a glance at Alleyn or at her husband.

"Were you wanting to see me, sir?" Chubb asked woodenly. "I've just come in."

Alleyn explained about the cat and the medallion. Chubb listened impassively. "I was curious," Alleyn ended, "about the medallion itself and wondered if it was a badge."

He said at once and without hesitation, "That's correct, sir. It's a little social circle with an interest in E.S.P. and so forth. Survival and that."

"Mr. and Miss Sanskrit are members, aren't they?"

"That's correct, sir."

"And Mr. Sheridan?"

"Yes, sir."

"And you?" Alleyn said lightly.

"They was kind enough to make me an honorary member,

like. Seeing I go in and do the servicing for some of their meetings, sir. And seeing I was interested."

"In survival after death, do you mean?"

"That kind of thing."

"Your wife doesn't share your interest?"

He said flatly: "She doesn't come into it, does she? It's kind of complimentary to my services, isn't it? Like wearing a livery button used to be."

"I see. You must find a different place for it, mustn't you?" Alleyn said easily. "Out of reach of Lucy Lockett. Good afternoon to you, Chubb."

Chubb mouthed rather than sounded his response to this, and Alleyn left him, almost as bleached as his wife had been five minutes earlier.

Mr. Whipplestone was still sipping tea. Lucy was discussing a saucer of milk on the hearthrug.

"You must have some tea *at once,*" Mr. Whipplestone said, pouring it out. "And some anchovy toast. I hope you like anchovy toast. It's still quite eatable, I think." He tipped back the lid of the hot-server and up floated the smell that of all others recalled Alleyn to his boyhood days with the Boomer. He took a piece of toast and his tea.

"I can't stay long," he said. "I oughtn't to stay at all, in fact, but here goes."

"About the Chubbs?" Mr. Whipplestone ventured. Alleyn gave him a concise account of his visit upstairs. On the whole it seemed to comfort him. "As you suggested," he said, "the emblem of some insignificant little coterie, and Chubb has been made a sort of non-commissioned officer in recognition of his serving them sandwiches and drinks. Perhaps they think he's psychic. That makes perfectly good sense. Well, doesn't it?"

"Yes, of course. It's not without interest—do you agree?" Alleyn asked—"that Sanskrit is on the police records for fraudulent practice as a fortune-teller? *And* he's done time for the odd spot of drug trafficking."

"I am not in the least surprised," Mr. Whipplestone energetically declared. "In the realms of criminal deception he is, I feel sure, *capable de tout*. From that point of view, if from no other, I do of course deplore the Chubb connection."

"And there's Mrs. Cockburn-Montfort, who seems to be a likely candidate for the attempt-on-the-President stakes. Not a nice influence either, would you say?"

"Oh *drat!*" said Mr. Whipplestone. "Very well, my dear fellow. I'm a selfish, square old bachelor and I don't want anything beastly to happen to my Chubbs because they make life pleasant for me." His exasperated gaze fell upon his cat. "As for *you*," he scolded, "if you'd be good enough to keep your paws to yourself this sort of thing wouldn't happen. Mind that!"

Alleyn finished his tea and toast and stood up.

"Are you going, my dear chap?" Mr. Whipplestone asked rather wistfully.

"Needs must. Thank you for my lovely cuppa. Goodbye, my dear," he said to Lucy Lockett. "Unlike your boss, I'm much obliged to you. I'm off."

"To see Mrs. C.-M.?"

"On the contrary. To see Miss Sanskrit. She now takes precedence over the C.-M."

III

Alleyn had not come face-to-face with the Sanskrits at the Embassy. Like all the guests who had not been in or near the pavilion, they had been asked for their names and addresses by Inspector Fox, ticked off on the guest list, and allowed to go home. He didn't think, therefore, that Miss Sanskrit would recall his face or, if she did, would attach more importance to it than to any that she had seen among a hundred others at the reception.

He walked down Capricorn Mews, past the Napoli grocery shop, the flower shop and the garages. The late afternoon was warm, scents of coffee, provender, carnations and red roses drifted on the air, and for some reason the bells in the Basilica were ringing.

At the far end of the Mews, at its junction with the passageway into Baronsgate, was the converted stable now devoted to the sale of pottery pigs. It faced up the Mews and was, therefore, in full view for their entire length. Alleyn, advancing towards it, entertained somewhere in the back of his thoughts a prospect of stamping and sweating horses, industrious stablemen, ammoniacal fumes and the rumble of Dickensian wheels. Pigeons, circling overhead and intermittently flapping down to the cobbled passage, lent a kind authenticity to his fancies.

But there, as he approached, was the window legend THE PIGGIE POTTERIE and the nondescript sign-board: X. & K. SANSKRIT. And there, deep in the interior in a sort of alcove at the far end, was a faint red glow indicating the presence of a kiln and, looming over it, the dim bulk of Miss Sanskrit.

He made as if to turn off into the passageway, checked, and stopped to peer through the window at the exhibits ranked on shelves nearest to it. A particularly malevolent pig with forget-me-nots on its flanks lowered at him rather in the manner of Miss Sanskrit herself, who had turned her head in the shadows and seemed to stare at him. He opened the door and walked in.

"Good afternoon," he said.

She rose heavily and lumbered towards him, emerging from the alcove, he thought, like some dinosaur from its lair.

"I wonder," Alleyn said, as if suddenly inspired, "if you can help me by any chance. I'm looking for someone who could make castings of a small ceramic emblem. It's to be the badge for a newly formed club."

"We don't," rumbled an astonishingly deep voice inside Miss Sanskrit, "accept commissions."

"Oh. Pity. In that case," Alleyn said, "I shall do what I came to do and buy one of your pigs. The doorstop kind. You don't have pottery cats, I suppose? With or without flowers?"

"There's one doorstop cat. Bottom shelf. I've discontinued the line."

It was indeed the only cat: a baleful, lean, black, upright cat with blue eyes and buttercups on its haunches. Alleyn bought it. It was very heavy and cost five pounds.

"This is perfectly splendid!" he prattled while Miss Sanskrit busied her fat, pale hands in making a clumsy parcel. "Actually, it's a present for a cat. She lives at No. 1, Capricorn Walk, and is positively the double of this one. Except that she's got a white tip to her tail. I wonder what she'll make of it."

Miss Sanskrit had paused for a second in her wrapping. She said nothing.

He rambled chattily on. "She's quite a character, this cat. Behaves more like a dog, really. Retrieves things. Not above indulging in the odd theft, either."

She turned her back on him. The paper crackled. Alleyn waited. Presently she faced round with the parcel in her hands. Her embedded eyes beneath the preposterous beetroot-coloured fringe were fixed on him.

"Thank you," she growled, and he took the parcel.

"I suppose," he said apologetically, "you couldn't recommend anybody for this casting job? It's quite small. Just a white fish with its tail in its mouth. About that size."

There was something in the way she looked at him that recalled, however grotesquely, the interview with Mrs. Chubb. It was a feral look, that of a creature suddenly alarmed and on guard, and he was very familiar with it. It would scarcely be too fanciful to imagine she had given out a self-defensive smell.

"I'm afraid," she said, "I can't help you. Good afternoon." She had turned her back and begun to waddle away when he said:

"Miss Sanskrit."

She stopped.

"I believe we were both at the same party last night. At the Ng'ombwana Embassy."

"Oh," she said, without turning.

"You were with your brother, I think. And I believe I saw your brother a few weeks ago when I was in Ng'ombwana."

No reply.

"Quite a coincidence," said Alleyn. "Good afternoon."

As he walked away and turned the corner into Capricorn Place he thought: "Now, I wonder if that *was* a good idea. She's undoubtedly rattled, as far as one can think of blubber rattling. She'll tell Big Brother and what will they cook up between them? That I'm fishing after membership? In which case, will they get in touch with the other fish to see what *they* know? Or will she suspect the worst of me and start at once, on her own account, ringing round the circle to warn them all? In which case she'll hear I'm a cop in as short a time as it takes Mrs. Cockburn-Montfort to throw a temperament. And in *that* case we'll have to take damn' good care she and Big Brother don't shoot the moon. I don't mind betting," he thought as he approached No. 19, the Place, "that those dubious premises accommodate more than pottery pigs. Has Brother *quite* given up the drug connection? A nice point. Here we go again."

No. 19, Capricorn Place, although larger, was built in much the same style as Mr. Whipplestone's little house. The window-boxes, however, were more commonplace, being given over to geraniums. As Alleyn crossed the street he saw, behind the geraniums, Mrs. Cockburn-Montfort's bizarre face looking much the worse for wear and regarding him with an expression of horror. It dodged away.

He had to ring three times before the Colonel opened the door on a wave of gin. For a moment Alleyn thought, as he had with Chubb, that it might be slammed in his face. Inside the house someone was speaking on the telephone.

The Colonel said: "Yes?"

"If it's not inconvenient I'd like to have two words with Mrs. Cockburn-Montfort," Alleyn said.

"Out of the question, I'm 'fraid. She's unwell. She's in bed."

"I'm sorry. In that case, with you, if you'll be so good as to put up with me."

"It doesn't suit at the moment. I'm sorry. Any case we've nothing to add to what we said last night."

"Perhaps, Colonel, you'd rather come down to the Yard. We won't keep you long."

He glared, red-eyed, at nothing in particular and then said: "Damn! All right. You'd better come in."

"Thank you so much," said Alleyn and did so, pretty smartly, passing the Colonel into a hall with a flight of stairs and two doors, the first of which stood ajar.

Inside the room a voice, hushed but unmistakably Mrs. Cockburn-Montfort's, was speaking. "Xenny," she was saying. "It's true. Here! Now! I'm ringing off."

"Not that door. The next," shouted the Colonel, but Alleyn had already gone in.

She was dressed in a contemporary version of a garment that Alleyn had heard his mother refer to as a tea-gown: an elaborate confection worn, he rather thought, over pyjamas and held together by ribbons. Her hair had been arranged but insecurely, so that it almost looked more dishevelled than it would have if left to itself. The same appraisement might have been made of her face. She was smoking.

When she saw Alleyn she gestured with both hands rather as if something fluttered near her nose. She took a step backwards and saw her husband in the doorway.

"Why've you come down, Chrissy?" he said. "You're meant to stay in bed."

"I – I'd run out of cigarettes." She pointed a shaky finger at Alleyn. "You again!" she said with a pretty awful attempt at playfulness.

"Me again, I'm afraid," he said. "I'm sorry to pounce like this but one or two things have cropped up."

Her hands were at her hair. "I'm in no state—Too shaming!" she cried. "What *will* you think!"

"You'd better go back to bed," her husband said brutally. "Here! I'll take you."

"She's signalled," Alleyn thought. "I can't prevent this."

"I'll just tidy up a bit," she said. "That's what I'll do."

They went out, he holding her arm above the elbow.

"And now," Alleyn thought, "she'll tell him she's telephoned the Sanskrit. If it was the Sanskrit and I'll lay my shirt on it. They're cooking up what they're going to say to me."

He heard a door slam upstairs.

He looked round the drawing-room. Half conventional, half "contemporary." Different-coloured walls and "with-it" ornaments. One or two collages and a mobile mingled disconsolately with pouffes. Pimpering water-colours and martial photographs of the Colonel, one of which showed him in shorts and helmet with a Ng'ombwanan regiment forming a background. A lady-like desk upon which the telephone now gave out a click.

Alleyn was beside it. He lifted the receiver and heard someone dialling. The ringing sound set in. After a longish pause a muffled voice said, "Yes?"

"That you, Xenoclea?" the Colonel said. "Chrissy rang you a moment ago, didn't she? All right. He's *here*."

"Be careful." (The Sanskrit, sure enough.)

"Of course. This is only to warn you."

"Have you been drinking?"

"My dear Xenny! Look! He may call on you."

"Why?"

"God knows. I'll come round later. Or ring. 'Bye."

A click and then the dialling tone.

Alleyn hung up and walked over to the window.

He was gazing at the distant prospect of the Basilica when

the Colonel re-entered the room. Alleyn saw at once that he had decided on a change of manner. He came in jauntily.

"Ah!" he said. "There we are! Chrissy's insisting on making herself presentable. She'll be down in a moment. Says she feels quite equal to it. Come and take a pew. I think a drink while we wait is indicated, don't you? What shall it be?"

"Very civil of you," Alleyn said, speaking the language, "but it's not on for me, I'm afraid. Please don't let me stop you, though."

"Not when you're on guard duty, what? Bad luck! Well, just to show there's no ill-feeling," said the Colonel, "I think I will."

He opened a door at the far end of the room and went into what evidently was his study. Alleyn saw a martial collection of sword, service automatic and a massive hunting rifle hung on the wall. The Colonel returned with a bottle in one hand and a very large gin in the other.

"Your very good health," he said, and drank half of it.

Fortified and refreshed, it seemed, he talked away easily about the assassination. He took it for granted, or appeared to do so, that the spearman had killed the Ambassador in mistake for the President. He said that you never could tell with blacks, that he knew them, that he'd had more experience of them, he ventured to claim, than most. "Bloody good fighting men, mind you, but you can't trust them beyond a certain point." He thought you could depend upon it that when the President and his entourage had got back to Ng'ombwana the whole thing would be dealt with in their way and very little would be heard of it. "There'll be a new *mlinzi* on duty and no questions asked, I wouldn't wonder. On the other hand, he may decide to make a public example."

"By that do you mean a public execution?"

"Don't take me up on that, old man," said the Colonel, who was helping himself to another double gin. "He hasn't gone in for that particular exercise, so far. Not like the late lamented, f'instance."

"The Ambassador?"

"That's right. He had a pretty lurid past in that respect. Between you and me and the gatepost."

"Really?"

"As a young man. Ran a sort of guerilla group. When we were still there. Never brought to book but it's common knowledge. He's turned respectable of late years."

His wife made her entrance: fully clothed, coiffured and regrettably made up.

"Time for dinkies?" she asked. "Super! Give me one, darling: kick-sticks."

Alleyn thought: "She's already given herself one or more. This is excessively distasteful."

"In a minute," said her husband. "Sit down, Chris."

She did, with an insecure suggestion of gaiety. "What have you two been gossiping about?" she asked.

"I'm sorry," Alleyn said, "to bother you at an inopportune time and when you're not feeling well, but there is one question I'd like to ask you, Mrs. Cockburn-Montfort."

"Me? Is there? What?"

"Why did you fire off that Luger and then throw it in the pond?"

She gaped at him, emitted a strange whining sound that, incongruously enough, reminded him of Mrs. Chubb. Before she could speak her husband said: "Shut up, Chris. I'll handle it. I mean that. Shut up."

He turned on Alleyn. The glass in his hand was unsteady, but Alleyn thought he was in pretty good command of himself: one of those heavy drinkers who are seldom really drunk. He'd had a shock but he was equal to it.

He said: "My wife will not answer any questions until we have consulted our solicitor. What you suggest is obviously unwarranted and quite ridiculous. And 'stremely 'fensive. You haven't heard the last of this, whatever-your-rank-is Alleyn."

"I'm afraid you're right, there," Alleyn said. "And nor have you, perhaps. Good evening to you. I'll show myself out."

IV

"And the odd thing about that little episode, Br'er Fox, is this: my bit of personal bugging on the Cockburn-Montfort telephone exchange copped Miss Xenoclea Sanskrit—Xenny for short—in an apparently motiveless lie. The gallant Colonel said, 'He—' meaning me—'may call on you,' and instead of saying, 'He *has* called on me,' she merely growled, 'Why?' Uncandid behaviour from a comrade, don't you think?"

"If," said Fox carefully, "this little lot, meaning the Colonel and his lady, the Sanskrit combination, the Sheridan gentleman and this chap Chubb, are all tied up in some hate-the-blacks club, and *if*, as seems possible, seeing most of them were at the party, and seeing the way the lady carried on, they're mixed up in the fatality—" He drew breath.

"I can't wait," Alleyn said.

"I was only going to say it wouldn't, given all these circumstances, be anything out of the way if they got round to looking sideways at each other." He sighed heavily. "On the other hand," he said, "and I must say on the face of it this is the view I'm inclined to favour, we may have a perfectly straightforward job. The man with the spear used the spear and what else took place round about in the dark has little or no bearing on the matter."

"How about Mrs. C.-M. and her Luger in the ladies' loo?"

"Blast!" said Fox.

"The whole thing's so bloody untidy," Alleyn grumbled.

"I wouldn't mind going over the headings," Fox confessed.

"Plough ahead and much good may it do you."

"*A*," said Fox, massively checking it off with finger and thumb. "*A*. The occurrence. Ambassador killed by spear. Spearman stationed at rear in handy position. Says he was clobbered and his spear taken off him. Says he's innocent. *B*. Chubb. Ex-commando. Also at rear. Member of this secret society or whatever it is. Suggestion that he's a black-hater. Says *he* was clobbered by black waiter. *C*. Mrs. C.-M. Fires shot, probably blank, from ladies' conveniences. Why? To draw attention? To get the President on his feet so's he could be speared? By whom? This is the nitty-gritty one," said Fox. "If the club's an anti-black show would they collaborate with the spearman or the waiter? The answer is: unlikely. Very unlikely. Where does this take us?"

"Hold on to your hats, boys."

"To Chubb," said Fox. "It takes us to Chubb. Well, doesn't it? Chubb, set up by the club, clobbers the spearman and does the job on the Ambassador, and afterwards says the waiter clobbered *him* and held him down."

"But the waiter maintains that he stumbled in the dark and accidentally gabbed Chubb. If Chubb was the spearman what are we to make of this?"

"Mightn't it be the case, though? Mightn't he have stumbled and momentarily clung to Chubb?"

"Before or after Chubb clobbered the spearman and grabbed the spear?"

Fox began to look disconcerted. "I don't like it much," he confessed. "Still, after a fashion it fits. After a fashion it does."

"It's a brave show, Br'er Fox, and does you credit. Carry on."

"I don't know that I've all that much more to offer. This Sanskrit couple, now. At least there's a CRO on *him*. Fraud, fortune-telling and hard drugs, I think you mentioned. Big importer into Ng'ombwana until the present government turned him out. They're members of this club if Mr. Whipplestone's right when he says he saw them wearing the medallion."

"Not only that," Alleyn said. He opened a drawer in his desk and produced his black pottery cat. "Take a look at this," he said, and exhibited the base. It bore, as a trademark, a wavy X. "That's on the reverse of the medallions, too," he said. "X for Xenoclea, I suppose. Xenny not only wears a medallion, she makes 'em in her little kiln, fat witch that she is."

"You're building up quite a case, Mr. Alleyn, aren't you? But against whom? And for what?"

"You tell me. But whatever turns up in the ambassadorial department, I'll kick myself all round the Capricorns if I don't get something on the Sanskrits. What rot they talk when they teach us we should never get involved. Of course we get involved: we merely learn not to show it."

"Oh, come now! You never do, Mr. Alleyn."

"Don't I? All right, Foxkin, I'm talking through my hat. But I've taken a scunner on *la belle* Xenny and Big Brother and I'll have to watch it. Look, let's get the CRO file and have a look for ourselves. Fred Gibson wasn't all that interested at that stage. One of his henchmen looked it up for him. There was nothing there that directly concerned security and he may not have given me all the details."

So they called on the Criminal Records Office for the entry under Sanskrit.

Alleyn said, "Just as Fred quoted it. Fraudulent practices. Fortune-telling. Drug peddling, for which he did bird. All in the past before he made his pile as an importer of fancy goods in Ng'ombwana. And he did, apparently, make a tidy pile before he was forced to sell out to a Ng'ombwanan interest."

"That was recently?"

"Quite recently. I actually happened to catch sight of him standing outside his erstwhile premises when I was over there. He doesn't seem to have lost face—and God knows he's got plenty to lose—or he wouldn't have been asked to the party."

"Wouldn't you say it was a bit funny their being invited anyway?"

"Yes," Alleyn agreed thoughtfully. "Yes, I think I would."

"Would you reckon this pottery business of the sister's was a money-spinner?"

"Not on a big scale."

"Was she involved in any of the former charges?"

"She hasn't got a CRO. Wait a bit, though. There's a cross-reference. 'See McGuigan, O.' Fetch us down the Macs." The sergeant on duty obliged.

"Here you are," said Mr. Fox presently. "Take a look," and without waiting for Alleyn to do so he continued in the slightly catarrhal voice he kept for reading aloud: " 'McGuigan, Olive, supposed widow of Sean McGuigan, of whom nothing known. Sister of Kenneth Sanskrit q.v. Later assumed as first name, Xenoclea. Sus. drug traffic with brother. Charged with fortune-telling, for which fined, June, 1953. Reported to R.S.P.C.A. cruelty to cat, 1967. Charged and convicted. Fined with costs.' Fred Gibson's henchman left this out. He'll be getting some 'advice' on this one," said Fox.

"Ah. And Sam Whipplestone thinks she ill-treated his cat. Pretty little picture we're building up, aren't we? I must say I thought the 'Xenoclea' bit was too good to be true," Alleyn grunted.

"Is it a made-up job, then, that name?"

"Not by her at least. Xenoclea was a mythical prophetess who wouldn't do her stuff for Hercules because he hadn't had a bath. After his Augean stables job, perhaps. I bet *la belle* Xenny re-christened herself and reverted to her maiden name when she took to her fortune-telling lay."

"Where do they live?"

"Above the pottery pigs. There seems to be a flat up there: quite a sizable one by the look of it."

"Does the brother live there with her – wait a bit," said Fox, interrupting himself. "Where's the guest list we made last night?"

"In my office, but you needn't worry. I looked it up. That's their joint address. While we're at it, Br'er Fox, let's see, for the hell of it, whether there's anything on Sheridan, A. R. G., 1a, Capricorn Walk."

But Mr. Sheridan had no criminal record.

"All the same," Alleyn said, "we'll have to get him sorted out. Even if it comes to asking the President if there's a Ng'ombwanan link. He wasn't asked to the reception, of course. Oh well, press on."

They left the CRO and returned to Alleyn's rooms, where he managed to reach Superintendent Gibson on the telephone.

"What's horrible, Fred?"

"Nothing to report," said that colourless man. "All quiet inside the premises, seemingly. We've stopped the demolition. Routine precaution."

"Demolition?"

"Clearing up after the party. The Vistas people and the electrics. It's silly really, seeing we can't go in. If nothing develops they may as well get on with it."

"Any ingoings or outcomings of interest?"

"Post. Tradesmen. We looked over all deliveries, which wasn't very popular. Callers offering condolences and leaving cards. The media of course. One incident."

"What?"

"His Nibs, believe it or not."

"The President?"

"That's right. Suddenly comes out by the front entrance with a dirty great dog on a leash and says he's taking it for a walk in the park."

Alleyn swore vigorously.

"What's that?" asked Gibson.

"Never mind. Go on."

"My sergeant, on duty at the entrance, tries to reason with him. I'm doing a cruise round in a job car and they give me a shout and I come in and try to reason with him. He's very la-de-da, making out we're fussy. It's awkward," said Mr. Gibson drearily.

"How did you handle it, Fred?"

"I'm stuck with it, aren't I? So I say we'll keep with it, and he says if it's a bodyguard I'm worried about he's got the dog and his own personal protection, and with that the door opens and guess who appears?" invited Mr. Gibson without animation.

"The spearman of last night?"

"That's correct. The number one suspect in my book who we'd've borrowed last night, there and then, if we'd had a fair go. There he was, large as life."

"You don't surprise me. What was the upshot?"

"Ask yourself. In flocks the media, telly, press, the lot. He says 'No comment' and off he goes to his constitutional with the dog and the prime sus. and five of my chaps and a PANDA doing their best in the way of protection. So they all go and look at Peter Pan," said Mr. Gibson bitterly, "and nobody shoots anybody or lobs in a bomb and they come home again. Tonight it's the Palace caper."

"That's been scaled down considerably, hasn't it?"

"Yes. Nondescript transport. Changed route. Small party."

"At least he's not taking the spearman with him."

"Not according to my info. It wouldn't surprise me."

"Poor Fred!"

"Well, it's not what you'd pick in the way of a job," said Gibson. "Oh, yes, and there's another thing. He wants to see you. Or talk to you."

"Why? Did you gather?"

"No. He just chucks it over his shoulder when he walks away. He's awkward."

"The visit may be cut short."

"Can't be too short for me," said Gibson, and they took leave of each other.

"It's a case," Alleyn said when he'd replaced the receiver, "of 'Where do we go for honey?' I dunno, Br'er Fox. Press on, press on, but in what direction?"

"This Mr. Sheridan," Fox ruminated. "He seems to have been kind of side-tracked, doesn't he? I mean from the secret society or what-have-you angle."

"I know he does. He wasn't at the party. That's why."

"But he is a member of whatever they are."

"Yes. Look here, Fox. The only reason — the only tenable reason — we've got for thinking there was some hanky-panky based on this idiot-group is the evidence, if you can call it that, of Mrs. C.-M. having loosed off a Luger with a blank charge, in the ladies' loo. I'm quite convinced, if only because of their reaction — hers and the gallant Colonel's — that she's the girl who did it, though proving it will be something else again. All right. The highly suspect, the generally inadmissible word 'coincidental' keeps on rearing its vacant head in these proceedings, but I'll be damned if I accept any argument based on the notion that two entirely unrelated attempts at homicide occurred within the same five minutes at an ambassadorial party."

"You mean," said Fox, "the idea that Mrs. C.-M. and this little gang had something laid on and never got beyond the first move because the spearman hopped in and beat them to it?"

"Is that what I mean? Yes, of course it is, but blow me down flat if it sounds as silly as I expected it to."

"It sounds pretty silly to me."

"You can't entertain the notion?"

"It'd take a big effort."

"Well, God knows. You may have to make it. I tell you what, Foxkin. We'll try and get a bit more on Sheridan, if only for the sake of tidiness. And we'll take a long shot and give ourselves the dreary task of finding out how a girl of sixteen was killed in London on the first of May, 1969. Name Glynis Chubb."

"Car accident?"

"We don't know. I get the impression that although the word accident was used, it was not used correctly. Lurking round the fringe of my rotten memory there's something or another, and it may be so much nonsense, about the name Chubb in connection with an unsolved homicide. We weren't involved. Not on our ground."

"Chubb," mused Fox. "*Chubb,* now. Yes. Yes, there *was* something. Now, what was it? Wait a bit, Mr. Alleyn. Hold on."

Mr. Fox went into a glazed stare at nothing in particular, from which he was roused by Alleyn bringing his palm down smartly on his desk.

"Notting Hill Gate," Alleyn said. "May 1969. Raped and strangled. Man seen leaving the area but never knocked off. That's it. We'll have to dig it out, of course, but I bet you that's it. Still open. He left a red scarf behind and it was identified."

"You're dead right. The case blew out. They knew their man but they never got it tied up."

"No. Never."

"He was coloured," Fox said. "A coloured chap, wasn't he?"

"Yes," Alleyn said. "He was. He was black. And what's more – Here! We'll get on to the Unsolved file for this one and we'll do it now, by gum."

It didn't take long. The Unsolved Homicide file for May 1969 had a succinct account of the murder of Chubb, Glynis, aged sixteen, by a black person believed but never proved to be a native of Ng'ombwana.

VII

Mr. Sheridan's Past

When they had closed the file for unsolved homicide, sub-section rape and asphyxiation, 1969, Fox remarked that if Chubb hadn't seemed to have a motive before he certainly had one now. Of a far-fetched sort, Fox allowed, but a motive nevertheless. And in a sort of fashion, he argued, this went some way to showing that the society – he was pleased to call it the "fishy society" – had as its objective the confusion, subjection and downfall of the Black.

"I begin to fancy Chubb," said Fox.

At this point Alleyn's telephone rang. To his great surprise it was Troy, who was never known to call him at the Yard. He said: "Troy! Anything wrong?"

"Not really and I'm sorry about this," she said rapidly, "but I thought you'd better know at once. It's your Boomer on the blower."

"Wanting me?"

"Strangely enough, no. Wanting me."

"Oh?" said Alleyn with an edge in his voice. "Well, he'll have to wait. What for? No, don't tell me. It's about his portrait."

"He's coming. Now. Here. In full fig to be painted. He says he can give me an hour and a half. I tried to demur but he just roared roughshod over my bleating. He said time was of the essence because his visit is to be cut short. He said the conversation can be continued in a few minutes when he arrives, and with that he hung up and I think I hear him arriving."

"By God, he's a daisy. I'll be with you in half an hour or earlier."

"You needn't. It's not that I'm in the least flustered. It's only I thought you should know."

"You couldn't be more right. Stick him up in the studio and get cracking. I'll be there in a jiffy."

Alleyn clapped down his receiver and said to Fox: "Did you get the gist of that? Whistle me up a car, Fox, and see if you can get the word through to Fred Gibson. I suppose he's on to this caper, but find out. And you stay here in case anything comes through, and if it does call me at home. I'm off."

When he arrived at the pleasant cul-de-sac where he and Troy had their house, he found the Ng'ombwanan ceremonial car, its flag flying, drawn up at the kerb. A poker-faced black chauffeur sat at the wheel. Alleyn was not surprised to see, a little way along the street on the opposite side, a "nondescript," which is the police term for a disguised vehicle, this time a delivery van. Two men with short haircuts sat in the driver's compartment. He recognized another of Mr. Gibson's stalwarts sitting at a table outside the pub. A uniformed constable was on duty outside the house. When Alleyn got out of the police car this officer, looking self-conscious, saluted him.

"How long have *you* lot been keeping obbo on my pad?" Alleyn asked.

"Half an hour, sir. Mr. Gibson's inside, sir. He's only just arrived and asked me to inform you."

"I'll bet he did," Alleyn said, and let himself in.

Gibson was in the hall. He showed something like animation on greeting Alleyn and appeared to be embarrassed. The first thing he had heard of the President's latest caper, he said, was a radio message that the ambassadorial Rolls, with the Ng'ombwanan flag mounted, had drawn up to the front entrance of the Embassy. His sergeant had spoken to the driver, who said the President had ordered it and was going out. The sergeant reached Mr. Gibson on radio, but before he got to the spot the President, followed by his bodyguard, came out, swept aside the wretched sergeant's attempts to detain him, and shouting out the address to his driver had been driven away. Gibson and elements of the security forces outside the Embassy had then given chase and taken up the appropriate stations where Alleyn had seen them. When they arrived the President and his *mlinzi* were already in the house.

"Where is he now?"

"Mrs. Alleyn," said Gibson, coughing slightly, "took him to the studio. She said I was to tell you. 'The studio,' she said. He was very sarcastic about me being here. Seemed to think it funny," said Gibson resentfully.

"What about the prime suspect?"

"Outside the studio door. I'm very, very sorry, but without I took positive action I couldn't remove him. Mrs. Alleyn didn't make a complaint. I'd've loved to've borrowed that chap then and there," said Gibson.

"All right, Fred. I'll see what I can do. Give yourself a drink. In the dining-room, there. Take it into the study and settle down."

"Ta," said Gibson wearily. "I could do with it."

The studio was a separate room at the back of the house and had been built for a Victorian Academician of preposterous fame. It had an absurd entrance approached by a flight of steps with a canopy supported by a brace of self-conscious plaster caryatids that Troy had thought too funny to remove. Between these, in stunning incongruity, stood the enormous *mlinzi*, only slightly less impressive in a dark suit than he had been in his lion-skin and bracelets. He had his right forearm inside his jacket. He completely filled the entrance.

Alleyn said: "Good evening."

"Good day. Sir," said the *mlinzi.*

"I – am – going – in," said Alleyn very distinctly. When no move was made, he repeated this announcement, tapping his chest and pointing to the door.

The *mlinzi* rolled his eyes, turned smartly, knocked on the door and entered. His huge voice was answered by another, even more resonant, and by a matter-of-fact comment from Troy: "Oh, here's Rory," Troy said.

The *mlinzi* stood aside and Alleyn, uncertain about the degree of his own exasperation, walked in.

The model's throne was at the far end of the studio. Hung over a screen Troy used for backgrounds was a lion's skin. In front of it, in full ceremonials, ablaze with decorations, gold lace and accoutrements, legs apart and arms akimbo, stood the Boomer.

Troy, behind a four-foot canvas, was setting her palette. On the floor lay two of her rapid exploratory charcoal drawings. A brush was clenched between her teeth. She turned her head and nodded vigorously at her husband, several times.

"Ho-ho!" shouted the Boomer. "Excuse me, my dear Rory, that I don't descend. As you see, we are busy. Go away!" he shouted at the *mlinzi* and added something curt in their native tongue. The man went away.

"I apologize for him!" the Boomer said magnificently. "Since last night he is nervous of my well-being. I allowed him to come."

"He seems to be favouring his left arm."

"Yes. It turns out that his collar-bone was fractured."

"Last night?"

"By an assailant, whoever he was."

"Has he seen a doctor?"

"Oh, yes. The man who looks after the Embassy. A Dr. Gomba. He's quite a good man. Trained at St. Luke's."

"Did he elaborate at all on the injury?"

"A blow, probably with the edge of the hand, since there is no indication of a weapon. It's not a break—only a crack."

"What does the *mlinzi* himself say about it?"

"He has elaborated little on his rather sparse account of last night: that someone struck him on the base of the neck and seized his spear. He has no idea of his assailant's identity. I must apologize," said the Boomer affably, "for my unheralded appearance, my dear old man. My stay in London has been curtailed. I am determined that no painter but your wife shall do the portrait and I am impatient to have it. Therefore I cut through the codswallop, as we used to say at Davidson's, and here, as you see, I am."

Troy removed the brush from between her teeth. "Stay if you like, darling," she said, and gave her husband one of the infrequent smiles that still afforded him such deep pleasure.

"If I'm not in the way," he said, and contrived not to sound sardonic. Troy shook her head.

"No, no, no," said the Boomer graciously. "We are pleased to have your company. It is permitted to converse. Provided," he added with a bawling laugh, "that one expects no reply. That is the situation. Am I right, *maestro?*" he asked Troy, who did not reply. "I do not know the feminine of *maestro,*" he confessed. "One must not say *maestress.* That would be in bad taste."

Troy made a snuffling noise.

Alleyn sat down in a veteran armchair. "Since I am here, and as long as it doesn't disrupt the proceedings—" he began.

"Nothing," the Boomer interposed, "disrupts *me.*"

"Good. I wonder then if Your Excellency can tell me anything about two of your last night's guests."

"My Excellency can try. He is so ridiculous," the Boomer

parenthesized to Troy, "with his 'Excellencies.'" And to Alleyn: "I have been telling your wife about our times at Davidson's."

"The couple I mean are a brother and sister called Sanskrit."

The Boomer had been smiling, but his lips now closed over his dazzling teeth. "I think perhaps I have moved a little," he said.

"No," Troy said. "You are splendidly still." She began to make dark, sweeping gestures on her canvas.

"Sanskrit," Alleyn repeated. "They are enormously fat."

"Ah! Yes. I know the couple you mean."

"Is there a link with Ng'ombwana?"

"A commercial one. Yes. They were importers of fancy goods."

"Were?"

"Were," said the Boomer without batting an eyelid. "They sold out."

"Do you know them personally?"

"They have been presented," he said.

"Did they want to leave?"

"Presumably not, since they are coming back."

"What?"

"I believe they are coming back. Some alteration in plans. I understand they intend to return immediately. They are persons of little importance."

"Boomer," said Alleyn, "have they any cause to bear you a grudge?"

"None whatever. Why?"

"It's simply a check-up. After all, it seems somebody tried to murder you at your party."

"Well, you won't have any luck with them. If anything they ought to feel grateful."

"Why?"

"It is under my regime that they return. They had been rather abruptly treated by the previous government."

"When was the decision taken? To reinstate them?"

"Let me see – a month ago, I should say. More perhaps."

"But when I visited you three weeks ago I actually happened to see Sanskrit on the steps outside his erstwhile premises. The name had just been painted out."

"You're wrong there, my dear Rory. It was, I expect, in process of being painted in again."

"I see," said Alleyn, and was silent for some seconds. "Do you like them?" he asked. "The Sanskrits?"

"No," said the Boomer. "I find them disgusting."

"Well, then – ?"

"The man had been mistakenly expelled. He made out his case," the Boomer said with a curious air of restraint. "He has every reason to feel an obligation and none to feel animosity. You may dismiss him from your mind."

"Before I do, had he any reason to entertain personal animosity against the Ambassador?"

An even longer pause. "Reason? He? None," said the Boomer. "None whatever." And then: "I don't know what is in your mind, Rory, but I'm sure that if you think this person could have committed the murder you are – you are – what is the phrase – you will get no joy from such a theory. But," he added with a return to his jovial manner, "we should not discuss these beastly affairs before Mrs. Alleyn."

"She hasn't heard us," said Alleyn simply. From where he sat he could see Troy at work. It was as if her response to her subject was distilled into some sort of essence that flowed down arm, hand and brush to take possession of the canvas. He had never seen her work so urgently. She was making that slight breathy noise that he used to say was her inspiration asking to be let out. And what she did was splendid: a mystery was in the making. "She hasn't heard us," he repeated.

"Has she not?" said the Boomer, and added: "That, I understand. I understand it perfectly."

And Alleyn experienced a swift upsurge of an emotion that he would have been hard put to it to define. "Do you, Boomer?" he said. "I believe you do."

"A fraction more to your left," said Troy. "Rory – if you could move your chair. That's done it. Thank you."

The Boomer patiently maintained his pose, and as the minutes went by he and Alleyn had little more to say to each other. There was a kind of precarious restfulness between them.

Soon after half-past six Troy said she needed her sitter no more for the present. The Boomer behaved nicely. He suggested that perhaps she would prefer that he didn't see what was happening. She came out of a long stare at her canvas, put her hand in his arm and led him round to look at it, which he did in absolute silence.

"I am greatly obliged to you," said the Boomer at last.

"And I to you," said Troy. "Tomorrow morning, perhaps? While the paint is still wet?"

"Tomorrow morning," promised the Boomer. "Everything else is cancelled and nothing is regretted," and he took his leave.

Alleyn escorted him to the studio door. The *mlinzi* stood at the foot of the steps. In descending, Alleyn stumbled and lurched against him. The man gave an indrawn gasp, instantly repressed. Alleyn made remorseful noises and the Boomer, who had gone ahead, turned round.

Alleyn said: "I've been clumsy. I've hurt him. Do tell him I'm sorry."

"He'll survive!" said the Boomer cheerfully. He said something to the man, who walked ahead into the house. The Boomer chuckled and laid his massive arm across Alleyn's shoulders.

He said: "He really *has* a fractured collar-bone, you know. Ask Dr. Gomba or, if you like, have a look for yourself. But don't go on concerning yourself over my *mlinzi*. Truly, it's a waste of your valuable time."

It struck Alleyn that if it came to being concerned, Mr. Whipplestone and the Boomer in their several ways were equally worried about the well-being of their dependents. He said: "All right, all right. But it's you who are my real headache. Look, for the last time, I most earnestly beg you to stop taking risks. I promise you, I honestly believe that there was a plot to kill you last night and that there's every possibility that another attempt will be made."

"What form will it take, do you suppose? A bomb?"

"And you might be right at that. Are you sure, are you absolutely sure there's nobody at all dubious in the Embassy staff? The servants—"

"I am sure. Not only did your tedious but worthy Gibson's people search the Embassy but my own people did, too. Very, very thoroughly. There are no bombs. And there is not a servant there who is not above suspicion."

"*How* can you be so sure! If, for instance, a big enough bribe was offered—"

"I shall never make you understand, my dear man. You don't know what I am to my people. It would frighten them less to kill themselves than to touch me. I swear to you that if there was a plot to kill me, it was not organized or inspired by any of these people. No!" he said, and his extraordinary voice sounded like a gong. "Never! It is impossible. No!"

"All right. I'll accept that so long as you don't admit unknown elements, you're safe inside the Embassy. But for God's sake don't go taking that bloody hound for walks in the park."

He burst out laughing. "I am sorry," he said, actually holding his sides like a clown, "but I couldn't resist. It was so funny. There they were, so frightened and fussed. Dodging about, those big silly men. No! Admit! It was too funny for words."

"I hope you find this evening's security measures equally droll."

"Don't be stuffy," said the Boomer.

"Would you like a drink before you go?"

"Very much but I think I should return."

"I'll just tell Gibson."

"Where is he?"

"In the study. Damping down his frustration. Will you excuse me?"

Alleyn looked round the study door. Mr. Gibson was at ease with a glass of beer at his elbow.

"Going," Alleyn said.

He rose and followed Alleyn into the hall.

"Ah!" said the Boomer graciously. "Mr. Gibson. Here we go again, don't we, Mr. Gibson?"

"That's right, Your Excellency," said Gibson tonelessly. "Here we go again. Excuse me."

He went out into the street, leaving the door open.

"I look forward to the next sitting," said the Boomer, rubbing his hands. "Immeasurably. I shall see you then, old boy. In the morning? Shan't I?"

"Not very likely, I'm afraid."

"No?"

"I'm rather busy on a case," Alleyn said politely. "Troy will do the honours for both of us, if you'll forgive me."

"Good, good, good!" he said genially. Alleyn escorted him to the car. The *mlinzi* opened the door with his left hand. The police car started up its engine and Gibson got into it. The Special Branch men moved. At the open end of the cul-de-sac a body of police kept back a sizable crowd. Groups of residents had collected in the little street.

A dark, pale and completely bald man, well-dressed in formal clothes, who had been reading a paper at a table outside the little pub, put on his hat and strolled away. Several people crossed the street. The policemen on duty asked them to stand back.

"What *is* all this?" asked the Boomer.

"Perhaps it has escaped your notice that the media have not been idle. There's a front page spread with banner headlines in the evening papers."

"I would have thought they had something better to do with the space." He slapped Alleyn on the back. "Bless you," he roared. He got into the car, shouted, "I'll be back at half-past nine in the morning. Do try to be at home," and was driven off. "Bless *you,*" Alleyn muttered to the gracious salutes the Boomer had begun to turn on for the benefit of the bystanders. "God knows you need it."

The police car led the way, turning off into a side exit which would bring them eventually into the main street. The Ng'ombwanan car followed it. There were frustrated manifestations from the crowd at the far end, which gradually dispersed. Alleyn, full of misgivings, went back to the house. He mixed two drinks and took them to the studio, where he found Troy, still in her painting smock, stretched out in an armchair scowling at her canvas. On such occasions she always made him think of a small boy. A short lock of hair overhung her forehead, her hands were painty and her expression brooding. She got up, abruptly, returned to her easel, and swept down a black line behind the head that started up from its tawny surroundings. She then backed away towards him. He moved aside and she saw him.

"How about it?" she asked.

"I've never known you so quick. It's staggering."

"Too quick to be right?"

"How can you say such a thing? It's witchcraft."

She leant against him. "He's wonderful," she said. "Like a symbol of blackness. And there's something – almost desperate. Tragic? Lonely? I don't know. I hope it happens on that thing over there."

"It's begun to happen. So we forget the comic element?"

"Oh that! Yes, of course, he is terribly funny. Victorian music-hall, almost. But I feel it's just a kind of trimming. Not important. Is that my drink?"

"Troy, my darling, I'm going to ask you something irritating."

She had taken her drink to the easel and was glowering over the top of her glass at the canvas. "Are you?" she said vaguely. "What?"

"He's sitting for you again in the morning. Between now and then I want you not to let anybody or anything you don't know about into the house. No gas-meter inspectors or window cleaners, no parcels addressed in strange hands. No local body representatives. Nothing and nobody that you can't account for."

Troy, still absently, said, "All right," and then suddenly aware: "Are you talking about *bombs*?"

"Yes, I am."

"Good Lord!"

"It's not a silly notion, you know. Well, is it?"

"It's a jolly boring one, though."

"Promise."

"All right," Troy said, and squeezed out a dollop of cadmium red on her palette. She put down her drink and took up a brush.

Alleyn wondered how the hell one kept one's priorities straight. He watched her nervous, paint-stained hand poise the brush and then use it with the authority of a fiddler. "What she's up to," he thought, "and what I am supposed to be up to are a stellar-journey apart and yet ours, miraculously, is a happy marriage. Why?"

Troy turned round and looked at him. "I was listening," she said, "I do promise."

"Well—thank you, my love," he said.

II

That evening, at about the same time the Boomer dined royally at Buckingham Palace, Alleyn, with Fox in attendance, set out to keep observation upon Mr. Sheridan in his basement flat at No. 1, Capricorn Walk. They drove there in a "nondescript" equipped with a multi-channel radio set. Alleyn remembered that there had been some talk of Mr. Whipplestone dining with his sister who had come up to London for the night, so there was no question of attracting his attention.

They had been advised by a PANDA on Unit Beat that the occupant of the basement flat was at home, but his window curtains must be very heavy because they completely excluded the light. Alleyn and Fox approached from Capricorn Square and parked in the shadow of the plane trees. The evening was sultry and overcast and the precincts were lapped in their customary quietude. From the Sun in Splendour, farther back in the Square, came the sound of voices, not very loud.

"Hold on a bit. I'm in two minds about this one, Fox," Alleyn said. "It's a question of whether the coterie as a whole is concerned in last night's abortive attempt if that's what it was, or whether Mrs. C.-M. and the Colonel acted quite independently under their own alcoholic steam. Which seems unlikely. If it was a concerted affair they may very well have called a meeting to review the situation. Quite possibly to cook up another attempt."

"Or to fall out among themselves," said Fox.

"Indeed. Or to fall out."

"Suppose, for instance," Fox said in his plain way, "Chubb did the job, thinking it was the President: they won't be best pleased with *him*. And you tell me he seems to be nervous."

"Very nervous."

"What's in your mind, then? For now?"

"I thought we might lurk here for a bit to see if Mr. Sheridan has any callers or if, alternatively, he himself steps out to take the air."

"Do you know what he looks like?"

"Sam Whipplestone says he's dark, bald, middle height, well-dressed, and speaks with a lisp. I've never seen him to my knowledge." A pause. "He's peeping," said Alleyn.

A vertical sliver of light had appeared in the basement windows of No. 1a. After a second or two it was shut off.

"I wouldn't have thought," Fox said, "they'd fancy those premises for a meeting. Under the circs. With Mr. Whipplestone living up above and all."

"Nor would I."

Fox grunted comfortably and settled down in his seat. Several cars passed down Capricorn Walk towards Baronsgate, the last being a taxi which stopped at No. 1. A further half-dozen cars followed by a delivery van passed between the watchers and the taxi and were held up, presumably by a block in Baronsgate itself. It was one of those sudden and rare incursions of traffic into the quiet of the Capricorns at night. When it had cleared a figure was revealed coming through the gate at the top of the basement steps at No. 1: a man in a dark suit and scarf wearing a "City" hat. He set off down the Walk in the direction of Baronsgate. Alleyn waited for a little and then drove forward. He turned the corner, passed No. 1, and parked three houses further along.

"He's going into the Mews," he said. And sure enough, Mr. Sheridan crossed the street, turned right, and disappeared.

"What price he's making a call on the pottery pigs?" Alleyn asked. "Or do you fancy the gallant Colonel and his lady? Hold on, Fox."

He left Fox in the car, crossed the street, and walked rapidly past the Mews for some twenty yards. He then stopped and returned to a small house-decorator's shop on the corner, where he was able to look through the double windows down the

Mews past the Napoli and the opening into Capricorn Place, where the Cockburn-Montforts lived, to the pottery at the far end. Mr. Sheridan kept straight on, in and out of the rather sparse lighting, until he reached the pottery. Here he stopped at a side door, looked about him, and raised his hand to the bell. The door was opened on a dim interior by an unmistakable vast shape. Mr. Sheridan entered and the door was shut.

Alleyn returned to the car. "That's it," he said. "The piggery it is. Away we go. We've got to play this carefully. He's on the alert, is Mr. S."

At the garage where Mr. Whipplestone first met Lucy Lockett there was a very dark alley leading into a yard. Alleyn backed the car into it, stopped the engine, and put out the lights. He and Fox opened the doors, broke into drunken laughter, shouted indistinguishably, banged the doors, and settled down in their seats.

They had not long to wait before Colonel and Mrs. Cockburn-Montfort turned out of Capricorn Place and passed them on the far side of the Mews, she teetering on preposterous heels, he marching with the preternatural accuracy of the seasoned toper.

They were admitted into the same door by the same vast shape.

"One to come," Alleyn said, "unless he's there already."

But he was not there already. Nobody else passed up or down the Mews for perhaps a minute. The clock in the Basilica struck nine and the last note was followed by approaching footsteps on their side of the street. Alleyn and Fox slid down in their seats. The steps, making the customary rather theatrical, rather disturbing effect of footfalls in dark streets, approached at a brisk pace, and Chubb passed by on his way to the pottery.

When he had been admitted Alleyn said: "We don't, by the way, know if there are any more members, do we? Some unknown quantity?"

"What about it?"

"Wait and see, I suppose. It's very tempting, you know, Br'er Fox, to let them warm up a bit and then make an official call and politely scare the pants off them. It would stop any further attempts from that quarter on the Boomer unless, of course, there's a fanatic among them, and I wouldn't put that past Chubb for one."

"Do we try it, then?"

"Regretfully, we don't. We haven't got enough on any of them to make an arrest and we'd lose all chances of finally roping them in. Pity! Pity!"

"So what's the form?"

"Well, I think we wait until they break up and then, however late the hour, we might even call upon Mr. Sheridan. Somebody coming," Alleyn said.

"Your unknown quantity?"

"I wonder."

It was a light footstep this time and approached rapidly on the far side of the Mews. There was a street lamp at the corner of Capricorn Place. The newcomer walked into its ambit and crossed the road coming straight towards them.

It was Samuel Whipplestone.

III

"Well, of course," Alleyn thought. "He's going for his evening constitutional, but why did he tell me he was dining with his sister?"

Fox sat quiet at his side. They waited in the dark for Mr. Whipplestone to turn and continue his walk.

But he stopped and peered directly into the alleyway. For a moment Alleyn had the uncanny impression that they looked straight into each other's eyes, and then Mr. Whipplestone, slipping past the bonnet of the car, tapped discreetly on the driver's window.

Alleyn let it down.

"May I get in?" asked Mr. Whipplestone. "I think it may be important."

"All right. But keep quiet if anybody comes. Don't bang the door, will you? What's up?"

Mr. Whipplestone began to talk very rapidly and precisely in a breathy undertone, leaning forward so that his head was almost between the heads of his listeners.

"I came home early," he said. "My sister, Edith, had a migraine. I arrived by taxi and had just let myself in when I heard the basement door close and someone came up the steps. I daresay I've become hypersensitive to any occurrences down there. I went into the drawing-room and, without turning on the lights, watched Sheridan open the area gate and look about him. He was wearing a hat, but for a moment or two his face was lit by the head-lamps of one of some half-dozen cars that had been halted. I saw him very clearly. Very, very clearly. He was scowling. I think I mentioned to you that I've been nagged by the impression that I had seen him before. I'll return to that in a moment."

"Do," said Alleyn.

"I was still there, at my window, when this car pulled out of the square from the shadow of the trees, turned right, and parked a few doors away from me. I noticed the number."

"Ah!" said Alleyn.

"This was just as Sheridan disappeared up the Mews. The driver got out of the car and—but I need not elaborate."

"I was rumbled."

"Well—yes. If you like to put it that way. I saw you station yourself at the corner and then return to this car. And I saw you drive into the Mews. Of course I was intrigued, but believe me, Alleyn, I had no thought of interfering or indulging in any—ah—"

"Counter-espionage?"

"Oh, my dear fellow! Well. I turned away from my window

and was about to put on the lights when I heard Chubb coming down the stairs. I heard him walk along the hall and stop by the drawing-room door. Only for a moment. I was in two minds whether to put on the lights and say 'Oh, Chubb, I'm in' or something of that sort or to let him go. So uncomfortable has the atmosphere been that I decided on the latter course. He went out, double-locked the door, and walked off in the same direction as Sheridan. And you. Into the Mews."

Mr. Whipplestone paused, whether for dramatic effect or in search of the precise mode of expression, he being invisible, it was impossible to determine.

"It was then," he said, "that I remembered. Why, at that particular moment, the penny should drop I have no notion. But drop it did."

"You remembered?"

"About Sheridan."

"Ah."

"I remembered where I had seen him. Twenty-odd years ago. In Ng'ombwana."

Fox suddenly let out a vast sigh.

"Go on," said Alleyn.

"It was a court of law. British law, of course, at that period. And Sheridan was in the dock."

"Was he indeed!"

"He had another name in those days. He was reputed to come from Portuguese East and he was called Manuel Gomez. He owned extensive coffee plantations. He was found guilty of manslaughter. One of his workers—it was a revolting business—had been chained to a tree and beaten and had died of gangrene."

Fox clicked his tongue several times.

"And that is not all. My dear Alleyn, for the prosecution there was a young Ng'ombwanan barrister who had qualified in London—the first, I believe, to do so."

"The Boomer, by God!"

"Precisely. I seem to recollect that he pressed with great tenacity for a sentence of murder and the death penalty."

"What *was* the sentence?"

"I don't remember – something like fifteen years, I fancy. The plantation is now in the hands of the present government, of course, but I remember Gomez was said to have salted away a fortune. In Portugal, I think. It may have been London. I am not certain of these details."

"You *are* certain of the man?"

"Absolutely. And of the barrister. I attended the trial. I have a diary that I kept at that time and a pretty extensive scrap-book. We can verify. But I am certain. He was scowling in the light from the car. The whole thing flashed up most vividly those one or two minutes later."

"That's what actors call a double-take."

"Do they?" Mr. Whipplestone said absently, and then: "He made a scene when he was sentenced. I'd never seen anything like it. It left an extraordinary impression."

"Violent?"

"Oh, yes, indeed. Screaming. Threatening. He had to be handcuffed, and even then – It was like an animal," said Mr. Whipplestone.

"Fair enough," Fox rumbled, pursuing some inward cogitation.

"You don't ask me," Mr. Whipplestone murmured, "why I took the action I did. Following you here."

"Why did you?"

"I felt sure *you* had followed *Sheridan* because you thought, as I did, that probably there was to be a meeting of these people. Whether at the Cockburn-Montforts' or at the Sanskrits' flat. And I felt most unhappily sure that Chubb was going to join them. I had and have no idea whether you actually intended to break in upon the assembly, but I thought it might well be that this intelligence would be of importance. I saw

Chubb being admitted to that place. I followed, expecting you would be somewhere in the Mews, and I made out your car. So here I am, you see," said Mr. Whipplestone.

"Here you are and the man without motive is now supplied with what might even turn out to be the prime motive."

"That," said Mr. Whipplestone, "is what I rather thought."

"You may say," Fox ruminated, "that as far as motives go it's now one apiece. Chubb, the daughter. The Sanskrits, losing their business. Sheridan—well, ask yourself. And the Colonel and Mrs. C.-M.—what about them?"

"The Boomer tells me the Colonel was livid at getting the sack. He'd seen himself rigged out as a field marshal or as near as dammit. Instead of which he went into retirement and the bottle."

"Would these motives apply," Fox asked, "equally to the Ambassador and the President? As victims, I mean."

"Not in Sheridan's case, it would appear."

"No," Mr. Whipplestone agreed. "Not in his case."

They were silent for a space. At last Alleyn said: "I think this is what we do. We leave you here, Br'er Fox, keeping what I'm afraid may prove to be utterly fruitless observation. We don't know what decision they'll come to in the piggery-flat or indeed what exactly they're there to decide. Another go at the Boomer? The liquidation of the Klu-Klux-Fish or whatever it is? It's anybody's guess. But it's just possible you may pick up something. And Sam, if you can stand up to another late night, I'd very much like to look at those records of yours."

"Of course. Only too glad."

"Shall we go, then?"

They had got out of the car when Alleyn put his head in at the window. "The Sanskrits don't fit," he said.

"No?" said Fox. "No motive, d'you mean?"

"That's right. The Boomer told me that Sanskrit's been reinstated in his emporium in Ng'ombwana. Remember?"

"Now, that is peculiar," said Fox. "I'd overlooked that."

"Something for you to brood on," Alleyn said. "We'll be in touch."

He put his walkie-talkie in his pocket, and he and Mr. Whipplestone returned to No. 1, the Walk.

There was a card on the hall table with the word OUT neatly printed on it. "We leave it there to let each other know," Mr. Whipplestone explained. "On account of the door chain." He turned the card over to show IN, ushered Alleyn into the drawing-room, shut the door and turned on the lights.

"Do let's have a drink," he said. "Whisky and soda? I'll just get the soda. Sit down, do. I won't be a jiffy."

He went out with something of his old sprightly air.

He had turned on the light above the picture over the fireplace. Troy had painted it quite a long time ago. It was a jubilant landscape half-way to being an abstract. Alleyn remembered it well.

"Ah!" said Mr. Whipplestone, returning with a syphon in his hands and Lucy weaving in and out between his feet. "You're looking at my treasure. I acquired it at one of the Group shows, not long after you married, I think. Look out, cat, for pity's sake! Now: shall we go into the dining-room, where I can lay out the exhibits on the table? But first, our drinks. You begin yours while I search."

"Steady with the Scotch. I'm supposed to keep a clear head. Would you mind if I rang Troy up?"

"Do, do, do. Over there on the desk. The box I want is upstairs. It'll take a little digging out."

Troy answered the telephone almost at once. "Hello, where are you?" Alleyn asked.

"In the studio."

"Broody?"

"That's right."

"I'm at Sam Whipplestone's and will be most probably for the next hour or so. Have you got a pencil handy?"

"Wait a bit."

He had a picture of her feeling about in the pocket of her painting smock.

"I've got a bit of charcoal," she said.

"It's only to write down the number."

"Hold on. Right."

He gave it to her. "In case anyone wants me," he said. "You, for instance."

"Rory?"

"What?"

"Do you mind very much? About me painting the Boomer? Are you there?"

"I'm here all right. I delight in what you're doing and I deplore the circumstances under which you're doing it."

"Well," said Troy, "that's a straight answer to a straight question. Good night, darling."

"Good night," he said, "darling."

Mr. Whipplestone was gone for some considerable time. At last he returned with a large old-fashioned photograph album and an envelope full of press cuttings. He opened the connecting doors to the dining-room, laid his findings out on the table, and displaced Lucy, who affected a wayward interest in them.

"I was a great hoarder in those days," he said. "Everything's in order and dated. There should be no difficulty."

There was none. Alleyn examined the album, which had the faded melancholy aspect of all such collections, while Mr. Whipplestone looked through the cuttings. When the latter applied to items in the former, they had been carefully pasted beside the appropriate photographs. It was Alleyn who first struck oil.

"Here we are," he said. And there, meticulously dated and annotated in Mr. Whipplestone's neat hand, were three photographs and a yellowing page from the *Ng'ombwana Times* with the headline: GOMEZ TRIAL. VERDICT. SCENE IN COURT.

The photographs showed, respectively, a snapshot of a bewigged judge emerging from a dark interior; a crowd, mostly composed of black people, waiting outside a sun-baked court of justice; and an open car driven by a black chauffeur with two passengers in tropical kit, one of whom, a trim, decorous-looking person of about forty, was recognizable as Mr. Whipplestone himself. "Going to the Trial." The press photographs were more explicit. There, unmistakably himself, in wig and gown, was the young Boomer. "Mr. Bartholomew Opala, Counsel for the Prosecution." And there, already partially bald, dark, furious and snarling, a man handcuffed between two enormous black policemen and protected from a clearly menacing crowd of Ng'ombwanans. "After the Verdict. The Prisoner," said the caption. "Leaving the Court."

The letter-press carried an account of the trial with full journalistic appreciation of its dramatic highlights. There was also an editorial.

"And that," Alleyn said, "is the self-same Sheridan in your basement flat."

"You would recognize him at once?"

"Yes. I thought I'd seen him for the first time — and that dimly — tonight, but it turns out that it was my second glimpse. He was sitting outside the pub this afternoon when the Boomer called on Troy."

"No doubt," said Mr. Whipplestone drily, "you will be seeing quite a lot more of him. I don't like this, Alleyn."

"How do you think I enjoy it!" said Alleyn, who was reading the press cutting. "The vows of vengeance," he said, "are quite Marlovian in their inventiveness, aren't they?"

"You should have heard them! And every one directed at your Boomer," said Mr. Whipplestone. He bent over the album. "I don't suppose I've looked at this," he said, "for over a decade. It was stowed away in a trunk with a lot of others in my old flat. Even so, I might have remembered, one would have thought."

"I expect he's changed. After all — twenty years!"

"He hasn't changed all that much in looks and I can't believe he's changed at all in temperament."

"And you've no notion what became of him when he got out?"

"None. Portuguese East, perhaps. Or South America. Or a change of name. Ultimately, by fair means or foul, a British passport."

"And finally whatever he does in the City?"

"Imports coffee perhaps," sniffed Mr. Whipplestone.

"His English is non-committal?"

"Oh, yes. No accent, unless you count a lisp, which I suppose is a hangover. Let me give you a drink."

"Not another, thank you, Sam. I must keep my wits about me, such as they are." He hesitated for a moment and then said: "There's one thing I think perhaps you should know. It's about the Chubbs. But before I go any further I'm going to ask you, very seriously indeed, to give an undertaking not to let what I tell you make any difference — any difference at all — to your normal manner with the Chubbs. If you'd rather not make a blind commitment like this, then I'll keep my big mouth shut and no bones broken."

Mr. Whipplestone said quietly: "Is it to their discredit?"

"No," Alleyn said slowly, "not directly. Not specifically. No."

"I have been trained in discretion."

"I know."

"You may depend upon me."

"I'm sure I can," Alleyn said, and told Mr. Whipplestone about the girl in the photograph. For quite a long time after Alleyn had finished he made no reply, and then he took a turn about the room and said, more to himself than to Alleyn: "That is a dreadful thing. I am very sorry. My poor Chubbs." And after another pause: "Of course, you see this as a motive."

"A possible one. No more than that."

"Yes. Thank you for telling me. It will make no difference."

"Good. And now I mustn't keep you up any longer. It's almost midnight. I'll just give Fox a shout."

Fox came through loud, clear and patient on the radio.

"Dead on cue, Mr. Alleyn," he said. "Nothing till now but I think they're breaking up. A light in a staircase window. Keep with me."

"Right you are," said Alleyn, and waited. He said to Mr. Whipplestone: "The party's over. We'll have Sheridan-Gomez and Chubb back in a minute."

"Hullo," said Fox.

"Yes?"

"Here they come. The Cockburn-Montforts. Far side of the street from me. Not talking. Chubb, this side, walking fast. Hold on. Wait for it, Mr. Alleyn."

"All right."

Alleyn could hear the advancing and retreating steps.

"There he goes," Fox said. "He'll be with you in a minute, and now here comes Mr. Sheridan, on his own. Far side of the street. The C.-M.'s have turned their corner. I caught a bit of one remark. From her. She said: 'I was a fool. I knew at the time,' and he seemed to shut her up. That's all. Over and – hold on. Hold on, Mr. Alleyn."

"What?"

"The door into the Sanskrit premises. Opening a crack. No light beyond, but it's opening all right. They're being watched off."

"Keep with it, Fox. Give me a shout if there's anything more. Otherwise, I'll join you in a few minutes. Over and out."

Alleyn waited with Mr. Whipplestone for about three minutes before they heard Chubb's rapid step, followed by the sound of his key in the lock.

"Do you want to see him?" Mr. Whipplestone murmured. Alleyn shook his head. They heard the chain rattle. Chubb paused for a moment in the hall and then went upstairs.

Another minute and the area gate clicked. Mr. Sheridan could be heard to descend and enter.

"There he goes," said Mr. Whipplestone, "and there he'll be, rather like a bomb in my basement. I can't say I relish the thought."

"Nor should I, particularly. If it's any consolation, I don't imagine he'll be there for long."

"No?"

"Well, I hope not. Before I leave you I'm going to try, if I may, to get on to Gibson. We'll have a round-the-clock watch on Gomez-cum-Sheridan until further notice."

He roused Gibson, with apologies, from his beauty sleep and told him what he'd done, what he proposed to do, and what he would like Gibson to do for him.

"And now," he said to Mr. Whipplestone, "I'll get back to my patient old Fox. Goodnight. And thank you. Keep the scrapbook handy, if you will."

"Of course. I'll let you out."

He did so, being, Alleyn noticed, careful to make no noise with the chain and to shut the door softly behind him.

As he walked down Capricorn Mews, which he did firmly and openly, Alleyn saw that there were a few more cars parked in it and that most of the little houses and the flats were dark, now, including the flat over the pottery. When he reached the car and slipped into the passenger's seat, Fox said: "The door was on the chink for about ten seconds and then he shut it. You could just make it out. Light catching the brass knocker. Nothing in it, I daresay. But it looked a bit funny. Do we call off the obbo, then?"

"You'd better hear this bit first."

And he told Fox about the scrapbook and Mr. Sheridan's past.

"Get away!" Fox said cosily. "Fancy that now! So we've got a couple of right villains in the club. Him and Sanskrit. It's getting interesting, Mr. Alleyn, isn't it?"

"Glad you're enjoying yourself, Br'er Fox. For my part I — " He broke off. "Look at this!" he whispered.

The street door of the Sanskrits' flat had opened and through it came, unmistakably, the elephantine bulk of Sanskrit himself, wearing a longish overcoat and a soft hat.

"*Now* what's he think he's doing!" breathed Mr. Fox.

The door was locked, the figure turned outwards, and for a moment the great bladder-like face caught the light. Then he came along the Mews, walking lightly as fat people so often do, and disappeared down Capricorn Place.

"That's where the C.-M.'s hang out," said Fox.

"It's also the way to Palace Park Gardens, where the Boomer hangs out. How long is it since you tailed your man, Fox?"

"Well — "

"We're off on a refresher course. Come on."

VIII

Keeping Obbo

Fox drove slowly across the opening into Capricorn Place.

"There he goes. Not into the C.-M.'s, though, I'm sure," said Alleyn. "Their lights are out and he's walking on the opposite side in deep shadow. Stop for a moment, Fox. Yes. He's not risking going past the house. Or is he? Look at that, Fox."

A belated taxi drove slowly towards them up Capricorn Place. The driver seemed to be looking for a number. It stopped. The huge bulk of Sanskrit, scarcely perceptible in the shadows, light as a fairy, flitted on, the taxi screening it from the house.

"On you go, Fox. He's heading for the brick wall at the far end. We go left, left again into the Square, then right, and left again. Stop before you get back to Capricorn Place."

Fox executed this flanking manoeuvre. They passed by No. 1, the Walk, where Mr. Whipplestone's bedroom light glowed behind his curtains, and by the Sun in Splendour, now in eclipse. They drove along the far end of the Square, turned left, continued a little way farther and parked.

"That's Capricorn Place ahead," said Alleyn. "It ends in a brick wall with an opening into a narrow walk. That walk goes behind the Basilica and leads by an alleyway into Palace Park Gardens. It's my bet this is where he's heading, but I freely admit it's a pretty chancy shot. Here he comes."

He crossed the intersection rather like a walking tent with his buoyant fat-man's stride. They gave him a few seconds and then left the car and followed.

There was no sign of him when they turned the corner, but his light footfall could be heard on the far side of the wall. Alleyn jerked his head at the gateway. They passed through it and were just in time to see him disappear round a distant corner.

"This is it," Alleyn said. "Quick, Fox, and on your toes."

They sprinted down the walk, checked, turned quietly into the alleyway, and had a pretty clear view of Sanskrit at the far end of it. Beyond him, vaguely declaring itself, was a thoroughfare and the façade of an impressive house from the second-floor balcony of which protruded a flag-pole. Two policemen stood by the entrance.

They moved into a dark doorway and watched.

"He's walking up as cool as you like!" Fox whispered.

"So he is."

"Going to hand something in, is he?"

"He's showing something to the coppers. Gibson cooked up a pass system with the Embassy. Issued to their staff and immediate associates with the President's cachet. Quite an elaborate job. It may be, he's showing it."

"Why would he qualify?"

"Well may you ask. Look at this, will you?"

Sanskrit had produced something that appeared to be an envelope. One of the policemen turned on his torch. It flashed from Sanskrit's face to his hands. The policeman bent his head and the light, shone briefly up into his face. A pause. The officer nodded to his mate, who rang the doorbell. It was opened by a Ng'ombwanan in livery; presumably a night porter. Sanskrit appeared to speak briefly to the man, who listened, took the envelope if that was what it was, stepped back and shut the door after him.

"That was quick!" Fox remarked.

"Now he's chatting to the coppers."

They caught a faint high-pitched voice and the two policemen's "Goodnight, sir."

"Boldly does it, Br'er Fox," said Alleyn. They set off down the alleyway.

There was a narrow footpath on their side. As the enormous tented figure, grotesque in the uncertain darkness, flounced towards them it moved into the centre of the passage.

Alleyn said to Fox, as they passed it: "As such affairs go I suppose it was all right. I hope you weren't too bored."

"Oh, no," said Fox. "I'm thinking of joining."

"Are you? Good."

They walked on until they came to the Embassy. Sanskrit's light footfalls died away in the distance. He had, presumably, gone back through the hole in the wall.

Alleyn and Fox went up to the two constables.

Alleyn said: "Superintendent Alleyn, C. Department."

"Sir," they said.

"I want as accurate and full an account of that incident as you can give me. Did you get the man's name? You?" he said to the constable who had seemed to be the more involved.

"No, sir. He carried the special pass, sir."

"You took a good look at it?"

"Yes, sir."

"But you didn't read the name?"

"I—I don't—I didn't quite get it, sir. It began with S and there was a K in it. 'San' something, sir. It was all in order, sir, with his photograph on it, like a passport. You couldn't miss it being him. He didn't want to be admitted, sir. Only for the door to be answered. If he'd asked for admittance I'd have noted the name."

"You should have noted it in any case."

"Sir."

"What precisely did he say?"

"He said he had a message to deliver, sir. It was for the First Secretary. He produced it and I examined it, sir. It was addressed to the First Secretary and had "For His Excellency the President's attention" written in the corner. It was a fairly stout manilla envelope, sir, but the contents appeared to me to be slight, sir."

"Well?"

"I said it was an unusual sort of time to deliver it. I said he could hand it over to me and I'd attend to it, sir, but he said he'd promised to deliver it personally. It was a photograph, he said, that the President had wanted developed and printed very particular and urgent and a special effort had been made to get it done and it was only processed half an hour ago. He said he'd been instructed to hand it to the night porter for the First Secretary."

"Yes?"

"Yes. Well, I took it and put it over my torch, sir, and that showed up the shape of some rigid object like a cardboard folder inside it. There wasn't any chance of it being one of those funny ones, sir, and he *had* got a special pass and so we allowed it and—well, sir, that's all, really."

"And you," Alleyn said to the other man, "rang the bell?"

"Sir."

"Anything said when the night porter answered it?"

"I don't think he speaks English, sir. Him and the bearer had a word or two in the native language, I suppose it was. And then he just took delivery and shut the door and the bearer gave us a goodnight and left."

Mr. Fox, throughout this interview, had gazed immovably, and to their obvious discomfort, at whichever of the constables was speaking. When they had finished he said in a sepulchral voice to nobody in particular that he wouldn't be surprised if this matter wasn't Taken Further, upon which their demeanour became utterly wooden.

Alleyn said: "You should have reported this at once. You're bloody lucky Mr. Gibson doesn't know about it."

They said in unison: "Thank you very much, sir."

"For what?" Alleyn said.

"Will you pass it on to Fred Gibson?" Fox asked as they walked back the way they had come.

"The incident? Yes. But I won't bear down on the handling of it. I ought to. Although it was tricky, that situation. He's got the Embassy go-ahead with his special pass. The copper had been told that anybody carrying one was *persona grata.* He'd have been taking quite a chance if he'd refused." Alleyn put his hand on Fox's arm. "Look at that," he said. "Where did that come from?"

At the far end of the long alleyway, in deep shadow, someone moved away from them. Even as they glimpsed it, the figure slipped round the corner and out of sight. They could hear the soft thud of hurrying feet. They sprinted down the alley and turned the corner, but there was no-one to be seen.

"Could have come out of one of these houses and be chasing after a cab," Fox said.

"They're all dark."

"Yes."

"And no sound of a cab. Did you get an impression?"

"No. Hat. Overcoat. Rubber soles. Trousers. I wouldn't even swear to the sex. It was too quick."

"Damn," Alleyn said, and they walked on in silence.

"It would be nice to know what was in the envelope," Fox said at last.

"That's the understatement of a lifetime."

"Will you ask?"

"You bet I will."

"The President?"

"Who else? And at the crack of dawn, I daresay, like it or lump it. Fox," Alleyn said, "I've been visited by a very disturbing notion."

"Is that so, Mr. Alleyn?" Fox placidly rejoined.

"And I'll be obliged if you'll just listen while I run through all the disjointed bits of information we have about this horrid fat man and see if some kind of pattern comes through in the end."

"Be pleased to," said Fox.

He listened with calm approval as they walked back into the now deserted Capricorns to pick up their car. When they were seated in it Alleyn said: "There you are, Br'er Fox. Now then. By and large: what emerges?"

Fox laid his broad palm across his short moustache and then looked at it as if he expected it to have picked up an impression.

"I see what you're getting at," he said. "I think."

"What I'm getting at," Alleyn said, "is – fairly simply – this – "

II

Alleyn's threat to talk to the Boomer at the crack of dawn was not intended to be, nor was it, taken literally. In the event, he himself was roused by Mr. Gibson, wanting to know if it really was true that the President was giving Troy another sitting at half-past nine. When Alleyn confirmed this, Gibson's windy sighs whistled in the receiver. He said he supposed Alleyn had seen the morning's popular press, and on Alleyn's saying not yet, informed him that in each instance the front page carried a by-lined three-column spread with photographs of yesterday's visit by the Boomer. Gibson in a dreary voice began to quote some of the more offensive pieces of journalese. "Rum Proceedings? Handsome Super's Famous Wife and African Dictator." Alleyn, grinding his teeth, begged him to desist and he did so, merely observing that all things considered he wondered why Alleyn fancied the portrait proposition.

Alleyn felt it would be inappropriate to say that stopping the portrait would in itself be a form of homicide. He switched to the Sanskrit incident and learnt that it had been reported to Gibson. Alleyn outlined his and Fox's investigations and the conclusions he had drawn from them.

"It seems to look," Mr. Gibson mumbled, "as if things might be coming to a head."

"Keep your fingers crossed. I'm getting a search warrant. On the off-chance."

"Always looks 'active,' applying for a warrant. By the way, the body's gone."

"What?"

"The deceased. Just before first light. It was kept very quiet. Back entrance. 'Nondescript' van. Special plane. All passed off nice and smooth. One drop of grief the less," said Mr. Gibson.

"You may have to keep obbo at the airport, Fred. Outgoing planes for Ng'ombwana."

"Any time. You name it," he said dismally.

"From now. We'll be in touch," Alleyn said, and they rang off.

Troy was in the studio making statements on the background. He told her that yesterday's protective measures would be repeated and that if possible he himself would be back before the Boomer arrived.

"That'll be fine," she said. "Sit where you did before, Rory, would you, darling? He's marvellous when he focusses on you."

"You've got the cheek of the devil. Do you know that everybody but you thinks I'm out of my senses to let you go on with this?"

"Yes, but then you're you, aren't you, and you know how things are. And truly – it is – isn't it? – going – you know? Don't say it, but – isn't it?"

He said: "It is. Strange as it may sound, I hardly dare look. It's leapt out of the end of your brush."

She gave him a kiss. "I am grateful," she said. "You know, don't you?"

He went to the Yard in a pleasant if apprehensive state of mind and found a message from Mr. Whipplestone asking him to ring without delay. He put through the call and was answered at once.

"I thought you should know," Mr. Whipplestone began, and the phrase had become familiar. He hurried on to say that, confronted by a leaking water-pipe, he had called at his land agents, Messrs. Able and Virtue, at ten past nine o'clock that morning to ask if they could recommend a plumber. He found Sanskrit already there and talking to the young man with Pre-Raphaelite hair. When he saw Mr. Whipplestone, Sanskrit had stopped short and then said in a counter-tenor voice that he would leave everything to them and they were to do the best they could for him.

The young man had said there would be no difficulty as there was always a demand in the Capricorns. Sanskrit said something indistinguishable and rather hurriedly left the offices.

"I asked, casually," said Mr. Whipplestone, "if the pottery premises were by any chance to let. I said I had friends who were flat-hunting. This produced a curious awkwardness on the part of the lady attendant and the young man. The lady said something about the place not being officially on the market as yet and in any case if it did come up it would be for sale rather than to let. The present occupant, she said, didn't want it made known for the time being. This, as you may imagine, intrigued me. When I left the agents I walked down Capricorn Mews to the piggery. It had a notice on the door: Closed for stocktaking. There are some very ramshackle curtains drawn across the shop window but they don't quite meet. I peered in. It was very ill-lit but I got the impression of some large person moving about among packing cases."

"Did you, by George!"

"Yes. And on my way home I called in at the Napoli for

some of their pâté. While I was there the Cockburn-Montforts came in. He was, I thought, rather more than three sheets in the wind but, as usual, holding it. She looked awful."

Mr. Whipplestone paused for so long that Alleyn said: "Are you there, Sam?"

"Yes," he said, "yes, I am. To be frank, I'm wondering what you're going to think of my next move. Be quiet, cat. I don't habitually act on impulse. Far from it."

"Very far, I'd have thought."

"Although lately – However, I did act impulsively on this occasion. Very. I wanted to get a reaction. I gave them good-morning, of course, and then, quite casually, you know, as I took my pâté from Mrs. Pirelli, I said: 'I believe you're losing some neighbours, Mrs. Pirelli?' She looked nonplussed. I said: 'Yes. The people at the pig-pottery. They're leaving, almost at once, I hear.' This was not, of course, strictly true."

"I wouldn't be so sure."

"No? Well, I turned and was face-to-face with Cockburn-Montfort. I find it difficult to describe his look, or rather his succession of looks. Shock. Incredulity. Succeeded by fury. He turned even more purple in the process. Mrs. Montfort quite gasped out 'I don't believe it!' and then gave a little scream. He had her by the arm and he hurt her. And without another word he turned her about and marched her out of the shop. I saw him wheel her round in the direction of the piggery. She pulled back and seemed to plead with him. In the upshot they turned again and went off presumably to their own house. Mrs. Pirelli said something in Italian and then: 'If they go I am pleased.' I left. As I passed the top of Capricorn Place, I saw the C.-M.'s going up their steps. He still held her arm and I think she was crying. That's all."

"And this was – what? – half an hour ago?"

"About that."

"We'll discuss it later. Thank you, Sam."

"Have I blundered?"

"I hope not. I think you may have precipitated something."

"I've got to have a word with Sheridan about the plumbing – a genuine word. He's at home. Should I – ?"

"I think you might, but it's odds on the C.-M.'s will have got in first. Try."

"Very well."

"And the Chubbs?" Alleyn asked.

"Yes. Oh dear. If you wish."

"Don't elaborate. Just the news, casually, as before."

"Yes."

"I'll be at home in about a quarter of an hour if you want me. If I don't hear from you I'll get in touch myself as soon as I can," Alleyn said.

He checked with the man keeping observation and learned that Sanskrit had returned to the pottery after his visit to the land agents and had not emerged. The pottery was closed and the windows still curtained.

Five minutes later Alleyn and Fox found the entrance to the cul-de-sac, as on the former visit, cordoned off by police and thronged by an even larger crowd and quite a galaxy of photographers, who were pestering Superintendent Gibson with loud cries against constabular arrogance. Alleyn had a word with Gibson, entered his own house, left Fox in the study, and went straight to Troy in her studio. She had done quite a lot of work on the background.

"Troy," he said, "when he comes, I've got to have a word with him. Alone. I don't think it will take long and I don't know how much it will upset him."

"Damn," said Troy.

"Well, I know. But this is where it gets different. I've no choice."

"I see. O.K."

"It's hell but there it is."

"Never mind – I know. Here he is. You'd better meet him."

"I'll be back. Much more to the point, I hope he will."

"So do I. Good luck to whatever it is."

"Amen to that, sweet powers," Alleyn said, and arrived at the front door at the same time as the Boomer, who had his *mlinzi* in attendance, the latter carrying a great bouquet of red roses and, most unexpectedly, holding the white Afghan hound on a scarlet leash. The Boomer explained that the dog seemed to be at a loose end. "Missing his master," said the Boomer.

He greeted Alleyn with all his usual buoyancy, and then after a quick look at him said: "Something is wrong, I think."

"Yes," Alleyn said. "We must speak together, sir."

"Very well, Rory. Where?"

"In here, if you will."

They went into the study. When the Boomer saw Fox, who had been joined by Gibson, he fetched up short.

"We speak together," he said, "but not, it seems, in private?"

"It's a police matter and my colleagues are involved."

"Indeed? Good morning, gentlemen."

He said something to the *mlinzi,* who handed him the roses, went out with the dog, and shut the door.

"Will you sit down, sir?" Alleyn said.

This time the Boomer made no protest at the formalities. He said: "By all means," and sat in a white hide armchair. He wore the ceremonial dress of the portrait and looked superb. The red roses lent an extraordinarily surrealist touch.

"Perhaps you will put them down somewhere?" he said, and Alleyn laid them on his desk. "Are they for Troy?" he asked. "She'll be delighted."

"What are we to speak about?"

"About Sanskrit. Will you tell me what was in the envelope he delivered at the Embassy soon after midnight this morning? It was addressed to the First Secretary. With a note to the effect that it was for your attention."

"Your men are zealous in their performance of their tasks, Mr. Gibson," said the Boomer without looking at him.

Gibson cleared his throat.

"The special pass issued under my personal cachet evidently carried no weight with these policemen," the Boomer added.

"Without it," Alleyn said, "the envelope would probably have been opened. I hope you will tell us what it contained. Believe me, I wouldn't ask if I didn't think it was of great importance."

The Boomer, who from the time he had sat down had not removed his gaze from Alleyn, said, "It was opened by my secretary."

"But he told you what it was?"

"It was a request. For a favour."

"And the favour?"

"It was in connection with this person's return to Ng'ombwana. I think I told you that he has been reinstated."

"Was it, perhaps, that he wants to return at once and asked for an immediate clearance – visas, permits, whatever is necessary? Procedures that normally, I think, take several days to complete?"

"Yes," said the Boomer. "That was it."

"Why do you suppose he told the police officers that the envelope contained a photograph, one that you had ordered urgently, for yourself?"

For a second or two he looked very angry indeed. Then he said: "I have no idea. It was a ridiculous statement. I have ordered no photographs."

Alleyn said: "Mr. Gibson, I wonder if you and Mr. Fox will excuse us?"

They went out with a solemn preoccupied air and shut the door after them.

"Well, Rory?" said the Boomer.

"He was an informer," Alleyn said, "wasn't he? He was what

Mr. Gibson would call, so unprettily but so appropriately, a snout."

III

The Boomer had always, in spite of all his natural exuberance, commanded a talent for unexpected silences. He now displayed it. He neither moved nor spoke during a long enough pause for the clock in the study to clear its throat and strike ten. He then clasped his white gloved hands, rested his chin on them and spoke.

"In the old days," he said, and his inordinately resonant voice, taking on a timbre of a recitative, lent the phrase huge overtones of nostalgia, "at Davidson's, I remember one wet evening when we talked together, as youths of that age will, of everything under the sun. We talked, finally, of government and the exercise of power and suddenly, without warning, we found ourselves on opposite sides of a great gap – a ravine. There was no bridge. We were completely cut off from each other. Do you remember?"

"I remember, yes."

"I think we were both surprised and disturbed to find ourselves in this situation. And I remember I said something like this: that we had stumbled against a natural barrier that was as old as our separate evolutionary processes – we used big words in those days. And you said there were plenty of territories we could explore without meeting such barriers and we'd better stick to them. And so, from that rainy evening onwards, we did. Until now. Until this moment."

Alleyn said: "I mustn't follow you along these reminiscent byways. If you think for a moment, you'll understand why. I'm a policeman on duty. One of the first things we are taught is the necessity for non-involvement. I'd have asked to be relieved of this job if I had known what shape it would take."

"What shape has it taken? What have you—uncovered?"

"I'll tell you. I think that the night before last a group of people, some fanatical, each in his or her own degree a bit demented and each with a festering motive of sorts, planned to have you assassinated in such a way that it would appear to have been done by your spear-carrier—your *mlinzi:* it's about these people that I'd like to talk to you. First of all, Sanskrit. Am I right or wrong in my conjecture about Sanskrit? Is he an informer?"

"There, my dear Rory, I must plead privilege."

"I thought you might. All right. The Cockburn-Montforts. His hopes of military glory under the new regime came unstuck. He is said to have been infuriated. Has he to thank you, personally, for his compulsory retirement?"

"Oh, yes," said the Boomer coolly. "I got rid of him. He had become an alcoholic and quite unreliable. Besides, my policy was to appoint Ng'ombwanans to the senior ranks. We have been through all this."

"Has he threatened you?"

"Not to my face. He was abusive at a personal interview I granted. I have been told that in his cups he uttered threats. It was all very silly and long forgotten."

"Not on his part, perhaps. You knew he had been invited to the reception?"

"At my suggestion. He did good service in the past. We gave him a medal for it."

"I see. Do you remember the Gomez case?"

For a moment, he looked surprised. "Of course I remember it," he said. "He was a very bad man. A savage. A murderer. I had the pleasure of procuring him a fifteen-year stretch. It should have been a capital charge. He—" The Boomer pulled up short. "What of him?" he asked.

"A bit of information your sources didn't pass on to you, it seems. Perhaps they didn't know. Gomez has changed his name to Sheridan and lives five minutes away from your Embassy. He was not at your party but he is a member of this group, and from what I have heard of him he's not going to let one setback defeat him. He'll try again."

"That I can believe," said the Boomer. For the first time he looked disconcerted.

Alleyn said: "He watched this house from over the way while you sat to Troy yesterday morning. It's odds on he's out there again, now. He's being very closely observed. Would you say he's capable of going it alone and lobbing a bomb into your car or through my windows?"

"If he's maintained the head of steam he worked up against me at his trial—" the Boomer began and checked himself. He appeared to take thought and then, most unconvincingly, let out one of his great laughs. "Whatever he does," he said, "if he does anything, it will be a fiasco. *Bombs!* No, really, it's too absurd!"

For an alarming second or two Alleyn felt himself to be at explosion point. With difficulty he controlled his voice and suggested, fairly mildly, that if any attempts made upon the Boomer turned out to be fiascos it would be entirely due to the vigilance and efficiency of the despised Gibson and his men.

"Why don't you arrest this person?" the Boomer asked casually.

"Because, as you very well know, we can't make arrests on what would appear to be groundless suspicion. He has done nothing to warrant an arrest."

The Boomer scarcely seemed to listen to him, a non-reaction that didn't exactly improve his temper.

"There is one more member of this coterie," Alleyn said. "A servant called Chubb. Is he known to you?"

"Chubb? Chubb? Ah! Yes, by the way! I believe I *have* heard of Chubb. Isn't he Mr. Samuel Whipplestone's man? He came up with drinks while I was having a word with his master, who happened to mention it. You're not suggesting — !"

"That Sam Whipplestone's involved? Indeed I'm not. But we've discovered that the man is."

The Boomer seemed scarcely to take this in. The enormous creature suddenly leapt to his feet. For all his great size he was on them, like an animal, in one co-ordinated movement.

"What am I thinking of!" he exclaimed. "To bring myself here! To force my attention upon your wife with this silly dangerous person who, bombs or no bombs, is liable to make an exhibition of himself and kick up dirt in the street. I will take myself off at once. Perhaps I may see her for a moment to apologize and then I vanish."

"She won't take much joy of that," Alleyn said. "She has gone a miraculously long way in an unbelievably short time with what promises to be the best portrait of her career. It's quite appalling to think of it remaining unfinished."

The Boomer gazed anxiously at him and then, with great simplicity, said: "I get everything wrong."

He had made this observation as a solitary black schoolboy in his first desolate term and it had marked the beginning of their friendship. Alleyn stopped himself from saying: "Don't look like that," and instead picked up the great bouquet of roses, put them in his hands, and said: "Come and see her."

"Shall I?" he said, doubtful but greatly cheered. "Really? Good!"

He strode to the door and flung it open. "Where is my *mlinzi*?" he loudly demanded.

Fox, who was in the hall, said blandly: "He's outside Mrs. Alleyn's studio, Your Excellency. He seemed to think that was where he was wanted."

"We may congratulate ourselves," Alleyn said, "that he hasn't brought his spear with him."

IV

Alleyn had escorted the Boomer to the studio and seen him established on his throne. Troy, tingling though she was with impatience, had praised the roses and put them in a suitable pot. She had also exultantly pounced upon the Afghan hound, who, with an apparent instinct for aesthetic values, had mounted the throne and posed himself with killing effect against the Boomer's left leg and was in process of being committed to canvas.

Alleyn, possessed by a medley of disconnected anxieties and attachments, quitted the unlikely scene and joined Fox in the hall.

"Is it all right?" Fox asked, jerking his head in the direction of the studio. "All that?"

"If you can call it all right for my wife to be settled cosily in there painting a big black dictator with a suspected murderer outside the door and the victim's dog posing for its portrait, it's fine. Fine!"

"Well, it's unusual," Fox conceded. "What are you doing about it?"

"I'm putting one of those coppers on my doorstep outside the studio where he can keep the *mlinzi* company. Excuse me for a moment, Fox."

He fetched the constable, a powerful man, from the pavement and gave him his directions.

"The man doesn't speak much English, if any," he said, "and I don't for a moment suppose he'll do anything but squat in the sun and stare. He's not armed and normally he's harmless. Your job's to keep close obbo on him till he's back in the car with Master."

"Very good, sir," said the officer, and proceeded massively in the required direction.

Alleyn rejoined Fox.

"Wouldn't it be simpler," Fox ventured, "under the circumstances, I mean, to cancel the sittings?"

"Look here, Br'er Fox," Alleyn said. "I've done my bloody best to keep my job out of sight of my wife and by and large I've made a hash of it. But I'll tell you what: if ever my job looks like so much as coming between one dab of her brush and the surface of her canvas, I'll chuck it and set up a prep school for detectives."

After a considerable pause Mr. Fox said judicially: "She's lucky to have you."

"Not she," said Alleyn. "It's entirely the other way round. In the meantime, what's cooking? Where's Fred?"

"Outside. He's hoping for a word with you. Just routine, far as I know."

Mr. Gibson sat in a PANDA a little way down the cul-de-sac and not far from the pub. Uniform men were distributed along the street and householders looked out of upstairs windows. The crowd at the entrance had thinned considerably.

Alleyn and Fox got into the PANDA.

"What's horrible?" they asked each other. Gibson reported that to the best of his belief the various members of the group were closetted in their respective houses. Mrs. Chubb had been out-of-doors shopping but had returned home. He'd left a couple of men with radio equipment to patrol the area.

He was droning on along these lines when the door of Alleyn's house opened and the large officer spoke briefly to his colleague in the street. The latter was pointing towards the PANDA.

"This is for me," Alleyn said. "I'll be back."

It was Mr. Whipplestone on the telephone, composed but great with tidings. He had paid his plumbing call on Mr. Sheridan and found him in a most extraordinary state.

"White to the lips, shaking, scarcely able to pull himself together and give me a civil hearing. I had the impression that he was about to leave the flat. At first I thought he wasn't going to let me in, but he shot a quick look up and down the street and suddenly stepped back and motioned with his head for me to enter. We stood in the lobby. I really don't think he took in a word about the plumbers, but he nodded and—not so much grinned as bared his teeth from time to time."

"Pretty!"

"Not very delicious, I assure you. Do you know, I was transported back all those years, into that court of justice in Ng'ombwana. He might have been standing in the dock again."

"That's not an over-fanciful conceit, either. Did you say anything about the Sanskrits?"

"Yes. I did. I ventured. As I was leaving. I think I may say I was sufficiently casual. I asked him if he knew whether the pottery in the Mews undertook china repairs. He looked at me as if I was mad and shook his head."

"Has he gone out?"

"I'm afraid I don't know. You may be sure I was prepared to watch. I had settled to do so, but Mrs. Chubb met me in the hall. She said Chubb was not well and would I mind if she attended to my luncheon—served it and so on. She said it was what she called a 'turn' that he's subject to and he had run out of whatever he takes for it and would like to go to the chemist's. I, of course, said I could look after myself and *she* could go to the chemist's. I said I would lunch out if it would help. In any case it was only ten o'clock. But she was distressed, poor creature, and I couldn't quite brush her aside and go into the drawing-room, so I can't positively swear Sheridan—Gomez—didn't leave. It's quite possible that he did. As soon as I'd got rid of Mrs. Chubb I went to the drawing-room window. The area gate was open and I'm certain I shut it."

"I see. What about Chubb?"

"What, indeed! He *did* go out. Quite openly. I asked Mrs. Chubb about it and she said he'd insisted. She said the prescription took some time to make up and he would have to wait."

"Has he returned?"

"Not yet. Nor has Sheridan. If, in fact, he went out."

"Will you keep watch, Sam?"

"Of course."

"Good. I think I'll be coming your way."

Alleyn returned to the car. He passed Mr. Whipplestone's information on to Fox and Gibson and they held a brief review of the situation.

"What's important as I see it," Alleyn said, "is the way these conspirators are thinking and feeling. If I'm right in my guesses, they got a hell of a shock on the night of the party. Everything was set up. The shot fired. The lights went out. The expected commotion ensued. The anticipated sounds were heard. But when the lights went on again it was the wrong body killed by the right weapon wielded by they didn't know who. Very off-putting for all concerned. How did they react? The next night they held a meeting at the Sanskrits'. They'd had time to do a bit of simple addition and the answer had to be a rat in the wainscotting."

"Pardon?" said Gibson.

"A traitor in their ranks. A snout."

"Oh. Ah."

"They must at the very least have suspected it. I'd give a hell of a lot to know what happened at that meeting while you and I, Fox, sat outside in the Mews. Who did they suspect? Why? What did they plan? To have another go at the President? It seems unlikely that Sheridan-Gomez would have given up. Did any of them get wind of Sanskrit's visit to the Embassy last night? And who the devil was the shadow we saw sprinting round the alley-corner?"

"Come on, Mr. Alleyn. What's the theory? Who do you reckon?"

"Oh, I'll tell you *that,* Br'er Fox," Alleyn said. And did.

"And if either of you lot," he ended, "so much as mumbles the word 'conjecture' I'll put you both on dab for improper conduct."

"It boils down to this, then," said Fox. "They may be contemplating a second attempt on the President or they may be setting their sights on the snout whoever they reckon him to be, or they may be split on their line of action. Or," he added as an afterthought, "they may have decided to call it a day, wind up the Klu-Klux-Fish and fade out in all directions."

"How true. With which thought we, too, part company. We must be all-ways away, Br'er Fox. Some to kill cankers in the musk-rose buds—"

"What's all that about?" Gibson asked glumly.

"Quotations," Fox said.

"Yes, Fred," said Alleyn, "and you can go and catch a red-hipped humble-bee on the lip of a thistle while Fox and I war with reremice for their leathern wings."

"Who said all the bumph anyway?"

"Fairies. We'll keep in touch. Come on, Fox."

They returned to their own anonymous car and were driven to the Capricorns. Here a discreet prowl brought them into touch with one of Gibson's men, a plain-clothes sergeant, who had quite a lot to say for himself. The fishy brotherhood had not been idle. Over the last half-hour the Cockburn-Montforts had been glimpsed through their drawing-room window engaged in drinking and—or so it seemed—quarrelling in a desultory way between libations. Chubb had been followed, by a plain-clothes sergeant carrying artist's impedimenta, to a chemist's shop in Baronsgate, where he handed in a prescription and sat down, presumably waiting for it to be made up. Seeing him settled there, the sergeant returned to Capricorn Mews, where, having an aptitude in that direction, he followed a well-worn routine by sitting on a canvas stool and making a pencil sketch of the pig-pottery. He had quite a collection of sketches at home, some finished and prettily tinted with aquarelles, others of a rudimentary kind, having been cut short by an arrest or by an obligation to shift the area of investigation. For these occasions he wore jeans, a dirty jacket, and an excellent wig of the Little Lord Fauntleroy type. His name was Sergeant Jacks.

Mr. Sheridan, the Cockburn-Montforts and the Sanskrits had not appeared.

Fox parked the car in its overnight position under the plane trees in Capricorn Square, from where he could keep observation on No. 1, the Walk, and Alleyn took a stroll down the Mews. He paused behind the gifted sergeant and, after the manner of the idle snooper, watched him tinker with a tricky bit of perspective. He wondered what opulent magic Troy at that moment might be weaving, over in Chelsea.

"Anything doing?" he asked.

"Premises shut up, sir. But there's movement. In the back of the shop. There's a bit of a gap in the curtains and you can just get a squint. Not to see anything really. Nobody been in or out of the flat entrance."

"I'll be within range. No. 1, Capricorn Walk. Give me a shout if there's anything. You could nip into that entry to call me up."

"Yes, sir."

Two youths from the garage strolled along and stared.

Alleyn said: "I wouldn't have the patience, myself. Don't put me in it," he added. These were the remarks by bystanders that Troy said were most frequently heard. "Is it for sale?" he asked.

"Er," said the disconcerted sergeant.

"I might come back and have another look," Alleyn remarked, and left the two youths to gape.

He pulled his hat over his left eye, walked very quickly indeed across the end of Capricorn Place and on into the Walk. He had a word with Fox in the car under the plane trees and then crossed the street to No. 1, where Mr. Whipplestone, who had seen him coming, let him in.

"Sam," Alleyn said. "Chubb did go to the chemist."

"I'm extremely glad to hear it."

"But it doesn't necessarily mean he won't call at the piggery, you know."

"You think not?"

"If he suffers from migraine the stresses of the past forty-eight hours might well have brought it on."

"I suppose so."

"Is his wife in?"

"Yes," said Mr. Whipplestone, looking extremely apprehensive.

"I want to speak to her."

"Do you? That's – that's rather disturbing."

"I'm sorry, Sam. It can't be helped, I'm afraid."

"Are you going to press for information about her husband?"

"Probably."

"How very – distasteful."

"Police work is, at times, precisely that."

"I know. I've often wondered how you can."

"Have you?"

"You strike me, always, as an exceptionally fastidious man."

"I'm sorry to disenchant you."

"And I'm sorry to have been tactless."

"Sam," Alleyn said gently, "one of the differences between police work and that of other and grander services is that we do our own dirty washing instead of farming it out at two or three removes."

Mr. Whipplestone turned pink. "I deserved that," he said.

"No, you didn't. It was pompous and out of place."

Lucy Lockett, who had been washing herself with the zeal of an occupational therapist, made one of her ambiguous remarks, placed her forepaws on Alleyn's knee, and leapt neatly into his lap.

"Now then, baggage," Alleyn said, scratching her head, "that sort of stuff never got a girl anywhere."

"You don't know," Mr. Whipplestone said, "how flattered you ought to feel. The demonstration is unique."

Alleyn handed his cat to him and stood up. "I'll get it over," he said. "Is she upstairs, do you know?"

"I think so."

"It won't take long, I hope."

"If I — if I can help in any way — ?"

"I'll let you know," said Alleyn.

He climbed the stairs and tapped on the door. When Mrs. Chubb opened it and saw him, she reacted precisely as she had on his former visit. There she stood, speechless with her fingers on her lips. When he asked to come in she moved aside with the predictable air of terrified reluctance. He went in and there was the enlarged photograph of the fresh-faced girl. The medallion, even, was, as before, missing from its place. He wondered if Chubb was wearing it.

"Mrs. Chubb," he said, "I'm not going to keep you long and I hope I'm not going to frighten you. Yes, please, do sit down."

Just as she did last time, she dropped into her chair and stared at him. He drew his up and leant forward.

"Since I saw you yesterday," he said, "we have learnt a great deal more about the catastrophe at the Embassy and about the people closely and remotely concerned in it. I'm going to tell you what I believe to be your husband's part."

She moved her lips as if to say: "He never — " but was voiceless.

"All I want you to do is listen and then tell me if I'm right, partly right or wholly mistaken. I can't force you to answer, as I expect you know, but I very much hope that you will."

He waited for a moment and then said: "Well. Here it is. I believe that your husband, being a member of the group we talked about yesterday, agreed to act with them in an attack upon the President of Ng'ombwana. I think he agreed because of his hatred of blacks and of Ng'ombwanans in particular."

Alleyn looked for a moment at the smiling photograph. "It's a hatred born of tragedy," he said, "and it has rankled and deepened, I daresay, during the last five years.

"When it was known that your husband was to be one of the waiters in the pavilion, the plan was laid. He had been given detailed instructions about his duties by his employers. The group was given even more detailed information from an agent inside the Embassy. And Chubb's orders were based on this information. He had been a commando and was very well suited indeed for the work in hand. Which was this. When the lights in the pavilion and the garden went out and after a shot was fired in the house, he was to disarm and disable the spearman who was on guard behind the President, jump on a chair, and kill the President with the spear."

She was shaking her head to and fro and making inexplicit movements with her hands.

"No?" Alleyn said. "Is that wrong? You didn't know about it? Not beforehand? Not afterwards? But you knew something was planned, didn't you? And you were frightened? And afterwards you knew it had gone wrong? Yes?"

She whispered. "He never. He never done it."

"No. He was lucky. He was hoist— he got the treatment he was supposed to hand out. The other waiter put him out of action. And what happened after that was no business of Chubb's."

"You can't hurt him. You can't touch him."

"That's why I've come to see you, Mrs. Chubb. It may well be that we could, in fact, charge your husband with conspiracy. That means, with joining in a plan to do bodily harm. But our real concern is with the murder itself. If Chubb cuts loose from this group—and they're a bad lot, Mrs. Chubb, a really bad lot— and gives me a straight answer to questions based on the account I've just given you, I think the police will be less inclined to press home attempted murder or charges of conspiracy. I don't know if you'll believe this, but I do beg you, very seriously indeed, if you have any influence over him, to get him to make a complete break, not to go to any more meetings, above all, not to take part in any further action against anybody—Ng'ombwanan, white or what-have-you. Tell him to cut loose, Mrs. Chubb. You tell him to cut loose. And at the same time not to do anything silly like making a bolt for it. That'd be about the worst thing he could do."

He had begun to think he would get no response of any kind from her when her face wrinkled over and she broke into a passion of tears. At first it was almost impossible to catch the sense of what she tried to say. She sobbed out words piecemeal, as if they escaped by haphazard compulsion. But presently phrases emerged and a sort of congruence of ideas. She said what had happened five years ago might have happened yesterday for Chubb. She repeated several times that he "couldn't get over it," that he "never hardly said anything," but she could "tell." They never talked about it, she said, not even on the anniversary, which was always a terrible day for both of them. She said that for herself something "came over" her at the sight of a black man, but for Chubb, Alleyn gathered, the revulsion was savage and implacable. There had been incidents. There were times when he took queer turns and acted very funny with headaches. The doctor had given him something.

"Is that the prescription he's getting made up now?"

She said it was. As for "that lot," she added, she'd never fancied him getting in with them.

He had become secretive about the meetings, she said, and had shut her up when she tried to ask questions. She had known something was wrong. Something queer was going on.

"They was getting at him and the way he feels. On account of our Glyn. I could tell that. But I never knew what."

Alleyn gathered that after the event Chubb had been a little more communicative in that he let out that he'd been "made a monkey of." He'd acted according to orders, he said, and what had he got for it? Him with his experience? He was very angry and his neck hurt.

"Did he tell you what really happened? Everything?"

No, she said. There was something about him "getting in with the quick one according to plan" but being "clobbered" from behind and making a "boss shot of it."

Alleyn caught back an exclamation.

It hadn't made sense to Mrs. Chubb. Alleyn gathered that she'd felt, in a muddled way, that because a black man had been killed Chubb ought to have been pleased, but that he was angry because something had, in some fashion, been put across him. When Alleyn suggested that nothing she had told him contradicted the version he had given to her, she stared hopelessly at him out of blurred eyes and vaguely shook her head.

"I suppose not," she said.

"From what you've told me, my suggestion that you persuade him to break with them was useless. You've tried. All the same, when he comes back from the chemist's – "

She broke in: "He ought to be back," she cried. "It wouldn't take that long! He ought to've come in by now. Oh Gawd, where is he?"

"Now don't you go getting yourself into a state before there's need," Alleyn said. "You stay put and count your blessings. Yes, that's what I said, Mrs. Chubb. Blessings. If your man had brought off what he set out to do on the night of the party you *would* have had something to cry about. If he comes back, tell him what I've said. Tell him he's being watched. Keep him indoors and in the meantime brew yourself a strong cuppa and pull yourself together, there's a good soul. Good morning to you."

He ran downstairs and was met at the drawing-room door by Mr. Whipplestone.

"Well, Sam," he said. "Through no fault of his own your Chubb didn't commit murder. That's not to say—"

The telephone rang. Mr. Whipplestone made a little exasperated noise and answered it.

"Oh!" he said. "Oh, yes. He is. Yes, of course. Yes."

"It's for you," he said. "It's Mrs. Roderick."

As soon as she heard Alleyn's voice, Troy said: "Rory. Important. Someone with a muffled voice has just rung up to say there's a bomb in the President's car."

IX

Climax

Alleyn said: "Don't — " but she cut in.

"No, listen! The thing is, he's gone. Five minutes ago. In his car."

"Where?"

"The Embassy."

"Right. Stay put."

"Urgent," Alleyn said to Mr. Whipplestone. "See you later."

He left the house as Fox got out of the car under the trees and came towards him.

"Bomb scare," said Fox. "On the blower."

"I know. Come on. The Embassy."

They got into the car. On the way to the Embassy, which was more roundabout than the way through the hole in the wall, Fox said a disguised voice had rung the Yard. The Yard was ringing Troy and had alerted Gibson and all on duty in the area.

"The President's on his way back," Alleyn said. "Troy's had the muffled voice, too."

"The escort car will have got the message."

"I hope so."

"A hoax, do you reckon?"

"Considering the outlandish nature of the material we're

supposed to be handling, it's impossible to guess. As usual we take it for real. But I tell you what, Br'er Fox, I've got a nasty feeling that if it is a hoax it's a hoax with a purpose. Another name for it might be red-herring. We'll see Fred and then get back to our own patch. That Royal Academician in the Mews had better be keeping his eyes open. Here we are."

They had turned out of a main thoroughfare, with their siren blaring, into Palace Park Gardens, and there outside the Embassy, emerging from his police escort's car, was the Boomer, closely followed by his *mlinzi* and the Afghan hound. Alleyn and Fox left their car and approached him. He hailed them vigorously.

"Hullo, hullo!" shouted the Boomer. "Here are turn-ups for the books! You have heard the latest, I suppose?"

"We have," said Alleyn. "Where's the Embassy car?"

"Where? Where? Half-way between here and there, 'there' being your own house, to be specific. The good Gibson and his henchmen are looking under the seats for bombs. Your wife required me no longer. I left a little early. Shall we go indoors?"

Alleyn excused himself and was glad to see them off. The driver of the official police car was talking into his radio. He said: "Mr. Alleyn's here now, sir. Yes, sir."

"All right," Alleyn said and got into the car.

It was Gibson. "So you've heard?" he said. "Nothing so far but we haven't finished."

"Did *you* hear the call?"

"No. He or she rang the Yard. Info is that he probably spoke through a handkerchief."

"He *or* she?"

"The voice was peculiar. A kind of squeaky whisper. They reckon it sounded frightened or excited or both. The exact words were: *'Is that Scotland Yard? There's a bomb in the Black Embassy car. Won't be long now.'* Call not traced. They thought the car would be outside your place and a minute or so was lost ascertaining it was on the way back. All my chaps were alerted and came on the scene pronto. Oh, and they say he seemed to speak with a lisp."

"Like hell they do! So would they with a mouthful of handkerchief. Who's on the Capricorn ground?"

"A copper in a wig with coloured chalks."

"I know all about him. That all?"

"Yes," said Gibson. "The others were ordered round here," and added with a show of resentment, "My job's mounting security over this big, bloody black headache and a bloody gutty show it's turned out to be."

"All right, Fred. I know. It's a stinker. I'll get back there myself. What about you?"

"I'll stick here with the suspect car. Look!" said Gibson with the nearest approach to shrillness that Alleyn would have thought possible, "it's got to such a pitch that I'd welcome a straight case of bomb disposal and no nonsense. There you are! I'd welcome it."

Alleyn was forming what conciliatory phrases he could offer when he was again called to the radio. It was the gifted Sergeant Jacks.

"Sir," said the sergeant in some agitation. "I better report."

"What?"

"This bomb scare, sir. Just before it broke the military gentleman, Colonel Whatsit, beg pardon, came walking very rigid and careful up to the pig-pottery and leant on the bell of the door into their flat. And then the scare broke, sir. Mr. Gibson's chap, keeping obbo in a car near the entrance to Capricorn Passage, sir, came round and told me quick, through the driving window, that it was a general alert, sir. And while he was talking, a dirty great van pulled out of the garage and obscured my view of the pottery. Well, sir, I'd got my orders from you to stay where I am. And Mr. Gibson's chap drove off. Meanwhile a traffic jam had built up in the Mews behind the van. I couldn't get a sight of the pottery but I could hear the Colonel. He'd started up yelling. Something like: 'Open the bloody door, damn you, and let me in.' And then the drivers began sounding off on their horns. It was like that for at least five minutes, sir."

"Could anybody—could two enormous people—have got out and away while this lasted?"

"I reckon not, because it sorted itself out, sir, and when it had cleared, there was the Colonel still at the piggery door and still leaning on the bell. And he's leaning on it now. And yelling a bit but kind of fading out. I reckon he's so drunk he's had it. What'll I do, sir?"

"Where are you?"

"Ducked down behind my easel. It's a bit awkward but I thought I'd risk it. Could you hold on, sir?"

An interval of street noises. Alleyn held on and the voice returned. "I'm up the alleyway, sir. I had to duck. The gentleman from the basement of No. 1, the Walk, passed the end of the alleyway going towards the pottery."

"Get back to your easel and watch."

"Sir."

"I'm on my way. Over and out. Capricorn Square," Alleyn said to the driver. "Quick as you can make it but no siren."

"What was all that, then?" asked Fox. When he was informed he remarked that the painter-chap seemed to be reasonably practical and active even if he did get himself up like a right Charlie. Mr. Fox had a prejudice against what he called "fancy-dress coppers." His own sole gesture in that line was to put on an ancient Donegal tweed ulster and an out-of-date felt hat. It was surprising how effectively these lendings disguised his personality.

When they reached the Square, Alleyn said: "We'd better separate. This is tricky. Sheridan-Gomez is the only one of the gang that doesn't know me. The others might remember *you* from your checking out activities after the party. Have you got your nighty with you?"

"If you mean my Donegal ulster, yes I have. It's in the back."

"And the head-gear?"

"Rolled up in the pocket."

"When you've dolled yourself up in them you might stroll to the piggery by way of the Square and Capricorn Place. I'll take the Walk and the Mews. We'll no doubt encounter each other in the vicinity of the piggery."

Fox went off looking like a North of Ireland corn chandler on holiday, and Alleyn turned into Capricorn Walk looking like himself.

Lucy Lockett, taking the sun on the steps of No. 1, rolled over at him as he passed.

No doubt, Alleyn reflected, Gibson's men patrolling the Capricorns, who had been diverted to the Embassy on the bomb alarm, would soon return to their ground. At the moment there was no sign of them.

It was the busiest time of day in the Capricorns and a pretty constant two-way stream of traffic moved along the Walk. Alleyn used it to screen his approach to the house-decorator's shop on the corner of the Mews. From here, looking sideways through the windows, he had a view down the Mews to the pottery at the far end. Intermittently he had glimpses of the gifted Sergeant Jacks at his easel, but commercial vehicles backing and filling outside the garage constantly shut him off. The pottery flashed in and out of view like the fractional revelations of commercial television. Now it was Colonel Cockburn-Montfort, still at the pottery flat door, with Gomez beside him. And then, as if by sleight-of-hand, Chubb was there with them in consultation. Now a van drove into the Mews, fetched up outside the Napoli and began to deliver cartons and crates, and there was no view at all.

Between the Napoli and the garage, and next door to the flower shop, there was a tiny bistro, calling itself the Bijou. On fine days it put four tables out on the pavement and served coffee and patisseries. One of the tables was unoccupied. Alleyn walked past the van and flower shop, sat at the table, ordered coffee and lit his pipe. He had his back to the pottery but got a fair reflection of it in the flower shop window.

Gomez and Chubb were near the flat door. The Colonel still leant against it, looking dreadfully groggy. Chubb stood back a little way with his fingers to his mouth. Gomez seemed to be peering in at the curtained shop window.

He was joined there by Inspector Fox, who had arrived via Capricorn Place. He appeared to search for an address and find it in the pottery. He approached the shop door, took out his spectacles, read the notice *Closed for stocktaking* and evidently spoke to Gomez, who shrugged and turned his back.

Fox continued down the Mews. He paused by the talented Sergeant Jacks, again assumed his spectacles and bent massively towards the drawing. Alleyn watched with relish as his colleague straightened up, tilted his head appreciatively to one side, fell back a step or two, apologized to a passer-by and continued on his way. When he reached the table he said: "Excuse me, is that chair taken?" and Alleyn said: "No. Please."

Fox took it, ordered coffee, and when he had been served asked Alleyn the time.

"Come off it," Alleyn said. "Nobody's looking at you."

But they both kept up the show of casual conversation between strangers.

Fox said: "It's a funny set-up back there. They act as if they don't know each other. The Colonel seems to be on the blink. If you poked a finger at him, he'd fall flat."

"What about the premises?"

"You can't see anything in the shop. There's curtains almost closed across the window and no light inside."

He blew on his coffee and took a sip.

"They're in a funny sort of shape," he said. "The Gomez man's shaking. Very pale. Gives the impression he might cut up violent. Think they've skedaddled, Mr. Alleyn? The Sanskrits?"

"It would have to be after nine-ten this morning, when Sanskrit was seen to go home."

"That copper with the crayons reckons they couldn't have made it since he's been on the job."

"He dodged up the garage alley to talk to me, he might remember. Of course that damn bomb scare drew Fred Gibson's men off. But, no. I don't think they've flitted. I don't think so. I think they're lying doggo."

"What's the drill, then?" Fox asked his coffee.

"I've got a search-warrant. Blow me down flat, Br'er Fox, if I don't take a chance and execute it. Look," Alleyn said, drawing on his pipe and gazing contentedly at the sky. "We may be in a bloody awkward patch. You get back to the car and whistle up support. Fred's lot ought to be available again now. We'll move in as soon as they're on tap. Call us up on the artist's buzzer. Then we close in."

"What about Gomez and the Colonel? And Chubb?"

"We keep it nice and easy but we hold them. See you on the doorstep."

Fox put down his empty cup, looked about him, rose, nodded to Alleyn, and strolled away in the direction of Capricorn Walk. Alleyn waited until he had disappeared round the corner, finished his coffee, and at a leisurely pace rejoined Sergeant Jacks, who was touching up his architectural details.

"Pack up," Alleyn said, "and leave your stuff up the alley there. You'll get a shout from Mr. Fox in a matter of seconds."

"Is it a knock-off, sir?"

"It may be. If that lot, there, start to move, we hold them. Nice and quiet, though. All right. Make it quick. And when you get the office from Mr. Fox, come out here again where I can see you and we'll move in. Right?"

"Right, sir."

The delivery van from the Napoli lurched noisily down the Mews, did a complicated turn-about in front of the pottery, and went back the way it had come. Alleyn moved towards the pottery.

A police-car siren, braying in Baronsgate, was coming nearer. Another, closer at hand, approached from somewhere on the outer borders of the Capricorns.

Sergeant Jacks came out of the garage alleyway. Fox and Gibson had been quick.

Gomez walked rapidly up the Mews on the opposite side to Alleyn, who crossed over and stepped in front of him. The sirens, close at hand now, stopped.

"Mr. Sheridan?" Alleyn said.

For a moment the living image of an infuriated middle-aged man overlay that of the same man fifteen years younger in Mr. Whipplestone's album. He had turned so white that his close-shaved beard started up, blue-black, as if it had been painted across his face.

He said: "Yes? My name is Sheridan."

"Yes, of course. You've been trying to call upon the Sanskrits, haven't you?"

He made a very slight movement: an adjustment of his weight, rather like Mr. Whipplestone's cat preparing to spring or bolt. Fox had come up behind Alleyn. Two of Gibson's uniform men had turned into the Mews from Capricorn Place. There were more large men converging on the pottery. Sergeant Jacks was talking to Chubb and Fred Gibson loomed over Colonel Cockburn-Montfort by the door into the flat.

Gomez stared from Alleyn to Fox. "What is this?" he lisped. "What do you want? Who are you?"

"We're police officers. We're about to effect an entry into

the pottery and I suggest that you come with us. Better not to make a scene in the street, don't you think?"

For a moment Gomez had looked as if he meant to do so, but he now said between his teeth: "I want to see those people."

"Now's your chance," said Alleyn.

He glowered, hesitated, and then said: "Very well," and walked between Alleyn and Fox towards the pottery.

Gibson and the sergeant were having no trouble. Chubb was standing bolt upright and saying nothing. Colonel Cockburn-Montfort had been detached from the bell, deftly rolled round and propped against the door-jamb by Gibson. His eyes were glazed and his mouth slightly open, but like Chubb he actually maintained a trace of his soldierly bearing.

Four uniform men had arrived and bystanders had begun to collect.

Alleyn rang the bell and knocked on the top of the door. He waited for half a minute and then said to one of the policemen: "It's a Yale. Let's hope it's not double-locked. Got anything?"

The policeman fished in his breast pocket, produced a small polythene ready-reckoner of a kind used for conversion to metric quantities. Alleyn slid it past the tongue of the lock and manipulated it.

"Bob's your uncle," the constable murmured and the door was open.

Alleyn said to Fox and Gibson, "Would you wait a moment with these gentlemen." He then nodded to the constables, who followed him in, one remaining inside the door.

"Hullo!" Alleyn called. "Anyone at home?"

He had a resonant voice, but it sounded stifled in the airless flat. They were in a narrow lobby hung with dim native cloth of some sort and smelling of dust and the stale fumes of sandarac. A staircase rose steeply on the left from just inside the door. At the far end on the right was a door that presumably led into the shop. Two large suitcases, strapped and labelled, leant against the wall.

Alleyn turned on a switch and a pseudo-Oriental lamp with red panes came to life in the ceiling. He looked at the labels on the suitcases: *Sanskrit, Ng'ombwana.* "Come on," he said.

He led the way upstairs. On the landing he called out again.

Silence.

There were four doors, all shut.

Two bedrooms, small, exotically furnished, crowded and in disarray. Discarded garments flung on unmade beds. Cupboards and drawers open and half-emptied. Two small, half-packed suitcases. An all-pervading and most unlovely smell.

A bathroom, stale and grubby, smelling of hot wet fat. The wall-cupboard was locked.

Finally, a large, heavily furnished room with divans, deep rugs, horrid silk-shaded and beaded lamps, incense burners, and a number of ostensibly African artifacts. But no Sanskrits.

They returned downstairs. Alleyn opened the door at the end of the lobby and walked through.

He was in the piggery.

It was very dark. Only a thin sliver of light penetrated the slit between the heavy window curtains.

He stood inside the door with the two uniform men behind him. As his eyes adjusted to the gloom the interior began to emerge: a desk, a litter of paper and packing material, open cases, and on the shelves, dimly flowering, one pottery pig. The end of the old stable formed, as he remembered, a sort of alcove or cavern in which were the kiln and a long work table. He saw a faint red glow there now.

He was taken with a sensation of inertia that he had long ago learnt to recognize as the kind of nightmare which drains one of the power to move.

As now, when his hand was unable to grope about the dirty wall for a light switch.

The experience never lasted for more than a few seconds, and now it had passed and left him with the knowledge that he was watched.

Someone at the far end of the shop, in the alcove room, sitting on the other side of the work table, was watching him: a looming mass that he had mistaken for shadow.

It began to define itself. An enormous person whose chin rested with a suggestion of doggy roguishness on her arm, and whose eyes were very wide open indeed.

Alleyn's hand found the switch and the room was flooded with light.

It was Miss Sanskrit who ogled him so coyly with her chin on her arm and her head all askew and her eyes wide open.

Behind the table with his back towards her, with his vast rump upheaved and with his head and arms and barrel submerged in a packing case like a monstrous puppet doubled over its box, dangled her brother. They were both dead.

And between them, on the floor and the bench, were blooded shards of pottery.

And in the packing case lay the headless carcass of an enormous pottery pig.

II

A whispered stream of obscenities had been surprised out of one of the constables, but he had stopped when Alleyn walked into the alcove and had followed a short way behind.

"Stay where you are," Alleyn said, and then: "No! One of you get that lot in off the street and lock the door. Take them to the room upstairs, keep them there and stay with them. Note anything that's said.

"The other call Homicide and give the necessary information. Ask Mr. Fox and Mr. Gibson to come here."

They went out, shutting the door behind them. In a minute Alleyn heard sounds of a general entry and of people walking upstairs.

When Fox and Gibson arrived they found Alleyn standing between the Sanskrits. They moved towards him but checked when he raised his hand.

"This is nasty," Fox said. "What was it?"

"Come and see but walk warily."

They moved round the table and saw the back of Miss Sanskrit's head. It was smashed in like an egg. Beetroot-dyed hair, dark and wet, stuck in the wound. The back of her dress was saturated – there was a dark puddle on the table under her arm. She was dressed for the street. Her bloodied hat lay on the floor and her handbag was on the work table.

Alleyn turned to face the vast rump of her brother, clothed in a camel overcoat, which was all that could be seen of him.

"Is it the same?" Gibson asked.

"Yes. A pottery pig. The head broke off on the first attack and the rest fell in the box after the second."

"But – how exactly – ?" Fox said.

"Look what's on the table. Under her hand."

It was a sheet of headed letter paper. "The Piggie Potterie. 12, Capricorn Mews, S.W.3." Written beneath this legend was: "To Messrs. Able and Virtue. Kindly . . ." and no more.

"A green ball-point," Alleyn said. "It's still in her right hand."

Fox touched the hand. "Still warm," he said.

"Yes."

There was a checkered cloth of sorts near the kiln. Alleyn masked the terrible head with it. "One of the really bad ones," he said.

"What was *he* doing?" Fox asked.

"Stowing away the remaining pigs. Doubled up, and reaching down into the packing case."

"So you read the situation – how?"

"Like this, unless something else turns up to contradict it. She's writing. He's putting pigs from the bench into the packing case. Someone comes between them. Someone who perhaps has offered to help. Someone, at any rate, whose presence doesn't disturb them. And this person picks up a pig, deals two mighty downward blows, left and right, quick as you please, and walks out."

Gibson said angrily: "Walks out! When? And when did he *walk in*? I've had these premises under close observation for twelve hours."

"Until the bomb scare, Fred."

"Sergeant Jacks stayed put."

"With a traffic jam building up between him and the pottery."

"By God, this is a gutty job," said Gibson.

"And the gallant Colonel was on the doorstep," Alleyn added.

"I reckon *he* wouldn't have been any the wiser," Fox offered, "if the Brigade of Guards had walked in and out."

"We'll see about that," Alleyn said.

A silence fell between them. The room was oppressively warm and airless. Flies buzzed between the window curtains and the glass. One of them darted out and made like a bullet for the far end.

With startling unexpectedness the telephone on the desk rang. Alleyn wrapped his handkerchief round his hand and lifted the receiver.

He gave the number, speaking well above his natural level. An unmistakably Ng'ombwanan voice said: "It is the Embassy. You have not kept your appointment."

Alleyn made an ambiguous falsetto noise.

"I said," the voice insisted, "you have not kept your appointment. To collect the passports. Your plane leaves at five-thirty."

Alleyn whispered: "I was prevented. Please send them. Please."

A long pause.

"Very well. It is not convenient but very well. They will be put into your letter-box. In a few minutes. Yes?"

He said nothing and heard a deep sound of impatience and the click of the receiver being replaced.

He hung up. "For what it's worth," he said, "we now know that the envelope we saw Sanskrit deliver at the Embassy contained their passports. I'd got as much already from the President. In a few minutes they'll be dropping them in. He failed to keep his appointment to collect."

Fox looked at the upturned remains of Sanskrit. "He could hardly help himself," he said. "Could he?"

The front doorbell rang. Alleyn looked through the slit in the curtains. A car had arrived with Bailey and Thompson, their driver and their gear. A smallish crowd had been moved down the Mews into the Passage.

The constable in the hallway admitted Bailey and Thompson. Alleyn said: "The lot. Complete coverage. Particularly the broken pottery."

Thompson walked carefully past the partition into the alcove and stopped short.

"Two, eh?" he said and unshipped his camera.

"Go ahead," Alleyn said.

Bailey went to the table and looked incredulously from the enormous bodies to Alleyn, who nodded and turned his back. Bailey delicately lifted the checked cloth and said: "Cor!"

"Not pretty," Alleyn said.

Bailey, shocked into a unique flight of fancy, said: "It's kind of not real. Like those blown-up affairs they run in fun shows. Giants. Gone into the horrors."

"It's very much like that," Alleyn said. "Did you hear if they'd got through to Sir James?"

"Yes, Mr. Alleyn. On his way."

"Good. All right. Push on with it, you two." He turned to Gibson and Fox. "I suggest," he said, "that we let that lot upstairs have a look at this scene."

"Shock tactics?" Gibson asked.

"Something like that. Agreed?"

"This is your ground, not mine," said Gibson, still dully resentful. "I'm only meant to be bloody security."

Alleyn knew it was advisable to disregard these plaints. He said: "Fox, would you go upstairs? Take the copper in the hall with you. Leave him in the room and have a quiet word on the landing with the man who's been with them. If he's got anything I ought to hear, hand it on to me. Otherwise, just stick with them for a bit, would you? Don't give a clue as to what's happened. All right?"

"I think so," said Fox placidly and went upstairs.

Bailey's camera clicked and flashed. Miss Sanskrit's awful face started up and out in a travesty of life. Thompson collected pottery shards and laid them out on the far end of the work table. More exploratory flies darted down the room. Alleyn continued to watch through the curtains.

A Ng'ombwanan in civilian dress drove up to the door, had a word with the constable on guard, and pushed something through the letter-box. Alleyn heard the flap of the clapper. The car drove away and he went into the hall and collected the package.

"What's that, then?" Gibson asked.

Alleyn opened it: two passports elaborately stamped and endorsed and a letter on Embassy paper in Ng'ombwanan.

"Giving them the V.I.P. treatment, I wouldn't be surprised," Alleyn said and pocketed the lot.

Action known as "routine" was now steadily under way. Sir James Curtis and his secretary arrived, Sir James remarking a little acidly that he would like to know this time whether he would be allowed to follow the usual procedure and hold his damned post mortems if, when and where he wanted them. On being shown the subjects he came as near to exhibiting physical repulsion as Alleyn had ever seen him and asked appallingly if they would provide him with bull-dozers.

He said that death had probably occurred within the hour, agreed with Alleyn's reading of the evidence, listened to what action he proposed to take, and was about to leave when Alleyn said: "There's a former record of drug-pushing against the man. No sign of them taking anything themselves, I suppose?"

"I'll look out for it but they don't often, do they?"

"Do we expect to find blood on the assailant?"

Sir James considered this. "Not necessarily, I think," he said. "The size of the weapon might form a kind of shield in the case of the woman and the position of the head in the man."

"Might the weapon have been dropped or hurled down on the man? They're extremely heavy, those things."

"Very possible."

"I see."

"You'll send these monstrosities along then, Rory? Good day to you."

When he'd gone, Fox and the constable who had been on duty upstairs came down.

"Thought we'd better wait till Sir James had finished," Fox said. "I've been up there in the room with them. Chubb's very quiet but you can see he's put out."

This, in Fox's language, could mean anything from being irritated to going berserk or suicidal. "He breaks out every now and then," he went on, "asking where the Sanskrits are and why this lot's being kept. I asked him what he'd wanted to see them for and he comes out with it that he *didn't* want to see them. He reckons he was on his way back from the chemist's by way of Capricorn Passage and just ran into the Colonel and Mr. Sheridan. The Colonel was in such a bad way, Chubb makes out, he was trying to get him to let himself be taken home, but all the Colonel would do was lean on the bell."

"What about the Colonel?"

"It doesn't really make sense. He's beyond it. He said something or another about Sanskrit being a poisonous specimen who ought to be court-martialled."

"And Gomez-Sheridan?"

"He's taking the line of righteous indignation. Demands an explanation. Will see there's information laid in the right quarters and we haven't heard the last of it. You'd think it was all quite ordinary except for a kind of twitch under his left eye. They all keep asking where the Sanskrits are."

"It's time they found out," Alleyn said, and to Bailey and Thompson: "There's a smell of burnt leather. We'll have to rake out the furnace."

"Looking for anything in particular, Mr. Alleyn?"

"No. Well – no. Just looking. For traces of anything anyone wanted to destroy. Come on."

He and Fox went upstairs.

As he opened the door and went in he got the impression that Gomez had leapt to his feet. He stood facing Alleyn with his bald head sunk between his shoulders and his eyes like black boot-buttons in his white kid face. He might have been an actor in a bad Latin-American film.

At the far end of the room Chubb stood facing the window with the dogged, conditioned look of a soldier in detention, as if whatever he thought or felt or had done must be thrust back behind a mask of conformity.

Colonel Cockburn-Montfort lay in an armchair with his mouth open, snoring profoundly and hideously. He would have presented a less distasteful picture, Alleyn thought, if he had discarded the outward showing of an officer and – ambiguous addition – gentleman: the conservative suit, the signet ring on the correct finger, the handmade brogues, the regimental tie, the quietly elegant socks and, lying on the floor by his chair, the hat from Jermyn Street—all so very much in order. And Colonel Cockburn-Montfort so very far astray.

Gomez began at once: "You are the officer in charge of these extraordinary proceedings, I believe. I must ask you to inform me, at once, why I am detained here without reason, without explanation or apology."

"Certainly," Alleyn said. "It is because I hope you may be able to help us in our present job."

"Police parrot talk!" he spat out, making a great thing of the plosives. The muscle under his eye flickered.

"I hope not," Alleyn said.

"What is this 'present job'?"

"We are making enquiries about the couple living in these premises. Brother and sister. Their name is Sanskrit."

"*Where are they!*"

"They haven't gone far."

"Are they in trouble?" he asked, showing his teeth.

"Yes."

"I am not surprised. They are criminals. Monsters."

The Colonel snorted and opened his eyes. "What!" he said. "Who are you talking 'bout? Monsters?"

Gomez made a contemptuous noise. "Go to sleep," he said. "You are disgusting."

"I take 'ception that remark, sir," said the Colonel, and sounded exactly like Major Bloodknock, long ago. He shut his eyes.

"How do you know they are criminals?" Alleyn asked.

"I have reliable information," said Gomez.

"From where?"

"From friends in Africa."

"In Ng'ombwana?"

"One of the so-called emergent nations. I believe that is the name."

"You ought to know," Alleyn remarked, "seeing that you spent so long there." And he thought: "He really is rather like an adder."

"You speak nonsense," Gomez lisped.

"I don't think so, Mr. Gomez."

Chubb, by the window, turned and gaped at him.

"My name is Sheridan," Gomez said loudly.

"If you prefer it."

"'Ere!" Chubb said with some violence. "What is all this? *Names!*"

Alleyn said: "Come over here, Chubb, and sit down. I've got something to say to all of you and for your own sakes you'd better listen to it. Sit down. That's right. Colonel Cockburn-Montfort—"

"Cert'n'ly," said the Colonel, opening his eyes.

"Can you follow me or shall I send for a corpse-reviver?"

"'Course I can follow you. F'what it's worth."

"Very well. I'm going to put something to the three of you and it's this. You are members of a coterie which is motivated by racial hatred, more specifically, hatred of the Ng'ombwanan people in particular. On the night before last you conspired to murder the President."

Gomez said, "What is this idiot talk!"

"You had an informant in the Embassy: the Ambassador himself, who believed that on the death of the President and with your backing he would achieve a *coup d'état* and assume power. In return, you, Mr. Gomez, and you, Colonel Montfort, were to be reinstated in Ng'ombwana."

The Colonel waved his hand as if these statements were too trivial to merit consideration. Gomez, his left ankle elegantly poised on his right thigh, watched Alleyn over his locked fingers. Chubb, wooden, sat bolt upright on the edge of his chair.

"The Sanskrits, brother and sister," Alleyn went on, "were also members of the clique. Miss Sanskrit produced your medallion in her pottery downstairs. They, however, were double agents. From the time the plan was first conceived to the moment for its execution and without the knowledge of the Ambassador, every move was being conveyed by the Sanskrits back to the Ng'ombwanan authorities. I think you must have suspected something of the sort when your plan miscarried. I think that last night after your meeting here broke up, one of the group followed Sanskrit to the Embassy and from a distance saw him deliver an envelope. He had passed by your house, Colonel Montfort."

"I don't go out at night much nowadays," the Colonel said, rather sadly.

"Your wife perhaps? It wouldn't be the first time you'd delegated one of the fancy touches to her. Well, it's of no great matter. I think the full realization of what the Sanskrits had done really dawned this morning when you learned that they were shutting up shop and leaving."

"Have they made it!" Chubb suddenly demanded. "Have they cleared out? Where are they?"

"To return to the actual event. Everything seemed to go according to plan up to the moment when, after the shot was fired and the guests' attention had been deflected, you, Chubb, made your assault on the spear-carrier. You delivered the chop from behind, probably standing on a subsequently overturned chair to do so. At the crucial moment you were yourself attacked from the rear by the Ng'ombwanan servant. He was a little slow off the mark. Your blow fell, not as intended on the spearman's arm but on his collar-bone. He was still able to use his spear and he did use it, with both hands and full knowledge of what he was doing, on the Ambassador."

Alleyn looked at the three men. There was no change in their posture or their expressions, but a dull red had crept into Chubb's face, and the Colonel's (which habitually looked as if it had reached saturation point in respect of purple) seemed to darken. They said nothing.

"I see I've come near enough the mark for none of you to contradict me," Alleyn remarked.

"On the contrary," Gomez countered. "Your entire story is a fantasy and a libel. It is too farcical to merit a reply."

"Well, Chubb?"

"I'm not answering the charge, sir. Except what I said before. I was clobbered."

"Colonel?"

"What? No comment. No bloody comment."

"Why were you all trying to get in here half an hour ago?"

"No comment," they said together, and Chubb added his former statement that he'd had no intention of calling on the Sanskrits but had merely stopped to offer his support to the Colonel and take him home.

The Colonel said something that sounded like: "Most irregular and unnecessary."

"Are you sticking to that?" Alleyn said. "Are you sure you weren't, all three of you, going to throw a farewell party for the Sanskrits and give them, or at any rate, him, something handsome to remember you by?"

They were very still. They didn't look at Alleyn or at each other, but for a moment the shadow of a fugitive smile moved across their faces.

The front doorbell was pealing again, continuously. Alleyn went out to the landing.

Mrs. Chubb was at the street door demanding to be let in. The constable on duty turned, looked up the stairs, and saw Alleyn.

"All right," Alleyn said. "Ask her to come up."

It was a very different Mrs. Chubb who came quickly up the stairs, thrusting her shoulders forward and jerking up her head to confront Alleyn on the landing.

"Where is he?" she demanded, breathing hard. "Where's Chubb? You said keep him home and now you've got him in here. And with them others. Haven't you? I know he's here. I was in the Mews and I seen. Why? What are you doing to him? Where," Mrs. Chubb reiterated, "is my Chubb?"

"Come in," Alleyn said. "He's here."

She looked past him into the room. Her husband stood up and she went to him. "What are you doing?" she said. "You come back with me. You've got no call to be here."

Chubb said: "You don't want to be like this. You keep out of it. You're out of place here, Min."

"I'm out of place! Standing by my own husband!"

"Look – dear – "

"Don't talk to me!" She turned on the other two men. "You two gentlemen," she said, "you got no call because he works for you to get him involved stirring it all up again. Putting ideas in his head. It won't bring her back. Leave us alone. Syd – you come home with me. Come home."

"I can't," he said. "Min. I can't."

"Why can't you?" She clapped her hand to her mouth. "They've arrested you! They've found out – "

"*Shut up,*" he shouted. "You silly cow. You don't know what you're saying. *Shut up.*" They stared aghast at each other. "I'm sorry, Min," he said. "I never meant to speak rough. I'm not arrested. It's not like that."

"Where are they, then? Those two?"

Gomez said: "You! Chubb! Have you no control over your woman. Get rid of her."

"And that'll do from you," Chubb said, turning savagely on him.

From the depths of his armchair, Colonel Cockburn-Montfort, in an astonishingly clear and incisive tone, said: "Chubb!"

"Sir!"

"You're forgetting yourself."

"Sir."

Alleyn said: "Mrs. Chubb, everything I said to you this

morning was said in good faith. Circumstances have changed profoundly since then in a way that you know nothing about. You *will* know before long. In the meantime, if you please, you will either stay here, quietly, in this room –"

"You better, Min," Chubb said.

"– or," Alleyn said, "just go home and wait there. It won't be for long."

"Go on, then, Min. You better."

"I'll stay," she said. She walked to the far end of the room and sat down.

Gomez, trembling with what seemed to be rage, shouted: "For the last time – where are they? Where have they gone? Have they escaped? I demand an answer. Where are the Sanskrits?"

"They are downstairs," Alleyn said.

Gomez leapt to his feet, let out an exclamation – in Portuguese, Alleyn supposed – seemed to be in two minds what to say, and at last with a sort of doubtful relish said: "Have you arrested them?"

"No."

"I want to see them," he said. "I am longing to see them."

"And so you shall," said Alleyn.

He glanced at Fox, who went downstairs. Gomez moved towards the door.

The constable who had been on duty in the room came back and stationed himself inside the door.

"Shall we go down?" Alleyn said and led the way.

III

It was from this point that the sequence of events in the pig-pottery took on such a grotesque, such a macabre aspect that Alleyn was to look back on the episode as possibly the most outlandish in his professional career. From the moment the corpse of Miss Sanskrit received the first of her gentlemen visitors, they all three in turn became puppet-like caricatures of themselves, acting in a two-dimensional, crudely exaggerated style. In any other setting the element of black farce would have rioted. Even here, under the terrible auspices of the Sanskrits, it rose from time to time like a bout of unseemly hysteria at the bad performance of a Jacobean tragedy.

The room downstairs had been made ready for the visit. Bailey and Thompson waited near the window, Gibson by the desk, and Fox, with his notebook in hand, near the alcove. Two uniform police stood inside the door and a third at the back of the alcove. The bodies of the Sanskrits, brother and sister, had not been moved or shrouded. The room was now dreadfully stuffy.

Alleyn joined Fox. "Come in, Mr. Gomez," he said.

Gomez stood on the threshold, a wary animal, Alleyn thought, waiting with its ears laid back before advancing into strange territory. He looked, without moving his head, from one to another of the men in the room, seemed to hesitate, seemed to suspect, and then, swaggering a little, came into the room.

He stopped dead in front of Alleyn and said: "Well?"

Alleyn made a slight gesture. Gomez followed it, turned his head — and saw.

The noise he made was something between a retch and an exclamation. For a moment he was perfectly still, and it was as if he and Miss Sanskrit actually and sensibly confronted each other. And because of the arch manner in which the lifeless head lolled on the lifeless arm and the dead eyes seemed to leer at him, it was as if Miss Sanskrit had done a Banquo and found Mr. Gomez out.

He walked down the room and into the alcove. The policeman by the furnace gave a slight cough and eased his chin.

Gomez inspected the bodies. He walked round the work table and he looked into the packing case. He might have been a visitor to a museum. There was no sound in the room other than the light fall of his feet on the wooden floor and the dry buzzing of flies.

Then he turned his back on the alcove, pointed at Alleyn, and said: "*You!* What did you think to achieve by this? Make me lose my nerve? Terrify me into saying something you could twist into an admission? Oh, no, my friend! I had no hand in the destruction of this vermin. Show me the man who did it and I'll kiss him on both cheeks and salute him as a brother, but I had no hand in it and you'll never prove anything else."

He stopped. He was shaking as if with a rigor. He made to leave the room and saw that the door was guarded. And then he screamed out: "Cover them up. They're obscene," and went to the curtained window, turning his back on the room.

Fox, on a look from Alleyn, had gone upstairs. Thompson said under his breath, "Could I have a second, Mr. Alleyn?"

They went into the hallway. Thompson produced an envelope from his pocket and shook the contents out in his palm—two circular flattish objects about the size of an old sixpence, with convex upper surfaces. The under-surface of one had a pimple on it and on the other, a hole. They were blistered and there were tiny fragments of an indistinguishable charred substance clinging to them.

"Furnace?" Alleyn asked.

"That's right, sir."

"Good. I'll take them."

He restored them to their envelope, put them in his pocket, and looked up the stairs to where Fox waited on the landing. "Next," he said, and thought: "It's like a dentist's waiting-room."

The next was the Colonel. He came down in fairly good order with his shoulders squared and his chin up and feeling with the back of his heels for the stair-treads. As he turned into the shop he pressed up the corners of his moustache.

After the histrionics of Gomez, the Colonel's confrontation with the Sanskrits passed off quietly. He fetched up short, stood in absolute silence for a few seconds, and then said with an air that almost resembled dignity, "This is disgraceful."

"Disgraceful?" Alleyn repeated.

"They've been murdered."

"Clearly."

"The bodies ought to be covered. It's most irregular. And disgusting," and he added, almost, it seemed, as an afterthought: "It makes me feel sick." And indeed he perceptibly changed colour.

He turned his back on the Sanskrits and joined Gomez by the window. "I protest categorically," he said, successfully negotiating the phrase, "at the conduct of these proceedings. And I wish to leave the room."

"Not just yet, I'm afraid," Alleyn said as Gomez made a move towards the door, "for either of you."

"What right," Gomez demanded, "have you to keep me here? You have no right."

"Well," Alleyn said mildly, "if you press the point we can note your objection, which I see Inspector Fox is doing in any case, and if you insist on leaving you may do so in a minute. In that case, of course, we shall ask you to come with us to the Yard. In the meantime: there's Chubb. Would you, Fox?"

In its own succinct way Chubb's reaction was a classic. He marched in almost as if Fox were a sergeant-major's escort, executed a smart left turn, saw Miss Sanskrit, halted, became rigid, asked – unbelievably – "Who done it?" and fainted backwards like the soldier he had been.

And the Colonel, rivalling him in established behaviour, made a sharp exasperated noise and said: "Damn' bad show."

Chubb recovered almost immediately. One of the constables

brought him a drink of water. He was supported to the only chair in the room and sat in it with his back to the alcove.

"Very sorry, sir," he mumbled, not to Alleyn but to the Colonel. His gaze alighted on Gomez.

"You done it!" he said, sweating and trembling. "Din' you? You said you'd fix it and you did. You fixed it."

"Do you lay a charge against Mr. Gomez?" Alleyn said.

"Gomez? I don't know any Gomez."

"Against Mr. Sheridan?"

"I don't know what it means, lay a charge, and I don't know how he worked it, do I? But he said last night if it turned out they'd ratted, he'd get them. And I reckon he's kept 'is word. He's got them."

Gomez sprang at him like a released spring, so suddenly and with such venom that it took Gibson and both the constables all their time to hold him. He let out short, disjointed phrases, presumably in Portuguese, wetting his blue chin and mouthing at Alleyn. Perhaps because the supply of invective ran out, he at last fell silent and watchful and seemed the more dangerous for it.

"That was a touch of your old Ng'ombwanan form," Alleyn said. "You'd much better pipe down, Mr. Gomez. Otherwise, you know, we shall have to lock you up."

"Filth!" said Mr. Gomez, and spat inaccurately in Chubb's direction.

"Bad show. Damn' bad show," reiterated the Colonel, who seemed to have turned himself into a sort of Chorus to the Action.

Alleyn said: "Has one of you lost a pair of gloves?"

The scene went silent. For a second or two nobody moved, and then Chubb got to his feet. Gomez, whose arms were still in custody, looked at his hands with their garnish of black hair and the Colonel thrust his into his pockets. And then, on a common impulse, it seemed they all three began accusing each other incoherently and inanely of the murder of the Sanskrits, and would no doubt have gone on doing so if the front doorbell had not pealed once more. As if the sound-track for whatever drama was being ground out had been turned back for a replay, a woman could be heard making a commotion in the hallway.

"I want to see my husband. Stop that. Don't touch me. I'm going to see my husband."

The Colonel whispered, "No! For Chrissake keep her out. *Keep her out.*"

But she was already in the room, with the constable on duty in the hall making an ineffectual grab after her and the two men inside the door, taken completely by surprise, looking to Alleyn for orders.

He had her by the arms. She was dishevelled and her eyes were out of focus. It would be hard to say whether she smelt stronger of gin or of scent.

Alleyn turned her with her back to the alcove and her face towards her husband. He felt her sagging in his grasp.

"Hughie!" she said. "You haven't, have you? Hughie, promise you haven't. *Hughie!*"

She fought with Alleyn, trying to reach her husband. "I couldn't stand it, Hughie," she cried. "Alone, after what you said you'd do. I had to come. I had to know."

And as Chubb had turned on his wife, so the Colonel, in a different key, turned on her.

"Hold your tongue!" he roared out. "You're drunk."

She struggled violently with Alleyn and in doing so swung round in his grasp and faced the alcove.

And screamed. And screamed. And poured out such a stream of fatal words that her husband made a savage attempt to get at her and was held off by Fox and Thompson and Bailey. And then she became terrified of him, begged Alleyn not to let him get to her, and finally collapsed.

There being nowhere else to put her, they carried her upstairs and left her with Mrs. Chubb, gabbling wildly about how badly he treated her and how she knew when he left the house in a blind rage he would do what he said he would do. All of which was noted down by the officer on duty in the upstairs room.

In the downstairs room Alleyn, not having a warrant for his arrest, asked Colonel Cockburn-Montfort to come to the Yard, where he would be formally charged with the murder of the Sanskrits.

"And I should warn you that—"

X

Epilogue

"It was clear from the moment we saw the bodies," Alleyn said, "that Montfort was the man. The pig-pottery had been under strict surveillance from the time Sanskrit returned to it from the house-agents. The only gap came after Gibson's men had been drawn off by the bomb scare. The traffic in the Mews piled up between Sergeant Jacks and the flat entrance where Montfort leant against the doorbell, and for at least five minutes, probably longer, the façade was completely hidden by a van. During that time Montfort, who was beginning to make a scene in the street, had been admitted by one or other of the Sanskrits with the object, one supposes, of shutting him up.

"They were in a hurry. They had to get to the airport. They had planned to make their getaway within the next quarter of an hour and were packing up the last lot of pigs and writing a note for the agents. Leaving the drunken Colonel to grind to a halt, they returned to their jobs. Sanskrit put the penultimate pig in the case, his sister sat down to write the note. Montfort followed them up, found himself between the two of them, heaved up the last pig doorstop on the bench and in a drunken fury crashed it down left and right. The shock of what he'd done may have partly sobered him. His gloves were bloodied. He shoved them in the kiln, walked out, and had the sense or the necessity to lean against the doorbell again. The van still blocked the view, and when it removed itself there he still was."

"Who raised the false alarm about the bomb?" asked Troy.

"Oh, one of the Sanskrits, don't you think? To draw Gibson's men off while the two of them did a bunk to Ng'ombwana. They were in a blue funk over the outcome of the assassination and an even bluer one at the thought of the Klu-Klux-Fish. They realized, as they were bound to do, that they'd been rumbled."

"It would seem," Mr. Whipplestone said drily, "that they did not over-estimate the potential."

"It would indeed."

"Rory—*how* drunk was the wretched man?" Troy asked.

"Can one talk about degrees of drunkenness in an alcoholic? I suppose one can. According to his wife, and there's no reason to doubt her, he was plug-ugly drunk and breathing murder when he left the house."

"And the whole thing, you believe, was completely unpremeditated?" Mr. Whipplestone asked.

"I think so. No coherent plan when he leant on the doorbell. Nothing beyond a blind alcoholic rage to get at them. There was the pig on the work table and there were their heads. Bang, bang and he walked out again. The traffic block was just drunkard's luck. I don't for a moment suppose he was aware of it and I think he'd have behaved in exactly the same way if it hadn't occurred."

"He had the sense to put his gloves in the kiln," Mr. Whipplestone pointed out.

"It's the only bit of hard evidence we've got. I wouldn't venture a guess as to how far the shock of what he'd done sobered him. Or as to how far he may have exaggerated his condition for our benefit. He's been given a blood test and the alcoholic level was astronomical."

"No doubt he'll plead drunkenness," said Mr. Whipplestone.

"You may depend upon it. And to some purpose, I don't mind betting."

"What about my poor silly Chubb?"

"Sam, in the ordinary course of things he'd face a charge of conspiracy. If it does come to that, the past history—his daughter—and the dominance of the others will tell enormously in his favour. With a first-class counsel—"

"I'll look after that. And his bail. I've told him so."

"I'm not sure we've got a case. Apart from the *mlinzi*'s collarbone there's no hard evidence. What we would greatly prefer would be for Chubb to make a clean breast about the conspiracy in return for his own immunity."

Mr. Whipplestone and Troy looked uncomfortable.

"Yes, I know," Alleyn said. "But just you think for a bit about Gomez. He's the only one apart from Montfort himself who'd be involved, and believe me, if ever there was a specimen who deserved what's coming to him, it's that one. We've got him on a forged passport charge which will do to go on with, and a search of his pseudo coffee importing premises in the City has brought to light some very dubious transactions in uncut diamonds. And in the background is his Ng'ombwanan conviction for manslaughter of a particularly revolting nature."

"What about the Embassy angle?" Troy asked.

"What indeed! What happened within those *opéra bouffe* walls is, as we keep telling ourselves, their affair, although it will figure obliquely as motive in the case against Montfort. But for the other show—the slaughter of the Ambassador by the *mlinzi*—that's over to the Boomer and I wish the old so-and-so joy of it."

"He leaves tomorrow, I'm told."

"Yes. At two-thirty. After giving Troy a final sitting."

"*Really!*" Mr. Whipplestone exclaimed, gazing in polite awe at Troy. She burst out laughing.

"Don't look so shocked," she said, and to her own, Alleyn's and Mr. Whipplestone's astonishment dropped a kiss on the top of his head. She saw the pink scalp under the neat strands of hair turn crimson and said: "Pay no attention. I'm excited about my work."

"Don't ruin everything!" said Mr. Whipplestone with tremendous dash. "I'd hoped it was about me."

II

"By all the rules, if there were any valid ones," Troy said at half-past eleven the following morning, "it's an unfinished portrait. But even if you could give me another sitting I don't think I'd take it."

The Boomer stood beside her looking at her work. At no stage of the sittings had he exhibited any of the usual shyness of the sitter who doesn't want to utter banalities and at no stage had he uttered any.

"There is something African in the way you have gone about this picture," he said. "We have not portraitists of distinction at present, but if we had they would try to do very much as you have done, I think. I find it hard to remember that the painter is not one of my people."

"You couldn't have said anything to please me more," said Troy.

"No? I am glad. And so I must go. Rory and I have one or two things to settle and I have to change. So it is goodbye, my dear Mrs. Rory, and thank you."

"Goodbye," Troy said, "my dear President Boomer, and thank you."

She gave him her painty hand and saw him into the house, where Alleyn waited for him. This time he had come without his *mlinzi,* who, he said, was involved with final arrangements at the Embassy.

He and Alleyn had a drink together.

"This has been in some ways an unusual visit," the Boomer remarked.

"A little unusual," Alleyn agreed.

"On your part, my dear Rory, it has been characterized by the tactful avoidance of difficult corners."

"I've done my best. With the assistance, if that's the right word, of diplomatic immunity."

The Boomer gave him a tentative smile. Alleyn reflected that this was a rare occurrence. The Boomer's habit was to bellow with laughter, beam like a lighthouse, or remain entirely solemn.

"So those unpleasant persons," he said, "have been murdered by Colonel Cockburn-Montfort."

"It looks like it."

"They *were* unpleasant," the Boomer said thoughtfully. "We were sorry to employ them but needs must. You find the same sort of situation in your own service of course."

This being perfectly true, there was little to be said in reply.

"We regretted the necessity," the Boomer said, "to reinstate them in Ng'ombwana."

"In the event," Alleyn said drily, "you don't have to."

"No!" he cried gaily. "So it's an ill wind as the saying goes. We are spared the Sanskrits. *What* a good thing."

Alleyn gazed at him, speechless.

"Is anything the matter, old boy?" the Boomer asked.

Alleyn shook his head.

"Ah!" said the Boomer. "I think I know. We have come within sight of that ravine, again."

"And again we can arrange to meet elsewhere."

"That is why you have not asked me certain questions. Such as how far was I aware of the successful counterplot against my traitor-Ambassador. Or whether I myself dealt personally with the odious Sanskrits who served us so usefully. Or whether it was I, of my own design, who led our poor Gibson so far down the Embassy garden path."

"Not only Gibson."

An expression of extreme distress came over the large black face. His hands gripped Alleyn's shoulders and his enormous, slightly bloodshot eyes filled with tears.

"Try to understand," he said. "Justice has been done in accordance with our need, our grass-roots, our absolute selves. With time we shall evolve a change and adapt and gradually such elements may die out in us. At the present, my very dear friend, you must think of us – of me if you like – as – "

He hesitated for a moment, and then with a smile and a change in his huge voice: " – as an unfinished portrait," said the Boomer.

Coda

On a very warm morning in mid-summer, Lucy Lockett, wearing the ornamental collar in which she seemed to fancy herself, sat on the front steps of No. 1, Capricorn Walk, contemplating the scene and keeping an ear open on proceedings in the basement flat.

Mr. Whipplestone had found a suitable tenant and the Chubbs were turning out the premises. A vacuum cleaner whined, there were sundry bumps. The windows were open and voices were heard.

Mr. Whipplestone had gone to the Napoli to buy his Camembert, and Lucy, who never accompanied him into the Mews, awaited his return.

The cleaner was switched off. The Chubbs interchanged peaceful remarks and Lucy, suddenly moved by the legendary curiosity of her species and sex, leapt neatly into the garden and thence through the basement window.

The chattels of the late tenant had been removed but a certain amount of litter still obtained. Lucy pretended to kill a crumpled sheet of newspaper and then fossicked about in odd corners. The Chubbs paid little attention to her.

When Mr. Whipplestone returned he found his cat on the top step, *couchant*, with something between her forepaws. She gazed up at him and made one of her fetching little remarks.

"What have you got there?" he asked. He inserted his eyeglass and bent down to see.

It was a white pottery fish.